TH
LIA
SISTER

BOOKS BY SARAH A. DENZIL

Only Daughter

THE LIAR'S SISTER

SARAH A. DENZIL

bookouture

Published by Bookouture in 2019

An imprint of StoryFire Ltd.

Carmelite House
50 Victoria Embankment
London EC4Y 0DZ

www.bookouture.com

ISBN: 978-1-78681-738-9
eBook ISBN: 978-1-78681-737-2

Dear Rosie,

You'll never read this. Not while I'm still breathing. I don't even know why I'm writing it. All I know is that I need to get these words out of my head before they eat away at me. What I am about to say is unthinkable. And yet I have to say it. Just once. I will allow myself that.

I think you killed someone.

There, I said it. I've thought it for many years but I've never dared to write the words down, or say them out loud.

But I'll never tell. Remember when we'd spit on the stones near the bluebell field and make promises? I kept them all, didn't I? I'll spit on the stones again. I'll never tell.

Rosie, how can I look at your beautiful face and think this terrible thing? Sometimes, even if I'm with you, the thoughts scream at me, tearing through my mind until I can't hear anything else. It's a horrible thing to think about a person, let alone the person you love more than anyone else.

And I don't think you know what I'm thinking. I don't think you suspect. Do you wonder why we drifted apart? You think it's because of your addictions and your volatile behaviour, but it isn't. I would've helped you. I would've gone with you to rehab, held your hair back as you vomited, poured your booze down the drain and searched your tiny little flat for pills. But I didn't. I did the unforgivable. I turned away. For the first time ever.

We grew up inseparable as children, with the run of the land around us. And then the day came when we parted and we never found a way to fuse ourselves back to how we were before. It has always felt wrong, like throwing away the matching salt shaker to the pepper mill. But I can't blame everything on the night Samuel disappeared. It actually began a long time ago, before that night. Do you remember? When Grandad came to live with us we begged Mum and Dad not to force us to share a room. You even tried to convince Dad to convert the attic into a bedroom for you. Grandad could have the ground floor and I would take the room next to Mum and Dad. I know how much you hated the spiders in the attic. That was how much you didn't want to share a room with me at night. Now I know why you didn't want to, because you had places to go when darkness fell.

But Mum and Dad were the law, and two single beds were crammed into the ground-floor bedroom. Luckily for you, I was a deep sleeper. I had my own issues to deal with. You remember the sleepwalking, don't you? Remember when Grandad found me in the woods before breakfast? Sleeping on a blanket of dark-green mossy undergrowth. Nothing could wake me. I believed then, and still do when I occasionally sleepwalk now, that I could walk for miles in my sleep, possibly even hold a conversation, and never know about it. You hear of people wandering over cliffs or onto the motorway in their sleep. Maybe that could be me.

But this letter isn't about me, it's about you, and it's about that night ten years ago. You were seventeen and I was barely sixteen. No, I didn't wake up when you snuck out. Another stroke of luck was that Grandad had been too proud to take the ground-floor bedroom as Mum and Dad had planned. Which made it easier for you to climb out of the window at night and creep back in the same way.

What you don't know, because I've never told you, is that I saw you climbing back in through the window that morning. I caught a glimpse of your muddied clothes before I pulled the cover over my head and watched you through the thin sheets. It was sunrise and the room was bright, letting the light in through the weave of the old, worn cotton. You undressed quickly and shoved everything in a bag, which you hid at the back of the wardrobe. Then you used the tiny sink we had in the room to wash your hands and face. You were shaking. I thought about getting out of bed to comfort you, but I saw the way you kept glancing at my bed to make sure I didn't stir.

You didn't want me to see you.

Instead of helping you, I pretended to sleep until it was time for breakfast. Mum knocked on the door to wake us up around eight. I was cautious at first, waiting to see if you'd tell me where you'd been. Did you go to see a boyfriend? Did you sneak out to a party? Where did you go, Rosie?

We walked through to the kitchen in silence, and the whole time I expected you to pull me to the side and whisper your secrets in my ear. But you didn't. Mum asked if we'd both slept well, and you nodded your head as you picked the crust off your toast. She asked us what we wanted to do with our Saturday, and you just shrugged. Because the silence was making me uncomfortable, I told Mum that I was taking Lady out for a hack in the woods. I asked you if you wanted to come, but then the doorbell rang and you never got a chance to answer.

It was Lynn Murray, Samuel's mother, at the door. I heard her squeaky little voice as she started talking to Mum, and my body tensed. By this point, I'd come to expect bad news from any of the Murrays. After a moment or two, I knew something was wrong. Lynn's voice was even squeakier than normal, and I heard Mum gasp. It was weird that she would come to our house anyway, given what had happened a few weeks before. Why was she here? And what did she have to say?

When Mum came back to the kitchen, her face was as white as the milk in my cereal bowl. I'll never forget that moment. And I'll never forget the way you stared down at the table as though you knew what was about to happen.

'Samuel Murray is missing,' Mum said. Her words came out in a hurried, breathy whisper. She clamped a hand over her mouth. 'God! What if he's run away?'

You got up from the table then, and stormed out of the kitchen, back to our room. Mum sighed and leaned against the kitchen counter, shaking her head, with tears in her eyes.

I didn't know what to do. Part of me wanted to go after you, but I'd seen your reaction. You were not surprised by what Lynn Murray had had to say, and a freezing-cold fear penetrated my body. I stood up to go to Mum, but she was already gathering her things.

'I'm going over to the Murrays' farm,' she said. 'It's not my place, given everything that's happened between our families, but I need to go. Maybe I can help out.' She was frazzled, searching for her keys under a pile of laundry before finding them on top of the fridge. 'Your dad's working today, but you can stay with your sister or …' she glanced towards the kitchen door, 'your grandad.'

I remember standing awkwardly by the door as Mum hastily kissed me goodbye. She'd ruffled up my hair in the process and I had to straighten it out. I remember watching her push her feet into boots, yank open the door and disappear into the garden. And I remember thinking how strange it was that Samuel Murray was missing and you, my sister Rosie, had left the house last night. My stomach churned. I emptied out my bowl of cereal. I rinsed my pots and left them on the draining board. Slowly I walked through the hallway towards our bedroom, but I hesitated because my heart was pounding. He would come back, wouldn't he? Samuel wouldn't be missing for long. Someone would find him. He had to come back. My heart continued to thrum at an alarming speed. I didn't want to think about the alternative and what it would mean for me, and for you, Rosie.

Upstairs, I heard Grandad bumping around, swearing as always. I twisted my body around until I could see the stairs, and then back to our bedroom door. You were in there, keeping your secrets to yourself.

But I couldn't bring myself to ask you what you knew. The thought made me nauseous. If I asked, would I want to hear the answer?

Instead, I went outside to the shed and pulled down Lady's saddle and bridle. I went to the stable and stroked her soft muzzle, feeding her the morning mint I always put in my jeans pocket. She breathed hot steam into my ear as I fiddled with the tack until it was in place. We were almost too big for our ponies then, weren't we? In fact, we stopped riding them the year after. Dad wanted to sell them, but we cried until he agreed to keep them grazing in the paddock until a few years ago, when … Well, you know. You didn't come, but you know they had to be put down.

Lady swished her tail when I tightened the girth and flattened her ears when I pulled myself up into the saddle. I gave her a little pat on the neck to calm her, like I always did. She trotted politely out of the gate and towards the woods. That morning I wanted to gallop away, out of the village for good. I could feel the weight of this bad thing deep down in my bones. I wanted to get away from you and Mum and Dad and Grandad, but especially you. Even though I didn't understand the full extent of it, my instincts told me that I had a responsibility to keep your secret, but the burden was already a heavy one.

I didn't gallop, because I never do. Galloping is what *you* do, Ro. I'm the cautious one and you're the wild one. I slowed Lady down to a walk, despite her snorting unhappily at being reined back. We followed the bridle path into Buckbell Woods and I kept hold of her the entire time, keeping her steady for a better view. I was searching for Samuel, hoping he was hiding in the woods. Every part of me longed to see him. I needed to see him.

Lady finally relaxed and I extended the reins, allowing her to stretch out her neck. Beneath me her body moved rhythmically, left shoulder, then right shoulder, dipping and rising. Her ears, pricked forwards, bobbed up and down along with her steps. She pulled on the reins, trying to sneak in a bit of grazing if she couldn't stretch her legs and canter. It was when I leaned forward to shorten my reins again that I saw it.

So small and inconsequential. Maybe no one else would've noticed. But I did.

It was late April, the third Saturday in, and the bluebells had flowered that week. I was right on the edge of the field with Lady, halted on the bridle path, facing the clearing that eventually leads to that creepy little cabin we both hate. There on the ground, a few feet away from Lady's hooves, was a small object that caught the morning sun peeking through the branches overhead.

I leaned forward, took my feet out of the stirrups and swung my leg over the saddle, landing on damp ground. Carefully, ensuring that Lady did not step on the object, I pulled her forwards and moved towards it. I checked I was alone then. When I was sure there was no one else there, I picked it up and put it in my pocket. Then I climbed back onto Lady and let her gallop all the way home.

Your bracelet weighed heavily in my pocket. The silver charm bracelet that Mum gave you on your eleventh birthday. We have matching ones, don't we? Almost matching, anyway. Yours has little rose charms all the way around it. Mine has pendant charms with tiny images of heather in enamel. That's Mum, though, isn't it? Always so literal.

Lady needed a sponge-down when I got home, but I didn't do it right away. Instead I strode straight into the house, into our bedroom, where I found you on your bed, headphones on, eyes red. You watched me, face sullen, one knee up, the other leg straight. I went over to your chest of drawers, shoved my hand into my pocket and pulled out your bracelet. When I placed it on top of the cabinet, you never said a word.

You never spoke of it. And I never asked.

Samuel was my friend, my best friend, my only friend, and I never asked because I never wanted to know. For the first few years, I'd imagine another knock on the door, only this time it wouldn't be Lynn Murray, it would be Samuel. He would be back. But I shouldn't have been thinking those thoughts, should I? And you know why.

Do you remember the day you blurted out how you wished Samuel was dead? I can't stop thinking about it. I can't stop thinking about all the things you did in the weeks before he went missing. He remained missing. No one ever found him. Dead or alive. The police were involved, of course. He remained a missing sixteen-year-old boy, frozen in time. A face on a lamp post.

Deep down, I don't think I wanted to know the truth because I thought it might kill me. I've never been brave, have I, Ro? In the end, I didn't search for my friend and I didn't demand the truth from you. I gave up. I tried to move on and I failed, miserably.

Eventually the unanswered questions built up between us and pushed us apart. There was no more spitting on the stones. We grew up. We were practically grown then anyway.

You left to go to university just over a year later, and soon enough you weren't even coming home for summer. Then one year you skipped Christmas. You were drunk at Grandad's funeral. You arrived late with some guy, a fresh tattoo on your wrist, unwashed hair, and scarpered before the wake. It was even worse at Dad's funeral five years ago.

What have you been doing, Rosie? You went from a solid student to intern at an advertising agency, to working in a restaurant, to working in a bar, to borrowing money from Mum, to … I don't even know what. Who are you? What kind of person passes out behind the sofa at their dad's funeral?

Now Mum is dying, Rosie. And she wants to see you.

But the problem is, *I* don't want to.
Because I think you're a murderer.

Your little sister,
Heather

CHAPTER ONE

Heather

Now

Sometimes I feel as though my childhood happened to someone else. Buckthorpe could be an imaginary place that comes to me in my dreams, or a fantasy world in a book. The idyll of my rural upbringing is hazy, leaving me with little more than déjà vu when I stare at Ivy Cottage. I spent eighteen years growing up in this place. I opened and closed the red wooden door thousands of times. I cleaned out the stables at the back of the house. I helped Mum weed the garden until I had blisters on my hands. I waved Dad goodbye from the kitchen table every morning. But it's all a blur.

Perhaps that's a good way of viewing childhood, as though it's nothing more than a dream. Maybe none of it is real until we reach adulthood, and everything that happened before is just the breeze drifting through the curtains at night.

Unless I'm wishing that it wasn't real. Idle wishful thinking for the woman always stuck in the past, because there is one part of my childhood that isn't a blur, as much as I wish it was. My mind can't stop travelling back to ten years ago, almost to the day. To the disappearance of Samuel Murray. And to what my sister Rosie may or may not have done that night.

Ivy Cottage is a probably on the small side for a three-bedroom house. The kitchen and dining room are combined, the living room is snug and always resulted in many crossed-legged positions on the carpet for the family to watch TV together. A few years before Samuel went missing, Grandad moved into the bedroom next to my parents', and our house was about ready to burst. And yet it feels inexplicably enormous now that I'm the only one living in it.

On my way out of the familiar door, I grab my waterproof coat and my car keys and walk along the road towards the woods. Our nearest neighbours, Joan and Bob Campbell, are a couple of minutes' walk away from Ivy Cottage. They are quiet retirees who keep to themselves. He used to teach at the local primary school. I remember how we made fun of his expanding waistline, in the way only young children can get away with.

Past their cottage, I enter Buckbell Woods and follow the bridle path; the same path where I rode Lady ten years ago and where I found Rosie's bracelet. It hasn't changed a bit – the bluebells are in bloom as they always are in April and May. I wish seeing them brought me comfort, but it doesn't. At one time, this was my favourite place in the world, but now I find it hard to be here, and yet I'm forever drawn back to this spot. I stop for a moment and stare out into the darkness beyond. But I don't want to linger. Not in this place. Not when I know who is out there.

I am less than an hour's walk from the cottage; this is a good spot to turn around and head back. I glance out past the bluebell field once more before turning away.

My phone rings and a bird leaps into the air from a nearby tree. A robin. My heart flutters. I lean forward and catch my breath before answering.

'Hello? Heather?' I recognise the voice right away, and it does nothing to calm my startled heart. The woman on the line is one of the nurses taking care of Mum in hospital, and she could be calling me with bad news. Every minute of the day I find myself steeled for the possibility that Mum has slipped away in her sleep overnight, or that this is the moment I drop everything to go to her and keep her company through her last moments.

'Yes. Is everything okay?' I ask.

'Your mum's fine,' Susie says, understanding why I'm anxious. 'It's just that she was asking about you this morning. I told her you'd be coming in, but I just wanted to check.'

'I'll be there,' I say. 'I've popped out for some fresh air, but I'll be coming to the hospital this afternoon.'

'Oh good. I thought so, but ... Well, she's a little agitated today.'

'Are you sure she's okay?' My fingers grip the phone harder. Mum's cancer has reached the incurable stage, and she will never be okay again. And yet I continuously find myself asking that question.

'She's no worse,' Susie says in a gentle voice, answering as diplomatically as she can. 'But she has been asking after someone else too. Rosie? Does that name mean anything to you?'

'Yes,' I say, the air leaving my lungs. *Rosie*. 'She's my older sister.'

'Oh, wow, I didn't know you had a sister.'

'We haven't seen each other for a long time. Rosie has ... issues.'

'Ah,' she replies. 'That could be why your mum's thinking of her.'

I find myself nodding my head. 'You're probably right.'

'Anyway, I'll be working later, so I'll see you then.'

We say goodbye, I hang up and I then begin my walk back to the cottage.

When I arrive home, I have an hour to kill before visiting hours begin at the hospital. I think back to the call with Susie, to Mum asking for Rosie. When Mum's cancer worsened, I knew she'd want Rosie to come. Of course she would. Which means I have to do this for her. I suppose you could say I've been waiting for this moment. Sitting down at the kitchen table, I retrieve my mobile from my jeans pocket, scroll through my contacts until I find Rosie. Then I call.

A dialling tone. Then nothing. This number has been disconnected. Well, it was a long shot. I haven't seen Rosie since Dad's funeral. Five years is a long time in Rosie years. Some people rarely move anywhere in five years. They don't change their number; they stay in the same house, the same country at least. But not Rosie. She could be anywhere. The last place I remember her living was a bedsit in Brighton.

But Brighton is a long way away and Mum doesn't have a lot of time left. Even though I've tried this before, when Mum first became ill, I fire off a message to Rosie's last-known email address. After that I try Facebook, the ideal place for people to connect to each other but rarely used for that purpose. Instead we use it for our own vanity, while occasionally spying on our exes. I type Rosie's name into the search bar, and her profile is the first result. We're still friends on Facebook, which is a good thing, but I rarely log on, so I don't know what she's been up to. In fact this is the first time I've logged on since Simon broke up with me a few months ago. I daren't check to find out if he is still my friend, or worse, whether he's moved on to another woman. No, I concentrate on Rosie, resisting the toxic urge to know about Simon.

And then I hear Rosie's voice in my mind, crystal clear: *You always were good at delayed gratification.* The tips of my fingers tingle at the sound of her words in my head. She teased me a lot about my prim personality. We were opposites. She was the wild, daring one. I was the mouse. The obedient one. I should be the rose, correct and proper. Rosie should be heather, growing wild on the moors. Mum got us the wrong way round.

Rosie's profile contains a tagged photograph from a month ago, but aside from that she hasn't updated Facebook for a long time. I click on the photo. It's nondescript. Two young women drinking coffee in a café. Rosie smiles at the camera, her dark hair spilling over the table. The sight of her takes my breath away, because in this picture she's Mum's double. Her eyes that same shade of blue, her hair dark as the unending night sky above Buckthorpe village, her skin neither pale nor tanned, more of a creamy colour. The last time I saw her, she was at least two stone lighter than in this photo, her skin was a waxy yellow and her eyes were red-rimmed and bruised. In short, she was a mess.

But this Rosie glows with health. There is a genuine smile on her face, and that intelligence I always missed when she was deep into her addictions is there in her eyes.

I scroll through older photographs in reverse chronological order, tracking the journey from sobriety to addiction. But I soon stop myself, no longer able to cope with the pain emanating from the computer screen.

Will she come to visit us before Mum passes away? If she does, what will we talk about? It's been such a long time since I was in the same space as my sister. I hardly know her now. She could be a completely different person. The thought makes the hairs stand up on the back of my neck. I breathe deeply, trying to ground myself to stop my thoughts from spiralling. There's no time for that, I need to go to the hospital to see Mum.

As I stand up to start getting ready to go, a new email appears in my inbox. The sight of it makes me inhale sharply. I hadn't thought she would email me back. Not right away. This is so unlike Rosie. When Dad died, I had to track her down through friends at a youth hostel in Thailand. But this is Rosie checking her email straight away, as any regular person would. Rosie is not a regular person.

Even my heart responds to the name on the screen, reacting to the flood of emotions working their way through my body. First there's the joy of seeing my sister's name. The excitement of knowing Rosie has noticed me. As the younger sister, I'll always have that reaction. Then there's the sense of dread, the anticipation of allowing her back into my life. And finally there is the fear.

*

The email is still unopened when I climb into my Golf and make my way to the hospital. Same old timid Heather, needing her mother with her when she has a problem. A hard thump to my chest. Fist against ribs. That's the painful reminder that my mum has not got long left. The cancer, which began in her left breast three years ago, has spread to her organs and her blood. It's everywhere, and there's nothing anyone can do. It's time to make her comfortable before she slips softly away when it's her time.

Except that none of it is comfortable and none of it is soft. Even when her smile is fixed, she can't keep the pain out of her eyes. Her mind wanders often. This is the woman who has every Shakespeare sonnet memorised, who could recite Tennyson backwards, who could finish a Sudoku faster than anyone I know. Now she is addled by the painkillers, so that sometimes she doesn't even recognise me. Sometimes she calls me Lily, her mother's name, or Rosie.

After parking the car, I do the same thing I always do. I take a deep breath, close my eyes, open them and get out of the car. Sometimes I cry, making sure that I get it all out before I see her.

I make my way through the labyrinth of hospital corridors, say hello to the nurses at the station and hand them the Tupperware box of cookies I've baked.

'You're a bad, bad woman, Heather Sharpe,' chides Susie. 'Those are at least ten Syns on Slimming.'

'Have half now and half later. Then it's only half the Syns,' I reply with a shrug.

She takes a cookie and laughs.

I guess it's a nice gesture for them, but the real reason I bake the cookies is to give me something to do to keep me occupied while I'm alone in the cottage. Banging around the old-fashioned kitchen with the radio on full blast makes me feel less alone. I'm still acclimatising to the quiet after living in London for the last few years. Buckthorpe is eerily silent, and pitch black without street lamps on its tiny country roads.

The few hazy childhood memories I have of the village are full of life and noise. We had two ponies, a coop full of chickens, and Mum's golden retriever, Buster. None of them are around any more, and the emptiness adds to my sense of disconnect with the place. At least the hospital is full of bustle and noise.

My mum has a room to herself now. She's propped up with some pillows, her sunken face bearing little expression amidst the white fabric. Because her hair hasn't been dyed for a while, there are two inches of grey beneath the dark brown. Mum and Rosie always had the same colour hair, and even after mum's went grey, she kept on maintaining it. I always lusted over Mum and Rosie's thick dark manes. In contrast, my hair is mousy and fine.

'Is that you, Rosie?' she rasps.

I move over to the bed and take her hand, sinking into the chair already in place for the visit. I let my bag fall to the floor.

'It's Heather, Mum.'

'Hi, darling.' She reaches out to touch my face, and then her arm drops. I catch it a moment before it hits the bed to give her a softer landing.

'Susie says you've been asking after Rosie today.'

'She should be here,' Mum says. 'I want to talk to her.'

She *should* be here, I can't help thinking bitterly. But she never comes home. Before her response to my email today, there were several that went unanswered when Mum was first diagnosed. But I never told Mum I'd contacted her, so that she could be spared the knowledge that her elder daughter had ignored my requests for her to visit. Mum will never know the real reason why Rosie hates to come home. I think I might be the only person who does.

'I got an email from her today, Mum.' Gently letting go of her hand, I reach into my bag and find my phone.

'You did?' she says, a little life coming back, that raspy whisper filling out into the voice I remember hearing as a child.

I'm glad that I'm leaning away from her, because hearing even a hint of vitality come back to Mum's voice reminds me of the past. It reminds me of her calling us down for dinner, or shooing Buster out of the kitchen. It reminds me of her laugh, which I haven't heard for weeks now.

'Yes,' I say, quickly brushing away a tear. 'Do you want me to read it to you?'

'Yes,' she says, still excited.

The familiar sensation of prickling nerves makes its way up my skin as I open the email. At least being with Mum gives me the strength to finally look at it. I quickly scan it to make sure there's nothing in there that I need to keep from Mum – though I doubt Rosie would bother replying if she wasn't going to come – and then I begin to read it aloud. 'Hi, Heather, I'm so sorry that I didn't send you my new phone number. I didn't realise things were tough there and I'm sorry for not getting in touch sooner. I'm actually doing much better. I'm six months sober and I'm in a better place right now. I think I'm well enough to come to Buckthorpe. I've missed you and I've missed Mum. I need to see you both. Love, Rosie.'

Mum's mouth gapes open as I read the last line of the email. Her skin is remarkably delicate around her mouth, cracking at the corners. I pull some lip balm from my bag and gently apply it, and her eyes water with tears.

'Oh, Heather,' she says. 'You look just like your father.'

I shake my head a little. 'I guess I have his eyes.'

She twists away and tears trickle down her cheeks. 'You must make sure that Rosie comes. It's important.'

'I know,' I say. 'I'll do my best, Mum.'

She directs her gaze back to me. 'You don't understand, Heather. You can't be alone in that house after I pass on. You remember all the details I left, don't you?'

I place the cap back on the lip balm, frowning. 'Yes.'

'Everything is in the drawer in the desk. My will. The deeds to the house. Everything. Don't stay here, Heather. Just sell the house and move on. This place is …' She pauses, as though she wants to tell me more.

But as she fixes me with those piercing blue eyes, the nurse walks in and the moment is lost.

CHAPTER TWO

Rosie

Then

You could say that I'm guilty of it all because I set off an unfortunate series of events. It's all because I wanted to go faster. We were riding too slowly. I clamped my legs against Midnight's side and lifted my arms higher up his neck to give him the space to gallop. And he did. He pushed that little bit more until we were flying along the grass verge. I wished I hadn't put my riding hat on, because galloping with the wind in your hair was much more fun, but Mum had a heart attack every time I did it. She always thought I was going to fall off. I never did, though. Heather was the one who used to freak out and end up on the ground.

To be fair to Heather, I was forcing us to ride fast next to the road that swept around the side of Buckbell Woods. It wasn't a busy road, because not many travellers passed through Buckthorpe, but it still wasn't the safest place to be pegging it on skittish animals.

The grass verge came to an end and I reined Midnight back to a slow trot. He pulled against me for a moment until he realised the soft grass had ended and we were back on the hard road. With an unenthused snort, he steadied to a walk, puffing after the exertion of the gallop.

My name is Rose, and I've always hated it. A rose is too structured. It's a Valentine's Day cliché. Heather and I used to talk about how Mum should have swapped our names, because I'm more like heather and she's more like roses, but we're stuck with who we are. At least Dad chose our ponies correctly. Midnight, a grey gelding, fourteen hands and wilful, was always supposed to be mine. Lady, a red-flecked roan colour, brown-eyed and lazy, was always meant for Heather. She wasn't the one who wanted to gallop as fast as possible whenever we hit grass. That was always me.

'Well that was stupid.' Heather, red in the face, glared at me with that judgemental stare she still has. You wouldn't think she was the younger sister. Even back then she was an old soul. She used to tell me off more than Mum did.

'We were fine.' I rolled my eyes as Heather came up on my right-hand side with Lady.

'What if there'd been a car?' she said. 'Or a tractor? Midnight would've panicked.'

I remember wanting to tell her to stop being such a wimp, but then I noticed that her voice was shaking and there were tears in her eyes.

'I've never ridden Lady that fast before,' Heather said, quickly wiping away her tears. 'I couldn't stop her.'

'Sorry,' I said, kind of half genuinely, half sarcastically. I guess I didn't want her to know that I actually was sorry. Admitting any kind of emotion when you're thirteen years old is, of course, an impossibility.

'Didn't bother me,' Heather said quickly, turning her head away.

I'd unbuttoned the top of my shirt to let in some air. It was the second week of the summer holidays and the third day of a surprise heat wave that had everyone in shorts, wafting themselves with their hands. Midnight huffed and puffed beneath me, tired but also wound up from the run, snorting and chomping at the bit.

By the time we reached the bend in the road with the weirdly shaped tree, he had managed to steady his breathing, but I began to feel weary. The tree provided a canopy, with one large, gnarly branch hanging suspended in the air across the road. As soon as Heather saw it, she sat up as straight as a rod and shortened her reins. Lady was a mostly calm pony, but for some strange reason she hated that tree.

'Just relax,' I said. 'She can tell you're nervous.'

'I am relaxing,' Heather snapped, her body as rigid as a plank of wood.

I remember rolling my eyes at her again. Grandad, who had taught us to ride in the fields behind our house, had told her to loosen up about a hundred times, but she couldn't, especially when she saw that stupid tree. Poor old Lady always got so spooked by it, because Heather couldn't stop herself from stressing out. The roan tossed her head and began walking like a crab, half twisting herself away from the trunk. Her head bobbed up and down in distress, and Heather leaned forward, her breath coming out in quick, shallow rasps.

If I hadn't galloped Midnight, Lady wouldn't have worked herself up. It was at this point that I began to feel terrible about it.

'We can get off if you want,' I suggested. 'Lead them past the tree and then get back on. I'll take Lady for you.'

But Heather shook her head. She gripped hold of the saddle as Lady started to dance, snorting hot air out of her nostrils and lifting her knees up high. I considered grabbing Heather's reins in case Lady took off, but we were almost past the old tree and hopefully the episode would be over soon. Poor Heather was pale-faced and tense, with her reins as tight as a violin string.

'Deep breaths, Hev,' I said.

She nodded and slowly began to relax her shoulders. But I could see that Lady wasn't relaxing with her. Within just a few seconds I realised that Lady was about to blow, and I reached across to try and grab the rein. But Lady bucked, throwing Heather onto her neck. Heather let out a small whimpering sound as her body hit the saddle and her face connected with the hard muscle on Lady's neck. As Heather was tossed forwards, she lost her reins.

Lady panicked and burst into a canter, her shoes clattering against the tarmac as she ran away. I quickly pushed myself into action, collecting up my own reins and pressing my legs against Midnight's sides to chase my poor sister.

'Hold onto the saddle, Hev!' I called out.

Lady was out of control, galloping down the centre of the road with my little sister clinging on for dear life. I saw that she'd lost one stirrup and was half hanging over Lady's withers, but I couldn't see if she still had hold of the saddle or not. My heart was hammering. If anything happened to Heather … I was the older sister; I was the one who should be taking care of her. But I never did, did I? I went off on my own adventures and expected her to keep up, even though I knew she couldn't.

Every bad word Mum had told me not to say went racing through my mind. *Please let Heather be okay.* Lady showed no sign of slowing down, though, and now we were racing past the Murrays' farm. God, that place was noisy enough for our ponies on a good day. My mind raced with potential disasters. What if the tractor came out of the yard? That'd be it. Lady would lose it completely. At least Heather wasn't screaming. Somehow she maintained a stoic silence as she continued to cling on. I'm not sure I would have remained as calm if it'd been me out of control on a road.

Lady's hooves must have been making quite a racket, because Colin Murray came hurrying out onto the road from the farm courtyard with his son Samuel next to him. The farmer stepped into the middle of the road with a bucket in his hands, gently lifting the bucket up and down, shaking the contents. As I slowed Midnight down to a gentle canter, I heard the rattling of feed in the bucket and realised that Mr Murray must have known there was a panicked horse running along the road.

Even in her terrified state, Lady would never miss an opportunity to eat. I saw the pony's ears prick towards the sound. She broke into a trot, and then pulled up right in front of Mr Murray and shoved her nose in the bucket. Heather wasted no time swinging her leg over Lady's side and hopped onto the road. She stood next to the pony for a moment, catching her breath, her eyes open wide, her face a mask of fear. Then, after a moment, she handed the reins to Mr Murray and stepped away, closer to Samuel, who we both knew from the village school. He was a year younger than me and in Heather's class with the other twelve-year-olds. I was the year above them and didn't tend to hang around with the same group of people. Not that anyone was friends with Samuel. No one wanted to be seen dead with him at our school. Thirteen-year-old me thought he was a freak. But I wasn't a nice person then.

I slowed Midnight down to a trot, then a walk, then a halt, and leaped down.

'Are you okay?' Samuel was speaking softly to my sister, leaning slightly over her. He was tall even then.

'Hev?' I asked, hurrying closer.

'I'm all right,' she said, her voice trembling. I could tell that it was taking all of her willpower for her to not burst into tears. She wouldn't, though, not in front of strangers.

'Easy now,' Mr Murray said, gently stroking Lady's sweaty neck. There were froth marks from where the reins had rubbed against her sweaty coat. 'She's all worked up and needs to cool down. We've got a couple of empty stables at the farm. We can put her in one of them and let her rest for a while. I'll call your parents and let them know where you are.'

'All right,' I said.

I remember how Mr Murray was taller and skinnier than my dad, with less hair. He wore one of those blue overalls that all farmers appeared to wear. I've often wondered whether they shop at the same place. Farmers must bump into each other all the time.

'It might take a bit of time for your ponies to cool down,' Mr Murray said. 'Samuel could show you girls around. I know you all go to the same school.'

I was about to open my mouth to suggest we go inside the farmhouse, but Samuel started talking first.

'I'll show you my reptiles if you want,' he said eagerly. 'I have a few snakes and some lizards. They aren't scary.'

'Not sure that's going to make Heather feel any better,' I replied, leading Midnight into the courtyard.

'Why not? Snakes are cool,' he insisted, reminding me why no one at school wanted to be his friend.

'I want to see the snakes,' Heather said, a little brightness back in her voice. Her shell-shocked expression was ebbing away to bring colour to her cheeks again.

'As long as you don't tell anyone at school,' I said, annoyed that Heather seemed intrigued. I remember thinking that she was just pretending to want to see them to cover up her embarrassment over the incident with Lady. 'I don't want people knowing we saw your silly snakes.'

'They're not silly,' Samuel complained. His face scrunched up as though he might burst into tears.

Next to us, Mr Murray shook his head. 'Girls. Give me strength.'

We took the ponies into a block of stables, removed their saddles and bridles, and gave them some water. Lady glugged it down, still stressed and tired after her episode. Mr Murray had to stop her from drinking too fast, pulling her head up for a few moments and then letting it back down again.

'Calm down now, lass,' he said gently.

'What're their names?' Samuel asked, leaning against the stable door. He was wearing cords tucked into wellington boots, and a checked shirt rolled up at the sleeves. Heather was standing close to him, away from the ponies.

'Lady,' she said. 'And she usually behaves like a lady too. Not today, though.'

'Ladies run,' I said, annoyed by my sister's usual prim tone. 'There are loads of women sprinters.'

'Shut up, Rosie. You know what I mean,' she snapped.

Mr Murray backed away. 'When you're done, you can come into the house for a cup of tea and cake. I'm going to call your mum now. She might be worried.'

Heather shrugged. 'Doubt it.' But she whispered it, and I don't think Mr Murray heard as he walked away.

Samuel heard, though, and turned to her. 'Why won't your mum care?'

'She's too busy moping around,' Heather replied. 'She's always "going for a lie-down", unless she's at work.'

I found myself nodding along. 'She does lie down a lot. But not all the time. You're just in a bad mood.'

Heather shot me a glower before picking up one of Mr Murray's curry combs to brush out Lady's coat. The foamy sweat had begun to harden now that she'd cooled down.

'This is all your fault, Rosie,' Heather said as Lady munched on a pile of hay. 'If you hadn't made us gallop up on the grass verge, she wouldn't have thrown a wobbly.'

'No, you should get her used to the tree,' I replied. 'Instead you tense up every time and she freaks out. You should learn how to help her.'

Samuel gazed at us, an expression of frozen awkwardness on his face. 'Do you two always argue?'

We both shrugged at the same time.

'When you're done, I'll show you round the farm if you want,' he said.

'Are you still showing us the snakes?' Heather asked.

'What is it with you and snakes?' I snapped.

'Stop being a wimp, Rosie.'

My jaw dropped. It was bloody rich of Heather to call me a wimp. I had half a mind to push her down for that. But I didn't, because I didn't want to scare Lady again.

'What's your pony called?' Samuel asked, turning to me.

I reached out and stroked Midnight's soft muzzle, proud of my boy. 'Midnight.'

'But he's white,' Samuel said.

'He's grey. See? His muzzle is dark. And he's called Midnight because when the moon is full at night, it's bright white like his coat.'

Samuel frowned as though not getting the logic at all.

'Let's go for that walk around the farm,' Heather suggested, falling into step with Samuel.

I didn't understand what had got into her, or it's possible part of me was jealous of this new secret smile on her lips. All of a sudden it was as though the scary business with Lady had never happened. I was used to Heather following me around, trying to butt into conversations with my friends. Now I was the third wheel, trying to keep up with the two of them, though Samuel intermittently directed the conversation to me, to make sure I wasn't left out.

We went around the milking barns and he showed us the strange equipment that attached to the cows' udders. Then we visited the sheep, and he told us all about lambing season and their border collie who kept the flock together. I remember thinking that he was nicer outside of school, not that I paid much attention to him *at* school. What I had noticed about him was that he tended to play too rough with the younger kids, especially the girls. In fact, I was pretty sure I'd seen him in detention at lunchtime for hurting a girl. His dad had had to come and take him home once. I'd always assumed it was because Samuel didn't get on with anyone in his own year. When he wasn't around the younger kids, he was alone.

'There you are,' Mr Murray said, striding up to the coop where we'd been investigating the chickens. 'I've spoken to your mother, and she's going to come and pick you up with the trailer for the ponies and drive you home. Don't worry,' he said, eyes flicking in Heather's direction, 'you won't have to ride them back. Now, she's going to be an hour or so. Would you like to come in for a drink? Mrs Murray baked a Bakewell tart yesterday.'

As we both nodded our heads enthusiastically, a young boy, about nine or ten, came walking up, dragging his wellies across the grass.

'Who're you?' he said rudely.

I remembered him from school too. Peter Murray. Always scruffy. Light-brown hair that fell into his eyes, and a sullen expression on his face.

'Go away, Peter,' Samuel said, spitting out the words.

'Hey!' The sudden rise in Mr Murray's voice made us all stand up straighter. There was no humour in that tone. 'I've told you not to snap at your brother.'

Samuel dropped his gaze to the grass. 'Sorry.'

'Now come on, let's go inside and wait for your mum.'

The thought of cake made us all forget the little outburst. Heather started walking first, and I joined her.

'You girls should spend some time here this summer if you want,' Mr Murray said. 'Earn some pocket money for helping out.'

Heather's head practically fell off as she nodded enthusiastically.

'We'll have to check with your mum and dad first, though,' he added.

CHAPTER THREE

Heather

Now

When I got back from the hospital yesterday, I wrote Rosie a letter I'll never send, and I put everything into it: all my fears and suspicions that I can't say out loud. They are weights I carry each day, and I thought that if I actually wrote them down, I could alleviate some of the burden. Because she can never know what's in my heart, especially now that she's coming home.

I cannot let go of the fact that there is, and always has been, a part of Rosie that frightens me. She was impulsive and wild as a girl, always running, never walking. She wasn't a tomboy, but she did have an adventurous streak, and her temper was ferocious. She was the kind of girl always in detention at school. She was usually the *only* girl in detention at school.

To distract my wandering thoughts, I go through the papers in the desk drawer that Mum was adamant I organise. In the exact spot Mum described, her will and all the details for the house are organised neatly in a cardboard wallet. The will leaves everything to me and Rosie for us to split equally. I suppose selling the house would be the easiest way to do it, but despite everything, I know I'll find it hard to give up this place.

Why did Mum tell me to sell the house as soon as she died? Was she worried that Rosie and I would fall out over money?

Perhaps it was the setting in the hospital, the fluorescent lights and the gravitas of Mum's condition, but those few words had left me with a sense of dread. A sense that something bad – other than her dying – was going to happen. But then everything said or done in a hospital has another layer of meaning. Whenever I'm with her, there's always the terrible possibility that any words spoken could be our last. Even so, I can't shake the feeling that she was hinting at a larger issue. I just don't understand why she wouldn't come out and say it.

I find myself drifting from room to room, trying to conjure up images from my childhood. The place is dusty and cluttered, which is pretty much how I remember it as a kid, despite the fact that Mum worked as a part-time cleaner. Since coming back to Buckthorpe, I've cleaned the house off and on, half-heartedly dragging a duster over the shelves and ornaments. I don't have the energy for it. Still, I force myself to do it because I hate dust. But I do love the clutter, mostly because it's Mum's clutter.

There are books on every stair of the house, stacked up at the edges in untidy, precarious piles. One thing I remember clearly is how those piles would grow and shrink depending on who was reading what at the time. When I was a child, the stacks were often full of poetry books that Mum would pick up and put down as she tidied the house. Ten minutes of housework, two hours of reading with her feet on the ottoman and a cup of tea in her hand. Then another two hours of writing her own poems, topped off with a last ten minutes of chores.

The walls are adorned with photographs. Me with my red rosette on Lady after winning first place at a gymkhana. Rosie next to me on Midnight, trophy in her hand after beating everyone at jumping. She was the little showjumper in the family, while I was far too cautious for anything dangerous. Then there are family photos of us outside a run-down rust bucket of a caravan, Grandad frowning into the camera lens at the back of the group. Rosie clutches a stuffed bear she won in the slot machines on Blackpool promenade. I have an ice-cream cone and a balloon.

None of the furniture matches in any of the rooms. Outrageous patterns compete for attention: floral sofas, striped curtains, flock wallpaper. There are brown carpets and off-white walls. Purple rugs and dark wooden cabinets. The place still smells of dog beds and old horse rugs. The utility-room shelf is piled high with old leather pieces from the bridles, a box full of metal bits, and at least half a dozen hoof picks.

In the corner, I see Dad's boots on old newspaper, now covered in cobwebs and dried flakes of mud. Mum's dressing gown hangs limply on a hook. I need to sort all of this out, and yet I don't even know where to begin. Part of me wants to preserve it as a strange museum dedicated to the unusual rural life of the Sharpes. *Here on your left you can see my torn wax coat from when I was fourteen, and on your right are Rosie's pink wellington boots with the missing butterfly clasp from when she was eight.*

My mobile-phone ringtone breaks the silence, and my heart jumps into my mouth. I accept the call and breathlessly say hello.

'Heather?'

The world shrinks down as though I'm caught in a vacuum-sealed bag. 'Rosie?'

'Yeah, it's me.'

I pause; I wasn't expecting to hear her voice today. 'Are you all right?'

'I'm okay. I got your email. How's Mum?'

'Not great. She doesn't have long left.' I take a deep breath. 'All she wants is to see you before—'

'I'm on my way,' she says. 'I'm actually on a train. Should be home this evening. That okay?'

'Yeah. Course it is.'

She pauses before she says, 'Good.'

Does she know? Can she hear it in my voice? All I can think about is that moment when I placed the bracelet on the cabinet.

'I'll see you later then,' I say.

'You will.'

We both hang up. I lean against the door frame in the utility room and remain still for a moment, trying to process my thoughts and feelings. There's always wariness when it comes to Rosie; the flickering of nerves in the pit of my stomach, the worry that we'll finally have a confrontation about Samuel's disappearance. And yet there's relief, too. Relief that I won't have to cope with all of this by myself any more. I won't be alone.

I spend the afternoon in the hospital. Because I now know that Rosie is visiting, I work with Susie to make Mum pretty, brushing her hair, painting her nails, moisturising her skin. She's not even sixty years old, and I'm already her carer. The world can be unfair at times, but even now we find moments of happiness. Her breath comes ragged and her arms are weak, but she laughs when Susie tells us a joke. Her eyes brighten when I tell her about my conversation with Rosie over the phone.

But I'm a terrible person, because the entire time we sit there preening and chatting, I feel jealous and resentful of my older sister. Rosie hasn't had to make round trips between London and Buckthorpe to take care of Mum every weekend. She hasn't taken Mum to her chemotherapy appointments and held her hand while the nurses try to find a vein. She hasn't cleaned the vomit from her clothes or painted her nails. And yet Rosie is the person Mum is excited to see.

This should make me happy, shouldn't it? Mum and Rosie reunited after five years. *Me* reunited with my long-lost sister, the girl I loved more than anyone.

But deep down amongst the numbness that has built up since Mum was first diagnosed, there's a wound yet to be healed, one that opened up ten years ago. To me, Rosie will always be the wild little girl with the temper who used to frighten me, and I'll never be able to stop convicting her of a crime in my head.

But I can't let Mum see any of that.

By the time I leave the hospital, the sun is setting over the dales, warming the green fields with an amber glow. This view has soothed me many times over the years, but today the reddish sunset chills my blood. Will Rosie be home when I get back? What are we going to talk about while we sit together in the cottage, alone?

A cool spring breeze whips my hair into my face as I get out of the car and head to the door. Rosie is coming by train – and, I assume, taxi – so I know not to expect another car on the drive. The curtains are as I left them. The door is closed. When I insert my key, it's still locked. I head in, my hands shaking. This is ridiculous. Whatever Rosie might have done to Samuel, she has never been a physical threat to me. I clear my throat and call out a hoarse, 'Hello?'

No answer.

Letting out a sigh of relief, I make my way into the kitchen, hang my coat on the hook and start putting away the few items I stopped for on the way home. Tea bags, milk, tins of soup, bread … things for quick and simple snacks and meals. It's as I have my back to the door, placing the milk in the refrigerator, that the air behind me seems to change. Trying not to panic, I wheel around, almost dropping the milk.

'Hey.' She pushes her hands into the pockets of her jeans. Her long dark hair falls partly over her face but doesn't quite hide her sheepish grin. My eyes travel down to see the suitcase at her feet. 'Sorry I didn't call out. You left the back door open.'

'I just got home,' I explain.

Her appearance has altered dramatically, in a good way, though I was already prepared for this after browsing her Facebook photos. Her face has filled out and her clothes fit snugly against her body.

The last time I saw her she was wearing a dress that hung from her skeletal frame, and her skin and hair were greasy and dull. She isn't wearing make-up, but then she never needed it, and her hair is long and thick, worn loose as it always was when we were teenagers. Her clothes are smart but inexpensive. They aren't the same vest tops and shorts that she wore at university, or the baggy trousers and dresses she wore after.

'Aren't you going to give me a hug?' she says, shrugging her shoulders awkwardly.

'Sure.' I close the fridge door and head over to where she stands by the door to the hallway.

The hug is brief but warm. She smells of the rose perfume she used to wear as a teenager. Mum bought it for her.

'It's the same perfume,' I say, stepping back.

'I bought a bottle on the way up here,' she replies. 'Thought Mum would like it.'

'She will.' Seeing her makes the fear fade away. Rosie isn't physically intimidating, she's just unpredictable, and her past is … worrying. But surely, no matter what she did all those years ago, she wouldn't hurt me. Would she? 'I've been sleeping in our old room, but you can take Grandad's if you want. Or … Mum's.'

Rosie swallows slowly and shakes her head. 'Grandad's.'

I nod, understanding. I wouldn't want to sleep in Mum's room either. It would be like admitting that soon she will be gone; that we're here to replace her.

'Right, well I'd better take my case up.' She gestures to the suitcase by her feet. It's small, the kind that people use as a carry-on when they fly abroad.

'Okay,' I reply. 'Do you want something to eat?'

'Sure,' she says. 'Is Pete's Pizza still open in the village?'

'Still does the pepperoni special, but it's ten quid now.'

She blows air through her lips in mock disgust. 'Used to be a fiver.'

'He reckons it's because of the recession. But we all know it's because there's nowhere else to get takeaway in Buckthorpe.'

Rosie shakes her head and grabs hold of the suitcase handle. 'God, this village. There's no life here, is there? Nothing living at all.'

While Rosie is upstairs settling in, I consider ordering the pepperoni special for old times' sake, but instead I shove some sausages in a frying pan and empty a tin of beans into a saucepan. Frozen oven chips complete the culinary masterpiece. Maybe the pizza would've been a better idea, but I don't have the cash on me, and Pete hasn't woken up to twenty-first-century technology yet. There's no ordering online in Buckthorpe, and only one delivery guy, Luke, who has been complaining about the steep drive to our house for the last decade.

As I'm cooking, I can't stop thinking about what Rosie said about Buckthorpe. Is she right? Has the village stalled and the life been sucked out of it? Maybe that's why those happy memories I have here are almost dreamlike. While I've grown up and moved on, Buckthorpe is stuck in the past. I've never been here for a wedding, because most of my old school friends have moved away and made their lives elsewhere. I only ever come back to Buckthorpe for Christmas and funerals. And now, to nurse Mum until she dies.

'That smells divine.' Rosie hovers in the kitchen doorway again. She's showered and dressed casually in cut-off jean shorts and a white T-shirt, making her look more like the Rosie I know, compared to the smart trousers and blouse she was wearing before. 'Are they from Murrays' farm shop?' She finally enters the room and saunters over to the cooker.

Hearing Rosie say that name sends a shiver down my spine. 'Yep.'

Her face pales as she stares down at the pan. 'Well, they do sell the best. I take back every bad word I said against ole Buckers.

The farm shops are incredible.' She climbs onto the breakfast-bar stool and lifts one foot to rest on the seat. Her other leg dangles, toes trailing the lino. It's like we're teenagers again, and I can hardly bear it.

'You all right?' she asks.

I throw down the spatula and she winces at the clatter. 'No, I'm not all right. For four months I've been coming here every weekend, and sometimes during the week as well. I'm barely hanging onto my job. I'm pretty sure they're going to fire me when I eventually go back. Oh, and Simon dumped me because we never saw each other. And do you know why?'

She cocks her head to one side, face stone cold. 'Did you throw spatulas at him, too?'

'Because I've been taking Mum to the hospital. I've done *everything* and you didn't even respond to my emails when Mum was diagnosed. You changed your phone number and fucked off as usual.'

For a few seconds her expression remains emotionless. I've gone too far, I know I have, but I couldn't stop it all from blurting out. I prepare myself for an angry outburst, but then her shoulders slump and her voice softens. 'I was in rehab, Hev. You know what I've been through, don't you?' She leans forward, reaching out over the pan, but then pulls her hand away as though burned by the heat from the stove. 'I'm ill.' She says it nonchalantly, with a shrug. 'Do you know what it's like to want to drink yourself to death every day?'

'No,' I mumble.

She raises her eyebrows in an 'I told you so' way. 'I have to fight to stop myself from doing just that.' As she clenches her fists, I see the long red welts on her forearms – her scars from self-harming. They started after Samuel went missing. She shakes her head a little, and her cheeks flush, reminding me of her temper tantrums as a child. Then she slams both fists down on the counter. 'You've never understood, have you? Because you're so *perfect* all the time!'

'That's not true,' I say, though with less conviction than my first outburst. The fighting has started early. It usually takes us at least two hours of being in each other's company before we row. 'I have my problems too, you know.'

'You mean the decent job? The nice flat? Being the favourite kid?' She straightens her leg and sits upright. 'You'll never be the fuck-up. You're not the one who passed out behind the sofa at Dad's wake.'

When a spit of fat burns my arm, I reduce the heat and let out a long sigh. 'Let's not talk about Dad.'

'Why? Because he killed himself? Maybe we *should* talk about it, Hev, because maybe whatever darkness drove him to it is in me.' I watch as the anger seeps out of her as quickly as it flared. She lowers her voice and relaxes her body. 'Listen, I'm serious. We should talk about it. Our family has a history of not talking about important things, doesn't it?'

I freeze. Is she referring to the night Samuel went missing?

'We always thought it was Mum who had that depressive side to her, didn't we?' Rosie says, her voice trailing off as though lost in thought. I wrap my arms around my body and frown. She might be sober, but her emotions are still unstable. 'But in the end, it was Dad who put the shotgun—'

'Don't.' I raise my hands. 'Please don't say it.'

She steps down from the stool and makes her way around the counter to stand by my side. 'Do you ever think that we blinkered ourselves from the signs on purpose?'

'What do you mean?'

'When I remember our childhood now, it seems obvious that Dad was in pain. Don't you think?'

'No.' I shrug. 'Not to me.'

'Really? All those jobs he took away from the family? The fact that he hardly talked to Mum when they were alone?'

'Mum and Dad talked,' I reply, hearing the note of uncertainty in my voice. It's true that Dad often worked away from home, but it was because he was providing for us. He did it to earn extra money and pay for our university tuition fees, not because he didn't want to be around us.

Rosie tucks a strand of hair behind my ear. 'Yeah. Maybe they did. Sorry, Hev, I'm rambling.'

She makes her way back to the stool and crosses one leg over the other. I stare down at the sausages and realise that I've lost my appetite. All I can think about is my dad in pain, with no one to help him. Rosie could be right about the darkness inside him. But what I don't know is how much darkness there is inside my sister, and how dangerous she might be.

CHAPTER FOUR

Rosie

Then

The day Heather almost fell off Lady wasn't the first encounter I'd had with one of the Murrays. For some reason, Samuel and I pretended we'd never met before, but that actually wasn't true. No, there was another occasion before the day at the Murrays' farm when I'd spent some time with Samuel outside of school.

It was about six months before that day, during a relatively mild February. I'd been reading lots of fantasy books about female warriors, and fancied myself a budding fierce girl like them. After an unsuccessful attempt at a fist fight in the playground, I decided I needed a weapon.

This, of course, was all completely logical to my thirteen-year-old self. And because we lived in Buckthorpe, where nothing bad ever happened, Mum and Dad allowed me to roam around as much as I wanted. Which meant that the first thing I did was wrap up in my winter coat and wellies and head into the woods for an appropriate stick. I was about to make myself a bow and arrow.

However, my knowledge of bows was minimal. All I knew was that I needed to make the wood curve or bend in some way to enable me to tie the string. Using the limited information from my fantasy books, as well as a memory of a TV version of Robin Hood, I began to whittle down a thin branch into what I thought resembled the limb of a bow. As I worked, I sat on a rock next to the path, smiling at the occasional dog walker as they passed. It was a quiet part of the forest. Most people go to see the famous gorge five miles out of Buckthorpe village, meaning that barely anyone who didn't live here walked this path.

'What're you doing?'

The boy's voice came from behind me. When I turned around, he was staring at the abandoned twigs on the ground that I'd ended up snapping.

'Making a bow,' I replied.

I knew Samuel was in Heather's year at school. I also knew that he was a weirdo who'd killed his pet lizard back in primary school; at least that was what everyone said.

He snorted as though he didn't believe me. 'Yeah, right.'

I frowned. 'Fuck off then.'

'No, wait,' he said in a gentle voice as I moved away from him. 'I want to see. Are you *really* making a bow? That's pretty cool.'

The compliment worked, because I stopped and showed him my work. 'It's supposed to be supple enough to bend when I tie the string on both sides. But they all keep snapping.'

'That's because you're using brittle wood,' Samuel said. 'See?' He picked up one of my abandoned twigs and snapped it. 'The wood is dead, so it'll never bend.'

'Oh,' I replied, feeling like a complete idiot. 'I guess it was a stupid idea anyway.'

'What do you want the bow for?'

'Hunting, I guess,' I replied. 'I don't know.'

He laughed and sat next to me on the rock. For the first time I noticed that he had dark-blue eyes, like the water deep down on the ocean floor. 'You're not supposed to hunt in these woods.'

'So?'

He was obviously impressed by my phoney rebelliousness.

'Hey, you could make a spear,' he suggested. 'You just need a long branch with a pointed end.'

We wandered further into the woods in search of the perfect branch to whittle into a spear. Neither of us had decided what we'd use the spear for if we actually completed it, but it was nice to have some company.

'Where's your sister today?' Samuel asked as we sat back down on the rock with the new piece of wood.

'I ditched her,' I admitted. 'She hangs around with me too much.'

'I know what you mean,' Samuel replied. 'I have a little brother who does that too. He's always whining. It gets on my nerves.'

'Heather isn't whiny,' I said. 'But she hates mucking about. She gets stressed out if I do anything that isn't allowed. She always follows the rules.'

Samuel grinned. I didn't get it then, but now I know it was because he thought of himself as someone who didn't follow the rules either, and he liked that about himself.

'My brother was adopted,' he said. 'So I guess we're not even related, even though it does feel like he's my brother.'

'I didn't know that,' I said. 'That's cool.'

'Yeah. Mum couldn't have any kids after me, but she wanted me to have a brother or sister, so they adopted Peter. I guess he loves it here, but he's kinda hard to get used to sometimes.'

'Does he know he's adopted?'

'Yeah,' Samuel said. 'We told him a couple of years ago. He wanted to know why he has brown eyes and we don't. Mum and Dad decided to tell him everything, but he seems okay with it.'

I nodded.

'Hey, that's pretty sharp now,' he said. 'You could definitely kill a rabbit with it.' But after Samuel said the words, his grin faded. 'Are you actually going to hunt anything?'

I gazed at the spear and pictured a dead, bloodied animal hanging from it. Suddenly I wasn't sure whether I wanted to be a warrior after all. But I couldn't deny that there was a certain power I enjoyed about having my own weapon.

Before I could answer, I heard a man's voice calling Samuel's name. His face dropped, and he kicked a stone with the toe of his boot.

'I've got to go. I was only supposed to be gone twenty minutes, and it's been at least forty, I reckon.' He stood up and dusted down his jeans. 'But it was nice to talk to you.'

I nodded back. 'See you then.'

'Yeah,' he said, with a hopeful note in his voice. 'See you at school.'

But I never acknowledged our encounter in the woods again. Back at school, I ignored him like I always did, even when he nodded a hello at me the Monday after. I think it was embarrassment that stopped Samuel from referencing our brief time in the woods. Looking back, I realise that I rejected Samuel by ignoring him at school. In his own way he was reaching out, searching for allies, hoping for a friend, and I rejected him.

It's possible that this made me especially complicit in changing him from a gentle boy to the person I feared just a few years later.

CHAPTER FIVE

Heather

Now

At six a.m., I get the call. It's *the* call. Mum is struggling to breathe, and the doctors don't think she has long left.

Rosie pulls on a top and a pair of jeans, doesn't bother brushing her hair. I rush to the car in my slippers and have to run back to get flat pumps. It's no time for footwear with complicated zips and laces; we need to be quick.

Rosie lets out a long, exhausted breath. 'I thought I'd have more time with her.'

I lean over to her in the passenger side of the car and squeeze her shoulder. 'So did I.' This must be terrible for her: to arrive one day to spend time with Mum, only to get the call the next morning.

When we arrive at the hospital, I'm grateful to see Susie on the ward. She pulls me into a quick hug and leads us into the room, all the time holding my hand. She's been with me from the first day Mum was admitted for palliative care. There's no time to explain who Rosie is, but I think she knows anyway.

'I'll get you both a tea,' she says.

I can't imagine wanting to drink tea, but at the same time I haven't eaten or drank anything since our quick meal of sausages and beans the night before. And I haven't even brushed my teeth.

'Mum, look who's here,' I say, somehow keeping the emotion out of my voice.

Rosie steps towards the bed with her chin wobbling and her eyes wide. She raises a hand to her mouth and her body goes rigid as she begins to cry. I find that I have to turn away, because there are tears in my eyes too. Watching her overcome with emotion transports me back to ten years ago, when I last saw that expression on her face. We were standing in the kitchen, just before our lives changed forever. Now Rosie is scrunched up in a girlish way, completely distraught and broken. My heart leaps around in my chest because I want to fix everything for both of them, but I don't know how.

Mum is pale, with flaky dark skin around her eyes. Out of habit, I take a little pot of moisturiser from my bag and dab it on. Her eyes are open, but they are misty and unfocused. Her chest rises and falls with shallow breaths. The change in her is significant compared to yesterday. I can hardly believe it. I smooth her hair and kiss her lightly on the forehead before moving away from the bed to allow her and Rosie space to reunite.

'Hey, Mum.' Rosie has finally managed to compose herself, and she sits down on the chair near Mum's head. 'It's good to see you.'

'Rosie,' Mum whispers.

I clear my throat, direct my gaze away from them, the tears stinging my eyes. I've always hated crying in front of other people, even my family.

'Is it really you?'

'It's me, Mum. Sorry I didn't come sooner,' she says, and I believe her. At least, I want to believe her, because she seems utterly heartbroken.

When I allow myself to look again, I notice Mum's fingers twitching.

'I think she wants to touch you, but she's too weak,' I say.

Rosie nods. She reaches out and takes Mum's hand. 'I've been in rehab, Mum. Getting better. I wanted to come sooner, but …' Her voice wobbles. 'Well, I was ill. I'm sorry.'

'Don't be.' Mum's voice is a raspy whisper.

'Do you want a drink, Mum?' I ask.

She shakes her head.

While Rosie talks about rehab, I find myself pacing back and forth, full of nervous energy. When Susie returns with the tea, I want it after all. God bless her. At least my mum has known kindness in the late stages of her life. Unselfish kindness.

'Hev.' Rosie's voice pulls me back from my thoughts. 'Mum wants to talk to you.'

I rush to the bedside, only remembering that I'm holding a mug of tea when I reach the chair. Rosie takes it and puts it on a nearby table. I hold Mum's hand and wait patiently for her to speak.

'I want you to know,' she says, the words causing her precious energy, 'that I never regretted anything, and that I love you very much.'

'I love you too, Mum.'

She slipped away in her sleep three hours later, and despite the four months of nursing, the weeks of build-up, and the knowledge that she could go at any time, it still felt sudden, as though I wasn't prepared for it. But it was in death that she appeared her age again. The cancer had crept up little by little, adding decades to her appearance, but now that she was at peace, she was back to how she looked before.

And it was at that moment that relief washed over me. It was brief, but it was there. After it went away, my stomach lurched.

Rosie placed her head in her hands and sobbed. I just sat there, staring at Mum, thinking about how beautiful she was now that she had passed away, wondering what was wrong with me.

We've been sitting by her now for almost thirty minutes, with Rosie crying and me silent.

'Take your time, girls,' Susie says. 'Stay with her as long as you need.' But there's an edge to her voice suggesting that it's time for us to leave this room. By telling us we can stay, she's reminding us that at some point we need to go.

I'm not sure Rosie can hear her over the sound of her own tears. But Susie's voice brings me back to reality, and I wrap an arm around Rosie's shoulder, holding her tight.

'What happens now?' I ask. My voice is so hoarse, it surprises me that Susie can even hear me.

'Well,' she says gently, 'we'll take her down to the mortuary. You can help us with that, or we can take care of everything. It's entirely up to you. Then we'll issue a certificate and you use that to register her death.' She continues giving her advice, and I nod along, but at the sound of the word 'death' I begin to hear a high-pitched ringing in my ears. She hands me a tissue and I realise that I'm crying too. 'I'm so sorry, girls. Iris was a wonderful woman. You can tell the kind people, the truly kind ones, from the way they are when they're in pain. Your mum was one of those.'

Rosie lifts her head and wipes away the tears on her cheeks. 'We were lucky to have her as our mum. Weren't we, Hev?'

All I can do is nod my head. I can't speak any more.

'I can't stand the thought of her in that horrible cold little room,' Rosie says.

My fingers wrap tightly around the steering wheel. 'It's just temporary. Once we get in touch with the funeral directors, she can be taken to the chapel of rest. It'll be … nicer there.'

'None of it's nice.'

'I guess it's the best we've got.' My tone is a little snappier than I intend it to be. But Rosie doesn't appear to notice. Despite the windy day, she rolls down the window and holds her hand out, spreading her fingers.

'Do you think we'll get it too?' she says. 'It's genetic, isn't it? Everyone dies young in our family.'

'You can be tested for the gene if you want. I think I'm going to do it.' I pause. 'Grandad didn't die young. And Dad killed himself.'

'I guess,' she says in an absent-minded tone. 'Grandad was one of those old codgers running on bitterness and old-man anger until his eighties.'

'I take it you miss him, then?'

We both exchange a glance with thin smiles. Mum's death happened sooner than I'd anticipated, but I had known it was going to happen. Still, the tiniest of jokes brings back the churning in my stomach. It reminds me of the relief I felt when Mum's face relaxed and she finally let go of life. It reminds me of the guilt.

It's almost an hour since we left the hospital, and we've both managed to get our emotions back under control. Maybe I shouldn't feel guilty about the relief I'd felt as she passed away. It wasn't relief that Mum was gone. No, I'll miss her every day for the rest of my life. The relief was for her, that she wasn't in pain any more. But it still feels strange to say anything lighthearted to each other. And yet at the same time, it wouldn't feel right to still be sobbing.

Rosie sighs. 'We should make everything perfect for her. The funeral, the wake. I know I ruined Dad's wake. I can never take that back. But I can help you with Mum's.'

'Thanks,' I reply. 'We'll organise it together if that's what you want.'

'What did she say to you at the end?'

'Oh, that she loved me.' I pause, considering holding back the rest. 'She also said that she didn't regret anything.'

'That's weird. Because she told *me* that she was sorry. She didn't say what for, though. It made me feel as though she did have some regrets.'

'I guess she wasn't quite herself, what with all the drugs,' I reply. 'Maybe her thoughts were jumbled up.'

'Yeah, you're probably right.' Rosie shakes her head. 'She might not have any regrets, but I do. I could build a whole new version of me just by stacking up all my regrets. During the rehab process I'm supposed to forgive myself. But I'm not sure I ever will.'

'I'm sure you ...' but I find my voice drifting off, because Rosie has done some unforgivable things. And while I know that she's been ill, I'm still struggling with the idea of forgiving her for them.

Silence fills the car. My silence, in particular, speaks loud and clear. It means that I think she's right. Moving my hand from the wheel, I stretch out my fingers towards the radio control, then think better of it. Maybe silence is better.

'It's okay,' Rosie says. 'I don't expect you to forgive me either.'

I shake my head. 'You're my sister.' *And I love you*. I'm not sure why I can't say that out loud. I'm too similar to Dad – terse to the point of making people uncomfortable. The occasional hug was as much emotion as you could get with him.

'That doesn't absolve me of anything.'

'It means that I'm here for you no matter what. It means we're a team.' But even as I say the words, I can't tell if I mean them. I want to, but there's always that night between us, acting as a wedge. A Samuel Murray-shaped wedge. Always making me wonder what my sister is capable of.

Right on cue, we pass the edge of the land belonging to the Murrays. It never changes here. There's still the rusting five-bar gate to the road, the dry-stone walls topped with barbed wire, the stretching fields of sheep. Further up, near where the weird tree used to be, is the entrance to the courtyard, with the sign on the road for fresh milk and eggs at the shop. In a few months there'll be a sign for Christmas-turkey bookings too.

And as my eyes roam the length of the estate, I see the three of us, young and innocent, running around chasing the chickens.

Just kids. Me, Rosie and Samuel. We started going to the Murrays' when I was barely twelve years old. The two of us hacked our ponies over to the farm and let them graze in the paddock as we collected eggs, mucked out the barns and swept up spilled hay for the cattle. Every summer we spent all our time there, racing each other through the yard with Samuel's younger brother Peter lagging behind, never truly part of the group. They were the happiest days of my life.

Until every day of that happiness became tainted by what happened next. A shiver runs down my spine as I think about Rosie standing in the kitchen, her clothes filthy, the tracks of tears in the dirt on her face. She was seventeen then, while I was sixteen, but up until that day we'd still been working on the farm every summer.

Rosie turns away from the Murrays' field, but I don't. I stare at it, and I think about the night she came home in tears. We never went to the farm again.

CHAPTER SIX

Rosie

Then

I never told Heather about meeting Samuel in the woods that day, and I'm not sure why I never told her. There was the fact that Samuel was hated at school, but there was another reason too. One I didn't quite understand at thirteen years old. It could be because I was trying to protect that experience. To make it mine and mine alone. Or it's possible I'd felt the burgeoning of an attraction towards Samuel but was too young to understand it. Perhaps it was a little of both.

When Samuel and Heather hit it off from the start, I realised I was grateful that he never mentioned our hour or so creating a weapon in the woods. And it made me feel as if we had a secret, though that also brought with it conflicting feelings of guilt. All these complicated teenage emotions could explain why I was snappy and off with him at the farm, because I knew he was keeping my secret for me, and I was oddly scared that he'd reveal it to my sister. Hev and I weren't supposed to have secrets. We'd spit on the stones near the bluebell field and make promises to each other. We never kept anything from each other.

And yet … I still loved having an experience she couldn't touch. Samuel was someone Heather knew from school. He was in her year and some of her classes, so when I spent time with him whittling a spear, I had a one-up on her and I enjoyed the fact that she knew nothing about it. Not that the feeling lasted. When Heather and Samuel became friends, I suddenly became the person on the outside looking in, and mine and Samuel's secret faded into insignificance.

Mum was in a terrible mood when she collected us from the Murrays' that first time. Our old Jeep dragged the rusting trailer behind it, rattling along the roads. Grandad was in the passenger seat, and he was enjoying the trip out, it seemed, because he'd taken up the offer of a cup of tea and a slice of Bakewell tart while we loaded the ponies into the trailer.

'She's not going to let you come back, is she?' Samuel had said, glancing first at Heather, then at me.

'Yeah,' I agreed. 'I doubt it.'

The truth is, I didn't want her to let us back there, not after watching my sister make friends with a boy I potentially liked.

'She will.' Heather was the most confident about it, and she was right.

The next day, we rode our ponies back to the farm, and this time Heather kicked Lady on as the weird tree came into view. Even though her body tensed with nerves, she gritted her teeth, pressed her heels into Lady's flanks and remained firm with her. I didn't say anything, but I was proud of her.

I remember not knowing what to expect when we got there, but we soon learned what was required of us. Mr Murray showed us where we could keep the ponies while we worked. Because they weren't as agitated this time, we decided to let them into the paddock to enjoy the sunshine and have a graze. He had already arranged for a trough to be set up with water, giving them everything they needed.

'Right then, girls,' he said. 'You can collect the eggs, fill the feeders with slop for the pigs, and muck out the cow shed while they're in the fields. What do you want to do first?'

'Let's do the eggs,' Samuel said.

'All right,' Heather said keenly.

He glanced over at me and twisted one corner of his mouth up in a tentative grin. 'That all right?'

'Guess so,' I said, my thoughts still on the day in the woods months ago. Still smarting that Heather was the one he usually talked to first. My bad mood was evident to Heather too, because she turned and glared at me. She wanted to have a day of fun and I was wrecking it all by being glum. She was right to be annoyed; I was being a moody cow.

We followed Samuel over to the chicken coop, which was behind the farmhouse. The hens clucked and pecked and moved in a comical way that made us all laugh. He picked one of them up, carefully holding its wings down, and showed us how you could move it all around and its head stayed in the same position.

'They have weird necks,' he said, chuckling as he lifted the hen up and down. 'It's hilarious.'

Still moody, I rolled my eyes, but Heather laughed and gently petted the bird as Samuel held it tight.

'Show me again how you pick them up,' she said.

Samuel demonstrated. The hen seemed to sense what was about to happen and lowered its little body towards the ground, clucking nervously. He gently wrapped his hands around it, clamping down the wings, and lifted it up.

Heather had a go next, but she was clumsy and the bird ran away when she moved too quickly. We all laughed at her attempt. Even me. The sweet little creatures were warming me up and I was starting to relax.

Samuel's dark-blue eyes fell on me. Even at twelve, he had a seriousness about his expression that meant you kind of enjoyed it when his attention fell on you. It was a strange sensation, being held in that attention. As a popular girl, I wasn't supposed to fancy a boy younger than me, and I especially wasn't supposed to fancy one who was mostly regarded as a freak. But there was definitely a prickle at the back of my neck when he glanced at me.

'What about you, Rosie?' he said in that quiet voice I remembered from the day in the woods. 'Do you want to have a go?' The chicken wriggled a little and he held it closer to his torso. I remember that he was wearing one of those awful black T-shirts with a rock band logo on the front. Some sort of death-metal band that did his reputation no good at our small village school. The first rule of a small school was to not make yourself a target, and thinking back, I've realised that Samuel failed miserably at that.

Samuel placed the hen back on the ground and I hovered over it, waiting for it to huddle down before gently placing my hands over its wings. The bird weighed almost nothing as I lifted it into the air. It bobbed its head and clucked, its suspended legs scrabbling.

'You're a natural,' he said.

When I felt the hen begin to struggle out of my hands, I placed it back down and rubbed my hands against my jodhpurs. The chickens had a sweet, putrid smell that I didn't particularly want to carry with me for the rest of the day.

'Shall we get the eggs, then?' Heather said. She had her arms crossed over her body and was glowering at me. Heather, someone who excelled at everything she put her mind to, hated it when anyone was better than her at anything.

'Yeah, come on,' Samuel said. 'We might even see one of the hens laying.'

Heather didn't look at me as she followed Samuel up the ramp into the coop. We'd forget about this moment later and spend the evening practising eyeshadow application with some of Mum's old collections, but at the time, it was a real betrayal. It made *me* the boring sister, dragging down the mood. With the funny little secrets and the boy I thought I might like, there was a strange atmosphere between the two of us.

And if I'm honest, it might have been that moment that changed a lot between the three of us.

CHAPTER SEVEN

Heather

Now

Spring presents Buckthorpe at its most glorious. Bluebells carpet the woods, golden hour touches the green dales outside the village and makes the place glow, and the mornings are cool enough for a long walk without breaking a sweat. I walk alone through Buckbell Woods, drinking it all in: the slight dampness of the earth after overnight rainfall, the silver bark of the birches, and the bobbing branches bending with the breeze. There is birdsong overhead and the throaty call of the occasional crow. I used to walk Buster here, watching as his nose trailed through the muddy ground, doggy saliva dripping on the forest floor. Or I would ride Lady, giving her the reins, leaning back to inhale the fresh scent of a spring morning. Before Rosie turned sixteen, she used to come with me too. But as soon as her sweet sixteen arrived, she changed. Having a dull little sister tagging along wherever she went annoyed her.

Not that we were completely inseparable before she turned sixteen. She would often sneak away for whatever mischief she was up to that day. She was clever enough to know that she couldn't break any rules around me, because I was a useless liar if Mum asked me a direct question. But it was when she was sixteen that I noticed her not wanting to spend any time with me at all.

Out of habit, I didn't even think to wake Rosie before I left the cottage. I also wanted to be alone. After a late night of food, talking and grieving, I assumed she'd want to sleep in. But I found myself awake at dawn, imbued with a ton of anxious energy. Being in the house only reminded me of the routine I'd become accustomed to while taking care of Mum. A routine that was no longer needed. There was the morning check-in with the hospital, the packed lunch I'd make myself to eat in her hospital room, the change of clothes that I'd take for her – not that she got dressed properly in the last week or so. The tissues and wipes I'd pack. The sensible shoes I'd wear for walking through the long, winding corridors.

But all that was over, and now it was time to move on to the other practical things relating to illness and death, the things I'm desperate to delay because it all feels too real. Calling work to request more compassionate leave. Registering the death. Choosing which funeral home to hire. The coffin. The service. The food. The newspaper announcement.

None of those scary tasks are here beneath the trees. Here, I can breathe. My spine tingles as I walk on towards the clearing where the bluebells flourish. They opened last week, and we're never sure how long they'll last. They are as stunning as I remember. A carpet of soft violet-blue spreads from my feet to the close-knit copse of trees beyond. I bend down, resting back on my heels in a low squat, and let out a long, deep breath. Then I allow myself to pick one perfect flower.

My mother's name was Iris. She named us both after flowers in the same way her mother had named her girls. I'm not sure how far back the naming ritual extends, but I know it's at least three generations of Lily and Iris and Hyacinth and Daisy and Rose and Azalea. Thank goodness I'm not a Daisy or an Azalea. No, I'm Heather, though that has always felt wrong for me, evoking the wild and windy moors of a Brontë novel.

I straighten up from my crouched position and examine the bluebell in my fingers. It calms me at first, because it reminds me of walks with Mum, where she'd identify the different kinds of flowers to me. Snapdragons and bluebells were my favourite, but daffodils were Mum's. Rosie claimed her favourite flower was a rose, but that was only because of her name. Her secret favourite flower is the orchid. It's as I think about Rosie that the cold seeps in under my jacket. Yes, it is spring, but the nip of winter hasn't left the air just yet. Also, this is where I found Rosie's bracelet all those years ago, and that chill has never gone away.

She'd gone to bed wearing that bracelet and woken up without it, and I'd found it in the woods on the same night Samuel disappeared. I've never told a single person.

As I leaned in to Mum at the hospital and heard her whisper her dying words to me, I had a thought that I kept to myself. On the way home, as Rosie and I talked about our last moments with Mum, I chose not to tell my sister what had been going through my mind as Mum uttered those last words.

She told me she didn't have any regrets, but I do have a regret. I wish I hadn't ignored what Rosie did the night Samuel went missing. I wish I'd at least tried to find out where she'd been.

But it isn't too late. We're here together in Buckthorpe for the first time since Dad died. I don't want to live my life with regrets; I want to finally find out what happened. Maybe it can be the last thing I do before I leave this place forever.

The hastily scribbled note on the fridge tells me that Rosie has gone out for eggs and bacon. When I check the back of it, I see that she tore the scrap from a bill I need to pay. No doubt she picked up whatever was to hand and scrawled on it without thinking. My sister never changes – always living the whirlwind approach to life, rarely slowing down to see how her actions affect the world around her.

It's ridiculous to resent her for that, but part of me does. When we were children I was forever righting her wrongs, clearing up what she'd spilled, fixing the clothes she'd torn and didn't want Mum to see.

Until I stopped doing those things for her and she fell apart.

I put the note back underneath a magnet of Blackpool Tower and make my way into the living room. There, atop the side table, is the phone. The sight of it reminds me of my tasks. The funeral home. My boss. The flowers … I can't. Instead I take myself up to Rosie's room, where Grandad used to sleep. Outside, I hesitate. Should I go in? The door is open a crack, with morning light filtering out onto the corridor. What would rummaging through her things even accomplish? She wouldn't be stupid enough to have kept any convenient evidence of a ten-year-old crime.

I lean away from the doorway and close my eyes for a moment. Impulsively diving into someone's belongings isn't who I am. As far as I'm concerned, rules exist for a reason. If I'm going to find out what happened to Samuel, I have to do it right, and I have to be logical. For one thing, he might have run away, or been killed by someone else, or even committed suicide. I roll my shoulders, uncomfortable with all of those thoughts. I open my eyes and hug my body for warmth.

Rather than trespass into my sister's space, I cross the landing and enter Mum's bedroom. The place is a mess. Boxes of medication are stacked in precarious towers along the top of the chest of drawers. They were all over the kitchen, but I moved them here when she went into hospital for her final weeks. The bedding is rumpled, though I did straighten it up a little last time I was in here. Everything clashes. The newish IKEA bed is an odd juxtaposition with the enormous antique wardrobe. I run my fingers along the dark mahogany. This wardrobe has been here forever. It was here before me, and I hate to imagine how it could ever be removed.

Opening the wardrobe for the first time since Mum died is something I should be doing with Rosie, but once it's done, it's done. My fingertips trail the length of Mum's clothes, as well as some of Dad's shirts. On the shelf above the rail are messy piles of jumpers and trousers. I reach up and touch the soft wool, then drop to my knees and part the dresses and shirts, because there is one item of my mother's that I've always wanted to see but was never allowed to as a child.

Beyond the sea of cotton and polyester, right at the back of the wardrobe, are several shoeboxes piled on top of each other. I pull out the first one and lift the lid. Inside are bundles of old photographs, which I thumb through quickly. Grandad with Rosie on his lap. Dad with a hammer in his hand fixing the fencing around the paddock. Mum wearing her glasses, a pen twisted into her hair. This is not the box I'm searching for. I delve back into the depths of the wardrobe to bring out more boxes. Once I have them all, I spread them out on the bed and begin removing the lids. I'm sure I'll want to examine all of these old photographs at some point, but for now I'm looking for something else.

The fourth box is filled with notebooks. Slim pocket notebooks that Mum used to slip into her old-fashioned farmer's-wife-style skirts. I begin opening them and reading. This is what I wanted to find – Mum's poetry.

What power it had over us all those years ago. Mum, cross-legged on the sofa, pen in hand, notebook on her lap, lost to her world. If we were desperate for attention during this time, we'd be shushed. She was entitled to a little peace and quiet every now and then, she would say, irritated and snappy. This was her way of de-stressing: to scribble words down in these books. There are dozens of them from over the years, each containing private thoughts that we were never privy to.

My heart flutters, like wings against my chest. *These are her words.*

Dreamlike light under green,
Hazy, low sun wants to be seen.
Our feet tread, crunch and slide,
I loved to walk by your side.

After all these years … after living with a woman who kept her thoughts and feelings tightly locked away, here they are. And I don't know what to feel now that I'm faced with these private thoughts. All I know is that a dull ache forms in my abdomen as I continue reading.

You were kind once,
I remember that,
Like an aftertaste
Turned sour …

Most of the poems are only a stanza or two. I wish I knew who she was writing about.

I long for the days
When regrets were simple.
You killed me.

Regrets again. What did you mean, Mum? Did you once have regrets but forgave yourself later? Did you come to terms with whatever you did? There are so many questions that can now never be answered. I mentally berate myself for not opening this box earlier. I was tempted to, of course, but that would have been sacrilege. I couldn't have faced her if I'd snooped through her poetry while she was alive.

But at the same time, if she hadn't wanted me to read her poems, wouldn't she have destroyed them when she found out she was ill? Why didn't she tell me more about who she was, about who the people in these verses were? Were the poems about Dad? *You were kind once.* I read on, skipping over the short lines of text. *Forbidden once and now lost, you were the one I wanted most.* Mum loved fiercely, something I never realised when I was young. Have I ever loved a man with this fervour? My face flushes at the thought of my parents involved in a passionate love affair with each other.

I dig deeper into the box and find a few scraps of paper with more verses scrawled on them. At some point Mum moved on to typing her poems on the computer, probably as arthritis set in, and one catches my eye:

Blame the blue,
Guilt the trees,
Curse the sleep,
We were complicit.

Yours to start,
Mine to end,
Dark to light,
In death illicit.

'What are you reading?'

The sudden voice at the door makes me bite my tongue as I inhale a gasp. I twist my body to see Rosie with her arms folded across her chest and a deep frown creasing her face. As soon as I recover from the shock – and the tongue bite – a flush of guilt warms my face.

'I was just—'

'It didn't take you long to start nosing through Mum's poetry.' There's a hard note to her voice that I can't ignore. And she's right, of course: I am poking around in our mum's personal belongings. Before I can say anything, though, she steps forward and leans over my shoulder. 'Who knew Mum was such an emo?' Her lips turn up into a half-smile, but I see a reticence in her expression. I didn't notice at first because I felt caught out with the poetry, but Rosie's skin is pale and waxy.

'Is everything all right?' I ask.

She nods. 'Yes, but we have an unexpected guest.'

CHAPTER EIGHT

Heather

Now

Mum's old-fashioned kettle begins to whistle as I follow Rosie down the stairs. She goes into the kitchen while at the same time giving me a sisterly shove towards the living room. She obviously doesn't want to deal with our visitor. I find myself stepping into the lounge to see Sergeant Ian Dixon sitting on the sofa.

He raises a hand. 'Hi, Heather.'

'Oh, hi,' I say. 'Is there something wrong?'

He's dressed in his uniform, which puts me on edge, but it's not as though he has never visited before. I wouldn't say he's a family friend, but he is well known in the village, having grown up here before joining the police. The station is located in Ingledown, the main town a few miles over, but all the villagers know him well. I suppose it's fair to say he's an authority figure in Buckthorpe, especially after being promoted to sergeant.

'Don't worry, I'm not here on official business.'

I sweep stray hairs away from my face and find a spot opposite Ian in one of the old floral armchairs. It's not the most comfortable seat in the house; in fact, as soon as I sit, a spring pokes through the fabric, prodding the flesh on my backside. Still, it's less awkward than sitting side by side on the sofa.

'Then what can we help you with?' I ask, attempting to sound comfortable with him being in the house, forcing too much cheer into my voice.

'Well, I heard that Rosie was visiting,' he says, smiling.

Right on cue, Rosie carries a tray of tea and biscuits into the room, and Ian watches as she places it on the coffee table. She kneels on the carpet and busies herself pouring the tea, not once glancing in his direction. I can't help but focus on the tension between them.

'That's right,' I say. 'As you know, Mum has been ill. Actually, she passed away yesterday.'

His smile fades, transforming into an earnest, sombre expression with lowered eyes. He shakes his head sadly. 'I'm so sorry. I shouldn't have come. I didn't realise.'

Rosie tilts her head in my direction, but I can't quite make out her expression. As she hands Ian his cup of tea, she keeps her gaze low. Even though her expression is unreadable, I can tell by the anxious way she taps one nail against the porcelain that she's hoping I'll get rid of him quickly.

'It's okay,' I reply. 'Feel free to stay and finish your drink.'

Rosie's eyes narrow. She's clearly pissed off that I've let a golden opportunity slip through my fingers. Why doesn't she want him in the house? But rather than say anything, she picks up her own cup and sits cross-legged on the floor, leaving me to get my own. I suppress the urge to roll my eyes as I lean forward for the last teacup.

'Your mum was a lovely lady,' Ian says, taking a cautious sip. Steam rises from the hot tea, catching the sunlight. When he leans back against the sofa, the light falls across his face. He's about ten years older than me and Rosie. When we were teenagers, he was a young PC living with his mum in the centre of Buckthorpe. She owned the newsagent before it was sold and converted into a café. 'She'll be missed around the village,' he adds.

'Thanks, we appreciate that,' I say.

'Why are you here, Ian?' Rosie asks, a little too rudely. She juts out her chin and shuffles against the carpet. 'You said you didn't know about Mum, so I guess you're not here to offer condolences.'

'That's right,' he says smoothly, as though not even noticing Rosie's bluntness. 'I just popped in to say hello to you, Rosie. You don't visit often.'

'Why, though? We're not friends.'

'Ro!' I warn. Now she's being blatantly rude.

'It's okay,' Ian says, smiling. 'I suppose we're not. But Buckthorpe is small and news travels.' He takes another sip of his tea. 'I like to keep up with what's going on in the village.'

The more he talks, the more my interest is piqued. Surely a sergeant, even one in a quiet rural location, is too busy to call on acquaintances while obviously on duty. And why would he want to see Rosie in particular? Also, why does he want to keep abreast of local events? Is he that nosy?

'I hear you're running the team in Ingledown now,' I say, attempting to change the subject but gather extra information while I'm at it. 'What's it called? A countryside initiative? I bumped into your mum a few weeks ago and she mentioned it.'

'That's right, Heather,' he says. 'We're aiming to keep the countryside crime-free.'

'Littering and loitering getting out of control, is it?' Rosie snipes.

I shoot her another warning glance. Rosie's obvious hostility is setting me on edge.

'Actually, there's been an increase in violent crime over the last few years. And unfortunately, rural areas like this are always vulnerable to animal cruelty. The Murrays found a slaughtered cow a few weeks back. The poor thing had cigarette burns all over its body.'

'Fuck.' Even Rosie appears taken aback by Ian's answer. She shakes her head sadly.

'That's horrible. Who would do such a thing?' I ask.

Ian drinks a little more of his tea, dragging out the suspense before giving us his professional opinion. 'Isolation can do funny things to folk, and Buckthorpe definitely feels isolated with the woods on most sides. I'm sure it was just kids on drugs. I'll be keeping an eye on the farm to make sure it doesn't happen again. Have you got any animals at the moment?'

'No,' I say. 'They're all gone now.'

'Ah,' he says. 'It's been a tough few years for you. You've said goodbye to a lot of family, as well as your pets.' He picks lint from his sleeve before lifting his head to meet my gaze. 'I suppose it means there isn't much tying you to Buckthorpe any more. Neither of you have kept in touch with many school friends, have you?' He picks up his teacup from the coffee table and sips again.

It takes me a moment to realise quite how odd that statement is. Rosie also frowns, absorbing Ian's words.

'Well, I suppose not. But this is our childhood home.' I glance up to the ceiling as though in explanation.

'With happy memories …' He raises his voice at the end of the sentence, making it into a question. Then he places his cup back down on the table. 'Or not so happy?' This time, he regards Rosie directly. 'Because I remember some not particularly happy memories, don't you?'

I don't appreciate the way he's staring at my sister, and I find myself bristling in response. 'We have many happy memories of our childhood home, Ian. The good outweighs the bad.'

'Does Rosie think so?' he asks, still staring at her.

Abruptly Rosie climbs to her feet and leaves the room in silence.

'I think you should go, Sergeant.' I slam my cup down on the coffee table and rise to my feet. 'We're grieving and we need some space.'

His eyes lazily find mine. 'Sorry. I didn't mean to upset you. It's just that … Well, the Murrays are acting a little agitated, what with Rosie back in the village.'

I'm taken aback by that. 'What did they expect? They know that Mum is – was – ill. Rosie has every right to come home and pay her respects.'

'Yes,' he says. 'But Rosie also accused their son of trying to rape her.'

It's been years since I've heard those words spoken out loud. They have the same power they did all those years ago. A jolt shoots up my spine and I let out a little gasp, and all the while Ian watches me carefully.

I steady myself before saying evenly, 'I know. I was there when she came home in tears, bruised and scratched.'

'Well, we know what happened after her accusation, don't we? They never saw Samuel again.' He raises his eyebrows. 'Look, I'm sorry, Heather.' His voice softens. 'I thought the world of your mum and dad, you know that. I don't mean to be an arsehole, especially so soon after your mum has passed away. But at the same time, the Murrays are still hurting. Their son went missing ten years ago and they never got any answers. It's been eating away at them for a decade, and Rosie being here is dragging it all up again. I'm just a copper, I know that, and it's not my place to be sticking my nose in where it's not wanted, but they might get antsy if you stay too long, that's all I'm saying.'

'You're suggesting that we leave?'

He shrugs. 'What's keeping you here? You've both got lives outside of Buckthorpe. Sell up and move on.'

He gets to his feet and follows me as I show him out, maintaining his calm and friendly demeanour. But I barely say goodbye, too lost in my own thoughts. Is he right? Do the Murrays not want us here because of the trouble between our families?

Mum insisted that I find the deeds to the house and sell up when she died. Did she know that the village wouldn't accept Rosie's presence here? My scalp tingles as I replay our conversation with Ian in my mind. He's right about one thing: isolation can have a strange effect on people. It's easy to get lost in your own trauma, to allow the past to consume you. I can only imagine the rage simmering deep down inside the Murrays, stoked by years of obsession.

We would never have started going to the Murrays' farm if Lady hadn't spooked at the weird tree. On my way to the farm now, I recall my memories of that day – Rosie's reckless gallop along the grass verge, the way I gripped the saddle until my knuckles went white, the feeling of pure helplessness as Lady took off up the road. The tree has since been cut down, and part of me wants to feel triumphant about the fact that I've outlived it. However much it frightened my pony, I'm the one still standing. And yet at the same time, it's a small part of my childhood chipped away, never to be restored, leaving me with the same strange dreamlike sense I felt when I first came back.

My stomach flutters with nerves as I pull into the driveway. The path to the farmhouse is gated off from the courtyard and the shop, which means that when I get out of the car I have to pull the stiff metal lever to open the gate. It makes a loud, rusty creak that makes my heart beat faster.

Rosie has no idea that I'm here, and I'm not sure what she'd say about it if she knew. After Ian left, I went to find her up in Grandad's old room, but she acted as though nothing had happened. Instead she started asking me about an outfit she'd brought with her, and whether it would be appropriate for the funeral.

The bizarre visit left me wondering whether Ian genuinely came to warn me that the Murrays weren't happy about us living here, or if there's more going on between him and my sister. Could it be possible that he knows something about what happened the night Samuel went missing? I thought about chasing him down to probe him with questions, but if he doesn't know anything and

I imply that I think Rosie has broken the law, he might decide to open the case, or at least take another glance at it. Which in turn made me consider my options if Rosie actually *was* involved in Samuel's sudden disappearance. Do I want my own sister to be arrested? If she did commit a crime, would I want her to go to prison for it? I've had years to think about this, and yet my thoughts are still jumbled.

A dog barks somewhere on the farm, and the smell of the animal barns catches the back of my throat. Acrid cow dung, sodden straw, the ammonia of horse urine. The Murrays always had a few horses around. Sometimes Samuel would go on a hack with us or ride around the fields on young, barely broken-in animals. Their wild behaviour made me nervous, and I stopped going. But then Rosie and Samuel went on a ride together without me, and I remember my petty jealousy and the childish conversations I made up in my head. Obviously they spent the entire time talking about me. After that, I always went with them, no matter how scared I was.

It has been ten years since Rosie accused Samuel of sexual assault, and the pain is still there, fresh in my mind. How could the boy I cared about do that to my sister?

It has been ten years, too, since I was last at the farmhouse, and the first time without Samuel. All around me, his ghost walks, haunting my memories of the place. It pains me to admit how much I miss him. Rosie can never know that I still think about him every day.

A chicken comes scratching around by my feet as I knock on the door. When Rosie and I were working here for pocket money, we used to walk in, sit at the kitchen table to chat, or put the kettle on. I'd take Mrs Murray her cup of tea and sit down on the carpet to play with their cat. Now I have to wait for an answer. What if they slam the door in my face? My palms begin to sweat and I consider setting off in the opposite direction for home. But now is a time to be brave. I need to know what's going on, and why

Ian Dixon came round to the house to vaguely insist we get the hell out of Buckthorpe.

The door opens and I find myself surprised to see Samuel's younger brother, Peter. For some reason I was expecting his mother, Lynn.

Peter smiles, and it lights up his expression. 'Heather! How nice to see you. Come in.' A warm welcome was the last thing I expected. Not based on Ian Dixon's visit, anyway. I haven't spoken to Peter since he was about thirteen years old, which would make him twenty-three now.

I shuffle awkwardly into the house behind him, trying to get my bearings. It could be because of his muscular bulk from the farm work, but he definitely looks older than twenty-three.

'I was expecting your mum to answer,' I admit.

'She's in,' Peter says. 'She's just on the phone. We're having a break and a cup of tea. Can I pour you one?'

'Um, sure. If it isn't any trouble.'

He glances back at me with a crooked grin. 'Course not.' There's a pot already on the table, covered in a rainbow-coloured cosy. Peter grabs a teacup from a cupboard and begins to pour. 'I'm sorry to hear about your mum. Is she doing any better?'

'Actually, she passed away yesterday.'

He splashes hot water on his hand and swears under his breath. 'Sorry. I mean, I'm so sorry for your loss, and for swearing.' His cheeks turn a pleasant, embarrassed red. 'Sorry.'

'No apology needed. We – I mean Rosie and me – are okay. We're devastated, obviously, but she was ill for a long time and she'd been in agony …' I find myself trailing off as my throat thickens with emotion. I take a moment before continuing. 'She's at peace now.'

Before I can steel myself, I feel a tear escaping. I brush it away with my fingertips as Peter reaches out to do the same thing. His hand drops when he realises what he was about to do, and his eyes widen with horror. I'm about to say that it's okay, it was a sweet gesture. But we haven't been friends since he was a young kid, and I know he had a crush on me back then. Has he just revealed his feelings to me by attempting such an intimate gesture? I open and close my mouth, settling on what I hope is a friendly smile. And it's at that moment that Lynn Murray walks into the kitchen.

She stops a few feet in, and her eyebrows lift in surprise. There's an awkward silence as our eyes lock.

Ten years has aged her. While I've seen Peter from a distance on a tractor, or walking around the village, somehow I haven't seen Lynn at all. The last time was not long after Samuel disappeared. Then, her eyes were red with tears, her skin flaky and pale, her figure wasting away. Now she's put some of the weight back on, but her face and bust have a deflated appearance, as though her weight has bounced up and down over the years. She was always a well-put-together woman; short and sturdy, with strong hands. Some of that power has withered away.

'Heather.' Her voice is breathy but has that high-pitched tone I remember. 'It's been a long time.'

I feel awkward, hovering by the kitchen table, my cup of tea cooling between me and her younger son, Lynn's hard eyes fixed on me. Did she notice Peter reaching out to touch me? That must have been terrifying for her to watch, given what happened between my sister and his older brother.

'I wanted to call in to let you know that Mum passed away yesterday,' I say, trying to keep the tremor out of my voice. 'I hope you don't think it was inappropriate for me to come.'

'Of course not.' Lynn finally moves, busying herself at the kitchen counter by rinsing Peter's teacup. I'm not sure he'd actually finished drinking the tea inside. 'When is the funeral? I'd like to pay my respects if that's all right.'

'We haven't actually arranged it yet,' I say. 'I'm in the process ...'

'That's right, it was only yesterday. You won't have had time yet.' Lynn shakes her head as though to berate herself. 'How are you holding up?'

'Oh, we're okay. It's hard, but ... she was in a lot of pain at the end and I think it was ... kinder that she slipped away.'

'I'm sorry.' Lynn stares down at her wet hands in the sink. 'That must have been hard to watch.'

'It was,' I admit. I pause for a moment, wondering whether to continue. The silence drags out, and I take a deep breath, deciding to say it even if it is a bad idea. 'Actually, there was another reason why I came here today.' But as I'm about to tell Lynn about Ian's visit, the front door is yanked open and I hear the sound of boots being brushed off and then removed. We all wait until Colin Murray enters the kitchen. When his eyes rest on me, his expression changes. His jaw clenches and his eyes narrow with suspicion.

'Heather,' he says simply.

Lynn clears her throat. 'Iris passed away yesterday. Heather came to let us know.'

Colin strides over to the sink and starts running the taps. 'I'm sorry to hear that,' he says as he squirts soap onto his hands.

I've seen this scene before: Mr Murray washing his hands, Mrs Murray moving to make way for him, a tea towel over her shoulder, Peter sitting quietly at the table. But everyone has changed. Colin's hairline has moved back from his forehead and his hair is grey. Lynn is a worn-out version of the woman she used to be. Even Peter has dark circles of tiredness around his brown eyes. And the strangest part of all is that Samuel isn't here.

'I should get going,' I say. 'Thank you for the tea.'

Peter frowns down at the untouched teacup.

'You came here for more than that, didn't you?' Lynn folds her arms and moves across to the opposite side of the room, giving her husband space to dry his hands. 'You were about to say something else.'

Nerves clog my throat. Now that Colin is here too, I just want to leave. I pictured speaking just to Lynn, us shedding a few tears together and making amends for the past. But now all the Murrays are here staring at me. Waiting.

'It's not that important. It's just … well, Ian Dixon called in at the cottage this morning and suggested that maybe you weren't happy about Rosie being here. I wanted to come and let you know that we don't want any trouble. We just want to give our mum the best send-off that we can.' I rub my sweaty palms against my jeans.

'What did Ian say, exactly?' Lynn frowns as though this is new information. 'We have no problem with Rosie being here.'

Peter glances from his mother to his father, and I wonder whether Lynn is telling the truth.

'It's just that Ian suggested we should sell the cottage and move on,' I say. 'And I think that's a little unfair.'

Lynn inhales at the last word, the air whistling through her teeth. 'Yes, I know a lot about things that are unfair … My boy being missing is one of them.' Her entire body stiffens, and I imagine a pulse of anger running through her. The sight makes the blood drain from my face. Even the large farmhouse kitchen is too small for Lynn Murray and her pain.

'Sorry. I didn't mean to offend. I know you've been through hell—'

'There's nothing keeping you here, though, is there?' Colin interrupts. 'I'm not saying you should go. The past is the past. It can't be changed, and any kind of feud is ridiculous. But at the same time, why would you want to stay here?' He places a hand on Lynn's shoulder, and she relaxes slightly.

'We haven't decided what we're doing yet,' I say. 'But I wanted to come and make sure there isn't any issue with it if we stay. We'll be here for a while sorting through Mum's things anyway. We certainly don't want to upset you.' I know that I'm rambling now and finally have the good sense to be quiet.

'You're always welcome here, Heather,' Peter says quietly.

Lynn sighs. 'You're not unwelcome, but the history between our families is intense, as you know. What Rosie did … well, it led to us never seeing our son again.' Her voice cracks as her emotions begin to pour out. 'And now he's lost out there somewhere.'

'You think he's still alive?' The words tumble out of my mouth before I can stop them.

'I know he is,' she says fiercely.

Colin places an arm over her shoulders. There are tears in his eyes, which makes me even more uncomfortable. Before Samuel disappeared, Colin always came across as the archetypal alpha male, tough and terse. 'We all know he's alive. We've known all along.'

'But how do you—' I begin.

'Hope,' Lynn says, her eyes bright with tears. 'Hope.'

CHAPTER NINE

Rosie

Then

At first, I hated going to the farm. From the early mornings tacking up ponies with bleary eyes, to the days of physical work. I'd get home with aching muscles and dung on my boots and all the while I was watching my sister become best friends with the boy I wanted to notice me. The place gave me anxiety. I wouldn't sleep properly the night before, but at the same time there was a sense of inevitability to it that I grew to accept.

After a few weeks, though, I began to enjoy it. Samuel's mum made homemade cakes, or fruit crumbles with proper custard, and gave us generous portions at lunchtime. I got to run around the fields inventing games for us to play, climbing over fences and rolling down hills.

Yes, it was strange watching Heather make a friend. She was the bookish one who rarely came out of her shell, even at home. I hadn't seen her hanging around with many people at school, either. Once I learned to accept that she and Samuel were close and there was nothing I could do about it, the three of us became something special. I'm not sure I realised how close they were back then. I can see now, with the benefit of hindsight, with knowing what happened after our idyllic jaunts at the farm abruptly stopped.

About a year after we started working at the farm, there was one day when Samuel was keen to take one of his father's new horses out for a ride. As well as working the farm, Mr Murray would on occasion buy colts to break in and sell on. While Samuel had always been a bit of a wimpy goth kid at school, on the farm he was actually pretty fearless and would get on horses even I would find intimidating.

There was a young stallion in particular that Samuel wanted to ride. The horse frightened Heather, especially after it had grabbed her ponytail with its teeth when she was walking past his stable. But Samuel didn't want to ride alone, and asked me to go with him. Heather's expression when I agreed could have curdled milk, as Grandad would have said, but I was bored and fed up of her and Samuel being in their own little club. She wasn't keen on our rides around the farmland anyway. Samuel and I loved racing each other, while Heather would trot Lady in the other direction to stop her getting the urge to join in. So she stayed in the courtyard sweeping up dropped hay and horse feed.

'She'll get over it,' I said to Samuel as we walked the horses out of the courtyard and into the field. The stallion was a fifteen-hand black beast with a thick mane that draped over its neck all the way down to its shoulder. Rather than walk, it pranced.

Samuel cast a glance behind him as he closed the gate, and then climbed into the saddle, gathering up his reins quickly to keep the stallion in check. 'I feel bad. I don't like making your sister unhappy.'

'She'll get over it,' I repeated more firmly, annoyed by how the attention always seemed to fall on Heather no matter what. 'It's a half-hour of her life.'

'I know, but …'

'But what?' I asked, twisting in the saddle to give him a fierce glare. We were still walking the horses because the ground was muddy after overnight rain. We were having a wet August and neither of us wanted our mounts to lose a shoe.

'She's hard on herself. She thinks of this as a failure. Don't you agree?' He lifted his dark eyebrows, making his eyes even brighter.

Shame rippled through my body like an annoying muscle spasm, lasting barely a second but making everything hurt. I knew he was right: in some ways Heather was much more vulnerable than I was at that age, even though in other ways she was stronger. But rather than admit to any of that, I pressed my heels into Midnight's flanks and pushed him into a canter. Always quick to go, he burst forth, and the stallion followed suit.

The ground hardened up the further away from the farm we went, and the two horses found their stride. Samuel leaned over the stallion's neck and loosened his reins, letting the horse have his head. Midnight was no match for the tall stallion, and though he tried, he couldn't keep up. Soon he was panting, and I slowed him down to a walk. We still had the hack home and I didn't want to tire him out.

Samuel eventually managed to rein in the stallion, and trotted back to where I was waiting with Midnight. There was steam rising from the black stallion's coat, which was gleaming in the midday sun. The horse's neck was arched, and he lifted his knees high. Samuel sat with a straight back, his cheeks flushed pink. I felt a squirming in my stomach and a vague sense that I was doing something wrong. I didn't want to look at him, but I couldn't stop myself.

'Well, I think it's safe to say I won that race.'

'You've got the faster animal,' I replied. 'It doesn't mean you're the best rider.'

He just laughed and patted the horse's shoulder. 'You should try him out some time. I know you could manage him. You're the best rider I know.'

The compliment made me grin with pride. Being a good rider was one of the things I liked the most about myself. It was part of my identity.

'What about Heather?' I asked.

'She's good too,' he said, but I could tell he was just being nice and didn't mean it. 'She's too cautious, though. I think I prefer girls willing to take a risk.'

My grin spread even wider, hurting my cheeks. I'd never felt so noticed as at that moment, and I wanted to be noticed even more. I brought Midnight closer to the stallion, until my knee almost touched Samuel's lower leg, then took one hand away from my reins and gently caressed the horse's dark, damp coat. The air smelled of sweat and sweet dewy grass. I was little more than fourteen years old, but even then I knew what I was feeling, and I knew what I wanted.

CHAPTER TEN

Heather

Now

I soon discover that the practical chores are the easy part. There's only one local funeral director, which makes that choice much more straightforward. Mum even left all her funeral preferences in her drawer of paperwork, and the director knows the family because he buried my father, too. All I need to do is tell him what she wanted. The flowers are easy as well. With Rosie's help, I choose a display of purple irises. We write a brief obituary for the local paper, speak to the local vicar, and hire the community centre for the wake.

The hard part is learning how to speak to my sister. Our conversations tend to be brief, skirting over anything significant about ourselves. We talk about the funeral arrangements, but we don't discuss our feelings or thoughts. We focus on the important tasks.

After Ian Dixon arrived at the house without warning, I somehow allowed an entire day to pass without asking Rosie why he was hostile towards her in particular. Then another day passed and I still didn't ask. I didn't even mention my visit to the Murrays, though part of me was dying to tell her about the awkward moment with Peter – not that it matters, when we have more important things to deal with.

Rosie does not open up easily; in fact she drifts further and further away with each day that passes. Even though we eat together and watch television together, as soon as it reaches about ten o'clock, she slips up to her room and closes the door. I spend the rest of the evening either staring at the television, barely concentrating on whatever show I'm watching, instead attempting to filter through the conflicting thoughts in my mind; or in bed, thinking about the letter I wrote, which is still inside the drawer of my old dressing table.

One thought that often pops into my mind is the idea that Samuel could still be alive. Lynn and Colin Murray both believe he is. Does that mean that one day I might see him again?

I push that thought out of my head. There's no way I could ever see him again, not after what he did to my sister.

On the third night after Mum's death, Rosie breaks the cycle. Rather than rushing upstairs at ten o'clock, she switches off the television and turns to me.

'Should we talk about it?' Her voice has a defensive tone to it. Her knees are pulled up to her chin, arms wrapped around them; a wall of limbs built around the core of her body. Are they there for protection? Or to keep me out?

'Talk about what?' I ask cautiously.

'You know what.' She gestures to the house. 'This. What are we going to do with it now that Mum's gone?'

'I don't know,' I admit. 'She left it to both of us, so I suppose the easiest thing is to sell it and split the money down the middle.'

She chews on her bottom lip. 'Is that what you want, though? You love it here.'

I shrug. 'Honestly, it doesn't feel the same as it did when we were kids. It's like it isn't real.'

Rosie's arms slowly unwrap from her body and she leans towards me. 'I didn't know you felt that way. I thought this place was … I dunno, some sort of shrine to your childhood.'

'Our childhood,' I correct. 'And it's not. There are loads of happy memories, but there are many unhappy ones too. Recently I keep thinking more about the unhappy ones.' I drop my gaze from hers as the night of Samuel's disappearance leaps into my mind. Rosie obviously notices, because her knees go back up to her chin.

'Do you agree with the great Sergeant Ian Dixon?' She curls her lip as though his name has an unpleasant taste.

'I can't stand that smarmy git either,' I say. 'But he had a point.' I pause, considering whether to tell her or not. Then I sigh and decide I should. 'I went to see the Murrays that day.'

'What? Why?'

'I felt awkward about what Ian had said. I wanted to clear the air.'

'And how are you going to do that?' she says with a derisive snort. 'Erase the past?'

'I know I can't do that. But it's been ten years. I thought they might see reason.'

Rosie shakes her head. 'That's a battle you're never going to win, little sis. They blame me for their son running away and nothing is ever going to change that.'

'Did he really run away?' I ask in a small voice.

The left side of her face twitches. 'What else could have happened?' She rubs her thumb slowly along her forefinger and stares over my head at the opposite wall.

'I don't know,' I say, my body growing hot all over. 'Maybe he's dead.'

'Maybe.' Her arms tighten around her legs, creating that barrier once again, and I can see her shutting down her emotions.

Even though I know Rosie is drifting away from me, I have to ask. 'Does Sergeant Dixon think you had some sort of … involvement in …' I clear my throat. 'You know … Samuel.'

Rosie taps her fingers against her legs. 'Probably. I don't know. He's a dick and he obviously wants to run this town. I've heard he's crooked.' Then in one fluid motion she stands up. 'I'm going to bed. See you in the morning.' And with that, she's gone.

April rain falls on the day of the funeral, but I don't mind. Mum always loved the rain. She said that it made the world come alive. Smells were more vivid. The sky felt closer. The sound of it blocked out all those annoying little distractions. And then she would tickle me, because I was one of those annoying little distractions.

It surprises me that Rosie cries in the car as we follow the hearse.

'I hate funerals,' she says between sobs. Then, after a pause, 'I'm going to miss her.'

Even though I take her hand, I can't stop the intrusive thought jumping into my head: *Then why didn't you visit more?* But I know it's unfair, and I'm only thinking it because I'm stressed and sad. This is my third funeral in six years, and my heart is heavy. Mum deserved more than a life cut off before her retirement. She deserved more time, grandkids, weddings. We gave her none of those things.

'We'll get through today together,' I say quietly. 'That's what Mum would've wanted.'

'She brought us together in the end,' Rosie replies. Then she sighs and stares out of the window towards Buckbell Woods.

Seeing her with tear-stained cheeks and a wistfulness to her expression makes me think of the person she was all those years ago.

'She'll miss the woods,' Rosie says. 'Maybe we should have arranged a cremation and scattered the ashes there.'

'She didn't want a cremation,' I remind her. 'We've given her exactly what she wanted, Ro.'

Rosie's face crumples in and I squeeze her hand. She wasn't this emotional at Dad's funeral; she was too out of it on some cocktail of drink and pills. Her tears remind me of the night I saw her running home from the woods, her clothes torn, blood on her face. *Blame the blue, Guilt the trees.* The bluebells were in bloom when Samuel disappeared. Mum's poem is undoubtedly about Buckbell Woods. Did she know the truth about everything before she died? It's a strange, intrusive thought that pops into my mind. Did Rosie confess a sin or a secret to her?

We're driving past the east side of the forest, and for a fleeting moment I consider asking her about that night, but then I let go of her hand instead, because I remember something from the previous evening. Ever since Samuel's disappearance, Rosie has always stated that she believes Samuel ran away. But every single time, she performs the same little tic she always does when she's lying. She rubs her forefinger with her thumb.

Another blow hits me, adding to my grief. No matter how much I want to believe her, I can't trust her, because she's lying to me.

The car continues on and soon the church comes into view. My thoughts return to Mum and how much I wish she was here with me now. There are mourners gathered around the entrance to the church, all in their smartest black outfits. Unfortunately, the first person I see is Ian Dixon, with his slim, long-faced wife standing next to him. I don't remember her name, but I know she's from Ingledown. There are a few others from the village: Reg Jackson, landlord of the Prince of Wales, our local pub; Susie, the nurse from the hospital; a builder my dad used to work with; some people from our old school; my mum's friend Beth. I'm surprised by how many shop owners and farmers have come out. Our neighbours, too, the Campbells. And then there's Peter Murray, who has dressed up in a black suit and smart boots.

As the coffin is carried towards the church, Rosie slips her hand into mine and I block away every thought not about Mum to allow me to say goodbye. She wasn't a perfect mother. Sometimes I wanted more from her. More attention. More love. But she gave me everything she had to give. That's the one thing I saw at the end, just how much she offered herself over to us. I think she always thought she was hollowed out and damaged inside, but she wasn't.

All the love she needed was in there; she just never learned to let it out. And while she struggled with those conflicting feelings, she gave so much to us that it drained her.

After the burial, a few of the mourners shake my hand and leave, but a handful come along to the village hall for sandwiches and tea. The afternoon goes by in a blur, and soon I find myself busy answering questions about what to do with the leftovers, while Rosie chats to some of her old school friends at the back of the hall.

Finally the caterer leaves me be, and as I go to hunt out a slice of cake, I find myself shoulder to shoulder with Peter Murray.

'Good spread,' he says.

'Thanks,' I reply, manoeuvring myself until we're face to face, my plate between us.

He shakes his head. 'I should've led with "sorry for your loss", shouldn't I?'

'It is customary.'

'I'm such an idiot. Your mum was a lovely lady.'

I nod. 'I'm going to miss her a lot.'

'I think the whole village will,' Peter says. 'Even Mum, though she's too stubborn to admit it. I'm sorry she isn't here today. I know she wanted to come, but Dad thought it would be too much for her.'

'I probably made things worse with my visit,' I admit. 'For some reason it seemed like a good idea at the time.'

'Yeah, well, the Capulets and the Montagues had a better relationship.'

I nibble at the cake and am grateful for the sustenance on such a long, emotionally draining day. Having Peter next to me isn't unpleasant either. The silence that follows is a comfortable one. I could be standing next to Samuel again. But that thought makes me cringe, and I put my plate down on the trestle table.

'God, I remember those girls from school,' Peter says, nodding towards Rosie, who is now in the centre of a circle of her old friends. 'Emily used to spit paper at me and the other younger kids at break time.'

'Emily once knocked me over with her bike when I was out walking. Then she laughed and called me Mud Face for an entire year. And Rhona told me I had a fat arse once, too.'

'They accused my brother of terrible things, too,' Peter says, his voice quieter, deeper.

I turn to him again, and try to find the right words to say next. But he holds his hands up in apology.

'That was tactless. I'm not trying to—'

'No, it's okay, it's all in the past.'

'I don't mean that I thought Rosie lied all those years ago,' he explains. 'But I never … God, this is going to sound awful. I just never believed the rest of them because the things they accused him of were … well, they were over the top and disgusting. They made him out to be some sort of *monster*, and I just …' He puts his plate down and steps away. 'I should go. I've … Dad wants me back at the farm this afternoon.'

I reach out for his arm but change my mind and retract my hand. I want to tell him that I never believed those other girls either, but that would betray something deep inside myself. It would be admitting, or confessing, a thought I've had for a decade. I let him go instead.

It takes less than thirty seconds for Ian Dixon to make his way over. 'Causing trouble already?'

I say nothing.

'I'm sorry for your loss,' he says. 'Your mother will be missed.' He rocks back on his heels and stares over my head. When I glance over my shoulder, I see that the person he's staring at is Rosie. 'But I'm not too sorry to tell you what you don't want to hear.'

'If it's something I don't want to hear, then maybe you shouldn't say it at my mother's funeral,' I snap.

He tilts his head and places his hands together in front of his waist, which reminds me of a detective on a TV show. I can imagine Ian Dixon moulding himself on a fictional detective, considering himself the Morse or Poirot of Buckthorpe.

'The village was never the same after your sister made that accusation,' he says. 'The whole sorry business tore this place apart and it'll never be mended, not while you're both still here. You can never fix the rift between your family and his. Don't start getting any airy-fairy ideas about making things right.'

'With all due respect, Sergeant, you should probably fuck off now.' I flash him a fierce glare. How dare he say these horrible things at a wake?

'Again, I'm sorry for your loss,' he says. 'Iris was a wonderful lady and we'll all miss her. I mean that from the bottom of my heart. But in a way, now that she's gone and it's only you and Rosie left, maybe Buckthorpe can move on.'

Those words sink deep, penetrating the flesh and going straight for the blood. But as I'm about to tell him that Buckthorpe has always been rotten and that removing my family won't fix anything, he walks away.

CHAPTER ELEVEN

Heather

Now

Rosie was the girl always in trouble, the girl who would come home drunk from a party, who would get detention, who would give some other girl a black eye. Seeing her with those bitchy school friends at the funeral reminded me of all of that. But what is it about Rosie that fuels this chaos? Mum and Dad were both pretty mild-mannered. Grandad used to shout a lot, but I never thought much of it when we were children. He was just bad-tempered and old. A little scary sometimes, but harmless.

The truth is, I don't know my sister as an adult. We've drifted so far apart that I can't imagine us as Hev and Ro any more. Since she's come home, we've barely been able to hold a conversation that lasts more than ten minutes. Yes, we are united in grief. We both miss our mother and we loved her deeply, but apart from that we're strangers.

Is there a stranger living in my house? Sharing my food? Lying to my face? Who is Rosie? Is she a murderer?

After the funeral, we pack away the food, go home and I finally get to step out of my smart black pumps. All I can think about is Ian Dixon and his insistence that we leave Buckthorpe. There was a definite atmosphere at the wake. Even Reg from the Prince of Wales pub asked me when we're putting the house on the market, a little gleam in his eyes suggesting he was excited about the prospect. Does he want to buy the cottage? Or does he just want us gone?

I believe what I wanted to say to Ian – there is a rotten core at the heart of Buckthorpe. It goes further than Samuel's disappearance. When Rosie stood in the kitchen and told us – with tears running down her face – that Samuel had hurt her, it only took a few days for the news to spread all the way around the village. She went to the police and made a statement, but outside the family, we told no one. In her statement, Rosie told the police that Samuel had followed her into the woods, pushed her down into the mud, and tried to force himself on her. Afterwards he ran off, and she walked round and round for hours in shock, ending up lost. As she tried to find her way home, she sensed someone following her.

At first, the village sided with Rosie. She was young and beautiful whereas Samuel was considered a strange outsider who listened to music that the older generation didn't understand, and occasionally painted his nails black. The gossip focused on Samuel's strangeness, as well as Rosie's outgoing nature and provocative fashion choices. *Not sure what she expected wearing those little shorts around the village and walking by herself in the woods.* Later, many of the villagers decided to pick sides. It split Buckthorpe in two.

Just days after Rosie's accusation, a Tumblr post by an anonymous female student from our school appeared accusing Samuel of many disgusting things. It was revealed later that the blog post was the work of Emily and Rhona. Emily told the police that she had seen Samuel drawing a pentagram on his hand. She said that he then grabbed her breast with the same hand and began speaking in a strange language. On another occasion, he pushed his hands into her knickers. Rhona had her own story. She said that she saw Samuel snap the neck of a cat when she was walking home from school. He swung the cat at her and taunted her before groping her and saying things in a demon language.

Ten years ago, I listened to these tall tales whispered behind hands across the tennis courts and the playing fields. Disgusting graffiti popped up in the girls' toilets. Someone took a photo of Samuel, then scratched out his eyes and drew devil horns on his head before pinning copies all over the school corridors. I watched in horror, with a heavy stone lodged in the pit of my stomach. This wasn't the Samuel I knew. Samuel was soft and gentle. He'd never …

The Samuel I knew was a good person, but I chose to believe my sister when she told me that he'd hurt her. I chose her over him.

Was it the wrong decision?

'Here, you sort through this box and I'll take the photo albums.' Rosie hands me another shoebox before stacking the albums on top of the bed.

'This one is photographs too,' I say, rummaging through the grainy old pictures. 'Grandad's about forty here, and he has a beard.'

Rosie leans over my shoulder and frowns. 'Huh. I thought that was Dad for a minute.' She snatches the photo out of my hand and examines it. 'There's one here that I remember.' She holds up a picture of us at a theme park. 'It was the day after Grandad found you sleepwalking in the woods. You were such a weird kid, Hev. You could walk for miles in your sleep without waking up.'

'I remember coming round in the living room with everyone staring at me, but I've never been able to remember being in the woods. I guess the brain shuts it all out when you're asleep.'

'Weren't you dreaming about anything?' Rosie drops the photograph back into the box. 'Why did your body want you to walk into the woods?'

'I don't know.' I move away from her and stare out of the window.

'How old were you then? About fifteen?'

'Can we talk about something else?' I say, turning back to face her. 'That whole sleepwalking in the woods thing creeps me out.'

Rosie shrugs and flips open an album. 'Okay.' But after a brief pause, she says, 'I know you don't want to talk about it, but I'll just say that it was weird how you used to sleepwalk all over the house when you were about ten, and then never did it again until you were fifteen. How did Grandad find you anyway? Are you hiding some sort of secret?'

'Would you shut up about it?' I let out a hollow laugh. 'You're one to talk about secrets.'

Rosie's jaw tightens. 'I don't have half as many as you think I do.' She stands up and walks over to the wardrobe, dropping to her hands and knees and reaching inside. 'What's this?'

When she straightens up, she's holding a long metal box, which she places on the bed.

Ice-cold needles prick my arms and legs, and my stomach flips over. 'It's the cabinet for Dad's shotgun. It must be empty, though, right?'

'Do you know where the key is?' Rosie asks.

I open the top drawer of the bedside table and take out a small key. 'Wait. Do we really want to find out what's inside?'

'Like you said,' Rosie replies, 'it can't be the actual gun.' She lifts one end. 'It's heavy, though.'

My heart beats faster as Rosie puts the key into the lock and turns it. The hinges squeak as she flips open the lid to reveal an object covered in an old pillowcase fastened with an elastic band. She lifts it, slips off the elastic band and pulls back the fabric to reveal the long barrel of a shotgun.

'Fuck,' I blurt out, feeling the blood drain from my face. Rosie lets out a gasp, then gently places the gun on the carpet and moves away, covering her mouth with her hand.

'Is that it?' she says. 'Is that what he used?'

'I don't understand why Mum would keep it,' I whisper, light-headed from the shock. 'What was she thinking?' I can't stop staring down at the gun my father used to kill himself. Did she request it back from the police? 'Is it definitely Dad's?' I ask. I'm not sure why Mum would buy a different gun, but I need to know for sure.

Slowly Rosie bends down and picks up the weapon. She rotates it in her hands. 'Yes, this is Dad's. I remember it. He never let us touch it, did he? I always wanted him to teach me how to shoot.' She leans over the box and produces two pieces of paper. 'Licences. One for Dad. One for Mum.'

I shake my head in disbelief. 'Mum had a licence?'

Rosie lets out a little laugh, as though not surprised at all. 'Everyone does in the countryside, don't they?'

'I guess she lived alone,' I mumble, thinking about Ian Dixon's hostility, and the Murrays', and the insistence that we should sell the house and leave. Perhaps Mum never felt safe after Dad died. How did I fail to see it?

Rosie swings the barrel around and I duck down.

'What if it's loaded?'

'It won't be,' she says. But after a moment of consideration, she adds, 'Do you know how to check?'

I shake my head.

With a flick of her finger, she pulls a lever and breaks open the gun, revealing the empty barrel.

'How did you know how to do that?' I ask.

'I once went clay-pigeon shooting with some friends on a hen do,' she says with a shrug. 'It's not that difficult to learn.' She examines the gun, eyes trailing along the length of it. 'There must have been blood. Who cleaned the blood away? Was it Mum?'

'I don't know. Please, Rosie. Put it back. I don't like seeing it.'

'Did you believe it when you heard?' Rosie finally pulls her eyes away from the gun and snaps it back together. I find it difficult to take my eyes from it: the lump of metal and wood that killed my father.

She leans down and picks up the old pillowcase. 'When Mum called me, I didn't believe her. Dad would never kill himself. He was too stubborn for that. He'd live to spite us, so that he could continue to make us feel inadequate all our lives.'

'He wasn't like that.'

She shoots me a hard stare. 'Not to you, maybe. But to everyone else he was.'

She positions the elastic band back over the pillowcase, then locks the gun in the metal cabinet and returns it to the wardrobe.

'He didn't want us, Hev. Don't you remember how much he used to work away? All those random building sites in the south of France. It wasn't for the money, it was to get away from *us*. You, me, Mum. He left us here with her and Grandad while he went on his jollies for weeks at a time.'

'He was working.'

'It was an excuse!'

The sudden rise in her voice and the way she moves towards me as she shouts makes me flinch away from her. There's that old bit of Rosie fire that I've always known. But when she sees the frozen expression of fear on my face, she takes a step away and rakes her fingers through her hair.

'Let's get out of here,' she suggests. 'Let's go for a coffee.'

'I don't know …'

'Come on, little sister.' She reaches down and pulls me to my feet.

I could be twelve years old again, following her wherever she leads.

'Do you remember that song we used to sing at school? "Watch your back, it's Buckthorpe Jack. Count to four, he's at your door."

And then everyone would run around the playground with an invisible knife, stabbing each other.'

'I remember.' I'm on edge as Rosie talks loudly in the café. There's only one in Buckthorpe, an odd little place decorated with vintage photo frames and tall candles.

'Poor Jack. Did he ever actually stab someone?' she says.

'I don't know,' I admit. No one knows.

'Anyway, all I'm saying is that no wonder Mum kept Dad's gun, with people like Buckthorpe Jack still living in the village.'

Buckthorpe Jack is a real person, surrounded by his own myths and legends. No one quite knows the truth about him. Some people believe he went to prison years ago for murder but had enough money when he was released to buy a run-down cabin. Since then he's lived mainly off the land, growing his own vegetables that he sells in the farm shop. I'm not sure anyone has ever had a full conversation with him. He's just there, in the background, existing but not living, and that makes most people pretty uncomfortable.

His cabin is a mile or so into the woods, near the bluebell field. He has lived there for as long as I can remember. He seemed old when we were kids but, in reality, he was probably only in his forties, just a little more wizened than the average person, especially with his long, straggly beard. He's still as much of a loner as always. Because he rarely comes into the village, many stories have been told about who he is and where he came from.

'You used to have nightmares about him,' Rosie says. 'I'd forgotten about that until now. You used to dream that he was going to kidnap you and take you to the woods to be his bride. Were you going to Jack that night, do you think?'

'What night?' I run a finger around the rim of my coffee cup. Behind me the coffee machine screeches and hisses.

'The night you were sleepwalking?'

I fold my arms tightly across my chest. 'I don't remember.'

She sighs. 'You're lucky that you don't remember the things you don't want to remember. There's a lot I wish I didn't remember.'

'Like what?' I ask, mind sharpened now that the conversation has moved on to her.

'Mum and Dad yelling at each other. Dad leaving us with Mum when she was being difficult. Grandad shouting at me all the time.'

'Mum and Dad hardly ever argued,' I protest. 'Apart from when Mum went loopy every once in a while.' There were fights and a few door-slamming occasions, but apart from that, I always considered our parents a normal couple. Both of them were quiet people in general, but maybe once a year Mum would scream at Dad until he'd storm out with promises that he was never coming back.

Rosie shakes her head. 'You were always on his side, weren't you? You never saw him for what he was.'

'Dad?' My jaw drops. The question has me reeling. 'What do you mean?'

'He wasn't the man you thought he was,' she says. 'You remember everything wrong, Heather. You're so naïve and you always have been.'

'I'm not naïve!'

'It must be nice,' she snaps, 'to be the favourite. The one everyone likes. Since I came home the entire village has already turned against me, and I've only been here a week. Mum dies, and I can't even grieve because they want me gone.'

'Can you blame them?' The words tumble out of my mouth before I can stop them.

Her expression is sharp when her gaze reaches mine. Afternoon sun dances across her chin and cheekbones, narrowing her face. 'Why? Why can't I blame them?' She stands. She has always been tall, and now she looms over me, speaking tightly through her teeth, body pulsating with anger.

'Nothing.' I glance back down at my coffee to avoid her icy-blue eyes.

'Say it,' she demands.

But I won't. I can't say the words and so they remain unspoken, as they have done since the day I put the bracelet back on her cabinet. She strides purposefully out of the café, leaving me there alone.

CHAPTER TWELVE

Rosie

Then

When I was fifteen, and Heather had just turned fourteen, Peter started to join in with us during our summer days at the Murrays' farm. He'd always been too young before, but now he was eleven, and Mr Murray said it was fine as long as Samuel kept a close eye on him. Soon Peter stopped following his brother around all day and started following Heather instead. It used to make me laugh how he'd sneak up on her in the stables when she least expected it. We called him Kitten Paws, because he was so skinny he didn't make a sound.

'Can I help you, Hev?' became his mantra. He called my sister 'Hev' as though they were best friends. Only I called her that, and occasionally, Samuel.

I started to tease Heather that Peter had a crush on her, which obviously annoyed her. But she tolerated Peter in a kind way that I never could. It was me who snapped at Peter when he got in the way of my wheelbarrow or startled the ponies when I brought them in from the paddock. I never had the patience for anyone or anything that slowed me down.

One day when Peter was following us around as we worked in the barns, I ended up breaking away to get a moment to myself. I'd had enough of his whiny voice asking Heather hundreds of questions – *Do you want to sit with me at lunch at school? Did you know I was adopted? Don't you think Samuel is annoying? Did I tell you I won the sprint race last sports day?*

While Heather bit her tongue and listened patiently as Peter regaled her with tales of his sprinting prowess, I slipped out of the barn and went to the paddock to check on Midnight and Lady. They were both grazing in the sun, occasionally lifting their noses from the grass to shake away flies. I made a mental note to remember their fly masks the next day.

Midnight eventually plodded lazily over to the gate, his tail swishing away horseflies. It was late July and the middle of a cloudy summer that would lead into a freezing winter. He allowed me to stroke his nose while I enjoyed time away from cow dung and boys with too many questions.

Out of the corner of my eye, I saw Samuel approaching. When he spotted me, he stopped, and I saw him considering walking in the opposite direction. I knew immediately that there was something wrong. He had been stomping rather than walking, and now he wiped his eyes with the back of his hand and sniffed. Then he came over but didn't speak. He just stroked Midnight's neck.

'You all right?' I asked eventually.

He nodded his head. 'My dad's being a dick again, that's all.'

'Oh,' I said. 'What did he do?'

'He says he can't afford to pay you and Heather any more. And he says you won't come to the farm unless we pay you.'

We didn't earn much from our work on the farm. There was no formal agreement and we certainly didn't earn minimum wage. It was a casual thing amongst people who knew each other in a close-knit community.

'I don't know about that,' I said. 'Heather would never stop coming here.' Which was true. She lived for it. Every morning during the holidays she woke me up already showered and forced me to get ready for the day. She was the one who saddled Midnight for me while I ate breakfast. If it wasn't for her, we'd be late every morning. 'I know you'd miss her if she did stop, but you'll still see her at school.'

Over the last few years, I'd noticed Heather and Samuel spending more and more time together at school. Samuel's bullying had calmed since we'd all got a little older and had more homework and GCSEs around the corner. I'd noticed that the two of them usually sat and ate lunch together, or came out of classrooms talking to each other. She used to have a small circle of nerdy girls to hang out with, but she didn't seem to spend that much time with them any more. It hadn't concerned me at the time, because I was preoccupied with my own group of friends.

'It's not the same, though, is it?' he said. 'I wouldn't get to see her for six weeks of the year.'

My heart sank a little. Of course this was more about Heather than me.

'I'd miss you too,' he added sheepishly. 'You won't even talk to me at school.'

His inclusion of me was too little too late, but I had to admit he was right about that. I didn't talk to him at school. I had a reputation to protect; I didn't want to lose the popularity that had been tough to earn, which meant that I generally ignored both Samuel and Heather. School was more my world than the farm was at this point. But it was then that I realised I'd still come to the farm without being paid, too. Because otherwise I'd never get to talk to Samuel. I had to come.

'If I talked to you at school, my friends would think I'd lost my mind.'

'I hate that school,' he said fiercely. 'All the girls are bitches.'

'You're just annoyed they won't go out with you.' I lifted my chin defensively. He was right, but I didn't want him to be, because I knew I was one of the bitches he was referring to.

'Yeah, well, I have standards anyway. Not like you, apparently. Who is it this week? Which idiot from the rugby team did I see you getting off with on the tennis courts?'

The elastic band that held my temper in check snapped and I slapped him hard around the face. Samuel gasped, lifted his hand to his cheek and stared at me.

We stood completely still for a moment, both of us silent, and my hands began to tremble. My face burned with heat, and I'm sure it was bright red with anger and shock. I opened my mouth to apologise, but I couldn't find the words. I'd regretted it immediately, but in a way, I still felt as though he'd deserved it.

Finally, I mumbled, 'Sorry.'

Samuel didn't say another word. He just walked away without looking back.

CHAPTER THIRTEEN

Heather

Now

What else have I forgotten about my past? My childhood with Rosie tends to blur into feelings and snapshots of the world I knew back then. There's a before and an after. Sometimes the before comes to me as clear as the sound of a bell. On other days, I think the after was terrible enough to mar everything that came before, twisting my memories.

What Rosie said to me plays on my mind as I walk back from the village. Is she right about everything? Am I truly as naïve and stupid as she makes out? No, I refuse to believe that our childhood was bad. No matter what she or Ian Dixon says, we were happy here. There was the day Dad came home with Lady and Midnight. Or when Rosie's dangerously fast bicycle raced down the hill from our primary school beating all the boys. The 50p choc ices from the village shop. Samuel showing me around the farm the day Lady spooked at the weird tree. Building forts out of hay bales on the Murrays' farm. Riding around the fields with the sheep and cows. Feeling that giggly, silly sensation of belonging somewhere, only to have it all ripped away.

Can it ever be mended? Can I ever trust my sister again?

The bushes rustle as I begin my walk home. There are no pavements on the narrow roads between the village and our cottage, making the footpaths through the fields a safer option. Luckily, it hasn't rained and the ground isn't too muddy. I hop over a stile and continue along a wider path between two fields, both blocked off by a tangle of weeds, bushes and trees.

I've always felt that the woods and the land around our village contain the kind of mysterious quality that makes it easy to believe that someone is watching you. When it's windy, like it is now, the trees whistle a low, eerie tune. The hair on the back of my neck stands on end, and the line *Watch your back, it's Buckthorpe Jack* plays through my mind on a loop.

I was hoping that I might catch up with Rosie on the way home if I walked quickly enough, but I can't see her. Then the breeze picks up, and the rustling of undergrowth becomes louder. I know it's ridiculous, but I find myself checking over my shoulder to see if I'm being followed. As that low hum of air tickles my skin, I move my feet more quickly until I'm almost jogging. Out of breath, with the Buckthorpe Jack warning in my mind, I wrap my arms around myself.

Drizzle begins to drip down from the sky. The whistle of the wind dies away, and my clenched muscles slowly relax. The drizzle becomes a light rain, and I pull my damp hair away from my face, wishing I'd tied it back before leaving. This is typical Rosie, hurrying us out of the house without checking the weather forecast or bothering to grab coats. Even so, I still feel guilty about our squabble in the café, and consider getting out my phone to call and see if she's okay.

I don't, though. She was the one who stormed out, after all. And yes, it's petty, but she did start it by prodding me with those stories of Buckthorpe Jack and my sleepwalking. I carry on, huddling up against the cold. The rain heightens the smells from the fields around me, but it also blocks out the sun with dark clouds, giving the impression that night is coming. The ground becomes slippery, and without realising, I stop paying attention to my surroundings and instead focus on my foot placement on the path. It's only when I sense a stirring behind me – whether it's a tree or a bush, I don't know – that I spin around to see some sort of movement far off between the trees.

The only sound comes from the pattering of the rain on the path. I wish Rosie hadn't brought up my dreams about Buckthorpe Jack, because now I can't stop thinking about him chasing me, even though I'm nowhere near Buckbell Woods.

'Is there someone there?' Despite attempting to say the words with confidence, my voice breaks slightly. I straighten my back and search the area with my gaze. Everything is quiet.

The movement could have been anything – a fox, a gust of wind making the bushes move, a trick of the light through the shadows – but my mind keeps going back to the idea that someone is following me. I need to get out of here. I turn around and set off at a slow jog, feeling partly ridiculous for letting such a small thing get to me, and partly terrified to my core.

Watch your back, it's Buckthorpe Jack.

I hurry over another stile and onto a narrower path that moves downhill towards the road. My feet slip on the wet ground and sweat begins to form between my shoulder blades, but I push on. Why did Rosie have to bring up my old fears? She was incredibly argumentative today, as though she was trying to goad me. Was she trying to scare me, too?

As I hurry towards the road, I cast another glance over my shoulder. The footpath is relatively silent apart from the rain, and no one is lurking in the shadows, but I'm still convinced I'm not alone.

My mind races as fast as my feet as I reach the road and make my way back to the cottage, thighs and lungs burning. I'm not a runner, and this is the most exercise I've done for months. Caring for an ailing mother and constant travelling doesn't give a person much time to work out.

I finally allow myself a little breathing time as I walk along the road, relieved to see the Campbells' cottage coming up. A few minutes later I can see the driveway of Ivy Cottage and know I'm almost there. As soon as I'm through the gate, I close it, place my hands on the top bar and suck in several long, deep breaths. Sweat stings my eyes, and my light clothing is sodden from rain. There's a hint of wet dog emanating from my hot body.

I need to calm down and apply some logic to this situation. Why would anyone be following me? To be sure they couldn't be seen, they would have had to move through the tangled weeds and bushes next to the footpath. Why would anyone do that? As far as I know, no one wants to do me any harm. Except maybe Rosie.

No, that's ridiculous. My sister wouldn't hurt me. Would she? I can't deny that she has been acting strangely today.

It's as I make my way up the drive that I notice the front door is wide open. My heart skips a beat until I remember that it's most likely Rosie arriving home before me.

'Ro?' I call, stepping into the house. 'Are you there?' I stoop down to pick up an envelope left on the doormat and throw it on the kitchen table to deal with later.

The house is still and silent as I make my way into the living room. Nothing is out of place. Everything is as I left it.

'You upstairs?' I shout, half expecting her long legs to come striding down, a towel drying her hair. But there's nothing.

What if someone has broken in? What if they're still upstairs? I grab a knife from the kitchen and make my way up, dripping on the carpet as I go. That same sensation of being watched lifts the hairs on the back of my neck. Halfway up, I find I have to check behind me again. Did I imagine a shadow moving through the hallway? Did someone slip out of the house?

Heart pounding, I come back down the stairs and check the kitchen, then the downstairs toilet. No one. The loo was the one room I hadn't checked before coming upstairs. What if they'd hidden down here and then sneaked along the corridor and out of the front door as I was walking upstairs? I keep hold of the knife as I lock the door then hurry up the stairs again, trying not to let myself be afraid. *There's no one here.* But then my mind jumps back to: *Watch your back, it's Buckthorpe Jack.*

My fingers tremble as I open the door to Mum and Dad's room. It's empty, but yet again, what I'm seeing sparks a visceral reaction. The room isn't quite how I left it.

When we went out, boxes and clothes were stacked up on the bed. There are still piles of boxes and clothes, but they're not in the same place. I know this because I remember the order I put the boxes of photographs in, the blue shoebox on top. Now all the shoeboxes and photo albums have been moved slightly. A leather-bound album is underneath the red scrapbook instead of on top of it. The box filled with recent photographs is next to a pile of skirts not underneath it.

Rosie?

I quickly work my way through the belongings on the bed, making sure that nothing is missing. It could be that she came home, resumed our sort-out, and then for some reason forgot to close the door when she left.

But why? And would she have had time to do all that before I arrived home? I walked quickly for most of the way and ran the last part of the footpath. She would have had to run all the way home to do this, which seems odd, but not impossible.

After checking through everything, I realise that there is a photo album missing. It was one of the large leather-bound albums that I hadn't opened yet. It's possible Rosie took it to her room to look at. Or out of the house.

Suddenly my back straightens. With my heart still racing, I move away from the bed and face the open wardrobe. The shotgun. I drop to my knees and part the remaining clothes, but find nothing but the wooden back of the wardrobe.

The shotgun is missing.

CHAPTER FOURTEEN

Heather

Now

Joan Campbell opens the door a crack and stares at me, unsmiling. Her short curly hair is now almost completely white, rather than the fiery red I remember as a child. The pink fur of her slippers peeks out from the gap between the door and the wall.

'Hello, Heather,' she says simply. 'Everything all right?'

'Actually, no,' I reply. 'I can't seem to find Rosie. She left the front door wide open and I don't know where she's gone. Have you seen her?'

'No,' Joan says, her jowls wobbling slightly as she shakes her head. 'But I'm sure you'll find her.' She steps back and begins to close the door.

'If you see her, can you call?' I say, but the door is already shut, leaving me bemused as I stand there on the step with the drizzle pattering behind me.

Joan and Bob Campbell have never been the friendliest of neighbours, but they have in the past been polite enough to invite Mum in for a cup of tea. Opening the door a mere crack was just odd. Shutting it in my face was plain rude.

Nowt so queer as folk, Dad used to say, hamming up his Yorkshire accent. The words resonate with me now, especially after my strange run-ins with Ian Dixon and the Murray family.

I decide to check if Rosie has returned. After another quick search of the house, which is still empty, the white envelope I dropped on the kitchen table catches my eye. It is hand-written, with no stamp on the front. Cautiously I slide a finger beneath the seal and tear it open.

Heather and Rosie,

It is unanimous. We do not want your presence here. Wherever you go, you bring destruction. Sell the house and get out.

We do things our own way here. You've been warned.

Sincerely,
Buckthorpe Village

My hands begin to shake. I read the note a second time, and a third, somehow hoping for a different outcome each time. *Sincerely, Buckthorpe Village*. Is this real? Did the village hold some sort of democratic meeting to vote on our fate? I know that a lot changed after Rosie's accusation, but I didn't realise they hated us this much. Why is it my family targeted by the wrath of these people? Why not the Murrays?

Because Samuel isn't here any more, that's why. Rosie is. They want this to be over, and they want us gone.

Did the person who left this letter also break in and steal the shotgun?

I don't want to be here on my own. Not after finding this note. I fold it up and stuff it into the pocket of my jeans, and hurry out to my car. There's no reply to the quick text message I sent Rosie, and I have no missed calls. Perhaps she just wants to be left alone. That could have been her slipping out of the house when I thought I saw a shadow, deciding to run away rather than deal with the argument we had in the café.

It wouldn't be the first time she's left without dealing with conflict.

But the missing gun and the threatening note makes this … sinister.

I sit in the car and force myself to consider every logical solution to what has just happened. Someone broke into the house, took the gun and left the note. Why would a stranger steal the gun, and how would they know it was there? As Rosie said earlier, we live in a place surrounded by farms and people who hunt. Many households have a rifle or shotgun of their own.

Alternatively, Rosie came home, didn't see the letter, and took the gun. Would she hurt herself? Someone else? Who would she even want to hurt?

Or Rosie wrote the letter, left it on the mat and took the gun.

I shiver at the thought of her orchestrating all of this to convince me to sell the house. I know she wants us to sell. She could be in debt. I conjure up an image of a seedy drug dealer in a white vest and baggy jeans, with dirty skin and missing teeth. I have to face the fact that I don't know Rosie's financial circumstances, meaning I might not be far from the truth.

I try calling one more time before starting the car and taking it out through the open gate. My only option is to drive around Buckthorpe and see if I can spot her. Not that I can imagine Rosie walking down the street carrying the long shotgun case. Another thought flashes across my mind. Could my sister be the kind of lone-wolf killer you see on the news? Terrorising a small neighbourhood after a mental breakdown? The thought makes my skin go cold, but I don't truly believe it. She was upset, but I saw no signs of a breakdown.

At the same time, she was in a strange, agitated mood. I find my mind drifting to the image of her holding the gun, knowing how to load and unload it. What I'm not sure about is whether there were any boxes of ammunition in the back of the wardrobe.

And if there were, would Rosie use the gun on herself? Or would she settle an old score?

A flood of emotion washes over me as my thoughts turn to Dad and what he did, but I push them back down. It all depends on Rosie's intentions in the end, and I have to admit that her orchestrating this to frighten me is more likely than her stealing the gun to use it.

For a while, I find myself driving aimlessly. At one point I head over to the Murrays' farm and park on the road next to the fields. Somehow I feel as though I should be here to make sure she doesn't turn up in a rage, armed with the gun, a wronged woman in a movie taking her revenge. It's ridiculous, and after a few minutes, I leave. As I drive away, I hate myself for even thinking that she might hurt them. But then maybe I should own up to the fact that I hate myself for believing she killed Samuel, too. I've hated myself for ten years. But I still can't let go of the suspicion …

Focus, Heather.

I drive along the road adjacent to our old school and look out for anything untoward, but the place seems empty. It was a long shot. I don't believe Rosie has any real connection to the building. Then I carry on into the village, driving past the newsagent, the café and the pub. That's where I decide to stop.

Rosie is a recovering alcoholic, and it would be remiss of me to not check the pub. Now that I've calmed down a little, I can see that my wild theories were just that: silliness from the shock and fear of the letter and the missing gun. Chances are she either moved the gun, or she didn't take it at all. It's possible that I misread her mood today, and that her strange argumentativeness was actually down to alcohol withdrawal. Or perhaps Mum's death has tipped her over the edge. Perhaps this is where she is.

I enter the Prince of Wales, still somewhat bedraggled from the walk in the rain, almost certainly resembling a complete mess. Reg is behind the bar as always, his tall, willowy frame leaning over the beer pumps. The expression on his face is somewhere between wary and hostile when he sees me, with a slight curl of the upper lip and his eyelids half closed. He nods to me with his mouth set tight. As grim a welcome as I'd expected.

Did you write the letter? Did you sign it 'Buckthorpe Village'? I glance around me, wondering if anyone else here contributed to the note. The place isn't packed, but it is humming with voices as people enjoy a drink on a Saturday afternoon. I turn and walk to the bar.

'Don't suppose you've seen my sister in here, have you, Reg?' I ask, attempting to keep those thoughts at bay.

'Nope. Sorry. You getting a drink?'

I shake my head. 'Not right now. If you do see Rosie, can you ask her to call me, please?'

He shrugs. 'Sure.'

On my way out, I cast him a final glance, less than convinced that he actually will ask her to call me. Dad once said that Reg failed to take Colin Murray's car keys one night after he got drunk, and that he didn't trust a man who failed to watch out for his mates. But I don't have many other options at present.

'Heather!' Peter Murray saunters up, pint in hand, cheeks flushed. 'Can I get you a drink?'

'Actually, I was just on my way out.'

His eyes flick up and down my face, taking in what must be a pale, tense woman with frizzy hair and damp clothing. 'Is everything okay?'

'I can't find Rosie. She's not answering her phone and I think she's taken some of my parents' things.' I lower my voice. 'Dad's shotgun is missing.'

Peter places his pint glass down on the nearest table and gently leads me to the exit. 'Come on. I'll help you find her.' I almost want to smile, because for the briefest of moments it's like we're back at the farm, and Peter is saying: *Can I help you, Hev?*

'Oh, I don't want to spoil your afternoon,' I say limply.

'Don't be ridiculous. This is important.'

It's at that moment, hearing him say those words, that everything inside me squeezes and releases. My stomach cramps up with fear.

'You all right?' He reaches out and touches my shoulder. 'Your clothes are wet. Have you been walking out in the rain?'

'I got caught in a downpour,' I admit.

'Do you want to go home and get changed?'

I shake my head and find my throat is thick with emotion when I reply. 'No, I just want to find Rosie.'

'Okay, come on then.'

We hurry back to my car and Peter climbs into the passenger side. 'I'm sorry I can't drive,' he says. 'I'm three pints in.' He casts me a sheepish glance, eyebrows up in puppy-dog fashion. 'It's Johnno's birthday.'

I don't have time to ask who Johnno is, but I nod as I reverse out of the parking spot. 'I've driven all around the village and I can't see her anywhere. What with her problems, I thought I might find her at the pub, but obviously she's not there either.'

'Let's just think for a minute. She took your father's gun. Do you think she might hurt herself or someone else?'

I bite down hard on my bottom lip. 'I don't know. She might not even have been the person who took it. When I came home, the door was wide open and the gun was gone. All I know is that we had an argument in the café and she left. But …' I take a left onto the village road, a little too sharply, and Peter grasps hold of the car door.

'What is it?' he asks.

'There was a note,' I say. 'From the village. It was left on the doormat.'

'What kind of note?'

'The unpleasant kind,' I reply. 'Telling us we're not welcome here because we're troublemakers.'

Peter rolls his eyes. 'Fucking hell. This place.'

'Yep.'

'You okay?'

'No, I'm not, if I'm honest,' I admit. 'Do you think I should be worried someone is going to hurt us? The letter and the missing gun are pretty serious. Maybe I should call the police.'

Peter is quiet for a moment. 'Do you think it's possible Rosie wrote the note?'

Even though I've already considered this as a feasible solution, I bristle at the accusation.

Peter seems to notice this and quickly adds, 'Sorry, that's stupid. Why would she do that?'

I let out a sigh. 'Maybe she wants to make sure I sell the house.'

He nods. 'That makes sense. What kind of mindset was she in during your argument?'

'It wasn't a huge fight. I've seen her lose her temper before and this wasn't anything like that. Even though she was upset, she didn't seem out of control. Her taking the gun doesn't make much sense. Unless ...' My fingers curl tightly around the steering wheel. 'Unless she just wanted to get rid of it. Before we left the house, we were sorting through Mum's things, arranging them into piles. Rosie found the gun at the back of the wardrobe. It's the same gun that Dad ...'

'Oh,' Peter says as he realises what I mean. 'Well, that makes sense. Seeing the gun must have been upsetting for you both. Maybe she wants some space to sort through everything.'

I pause. 'Maybe she's just left. I keep trying to fit the gun going missing and the note and Rosie together, but maybe she just decided to take off.'

'If she's run away, the train station at Ingledown might be a good place to start. She could've booked a taxi to take her there. Did she pack anything?'

I shake my head. 'Her room was exactly the same.' Before I walked over to the Campbells, I'd thoroughly checked her room, lifting out drawers and even opening her suitcase. My heart feels heavy as I take the turning towards the town. Is my relationship with my sister damaged enough that she would leave all her belongings behind in order to get away from me?

CHAPTER FIFTEEN

Rosie

Then

At that time, I wasn't sure exactly what I wanted from Samuel. I was attracted to him, despite the fact that he was bullied at school by the popular kids. A relationship would have been impossible, given who my school friends were and what they thought of him. There wasn't anything particularly handsome about him anyway. Emily always called him Weasel Boy, because he had such small features. I had to admit, though, he did have beautiful eyes – almost the opposite shade of blue to mine, dark as the bottom of a well – and a gentle way about him. That day he caught me making a bow in the woods, he winced when I mentioned hunting. He was always kind to the animals on his farm, and I once caught him arguing with his dad when Mr Murray wanted him to help slaughter a fox caught in the barbed wire in one of the fields.

I came to anticipate the summer holiday excitement because I knew it would mean spending every weekday at the farm with him, Heather and Peter. There was a sense of belonging and a sense of being wanted when I was there. Samuel practically begged us to come back once Mr Murray stopped paying us pocket money. Together we were a team, and we meant the world to each other. Well, except maybe Peter, who was mostly just annoying.

However, when I turned fifteen, I started dating boys, eventually losing my virginity to Rhys Turner. It was expected of me as part of the group I was in, and I did it without much thought or care given. Emily and Rhona had already done it at a house party a few months before. I decided to get it over with, and that was how the whole thing felt. Afterwards, I couldn't help thinking that had it been with someone I actually liked, someone like Samuel, it might have been different. Better. It might have meant something.

That afternoon on the farm, I'd slapped him because he'd disrespected me. I'd slapped him because he'd insulted me by putting Heather first. And I'd slapped him out of fear because of what it all might mean. Because I wasn't sure then. I didn't truly understand my feelings for Samuel or his feelings for Heather. It felt so forbidden to be with him that despite the gut attraction I had for him, in my head I kept repeating the word *friendship*. I was jealous of his *friendship* with Heather. In fact, I even told Mum about it once.

'Rosie, honey,' she'd said. 'Keep an eye on your sister. She's fragile.'

What about me? I'd thought. Am I not? What am I?

It was Dad who said we shouldn't go back to the farm unless we were receiving some pay. Mum agreed, but Heather whined, and in the end I joined in with her until Grandad couldn't stand the sight of our moping. The compromise was that we went three times a week instead of five – much to Heather's annoyance – and Mrs Murray had to feed us lunch. The Murrays also had to throw in the occasional pint of milk or carton of eggs from the farm shop when they could spare it. The day it was agreed, Mum had one of her migraines and was in a mood all day, or so Heather said. I was out with Emily in Ingledown the evening it happened. She said that Mum claimed we were too old to be spending our summers with the Murray boys.

But the year went on, and I turned sixteen. We resumed our friendships. We still did the same silly stuff we did when I was thirteen. Building a fort out of hay. Timing Peter as he sprinted round the paddock on foot, laughing when Midnight decided to chase him. Everything fell back into place, and even our parents relaxed.

I had decided to stay on and take my A levels at the village school, and after the summer holidays, normality resumed. I kept out of Samuel's way. Rhys Turner asked me out, and then I dumped him a couple of months later when he asked Rhona out behind my back. I ended up getting embroiled in this love triangle and forgot to keep an eye on my sister.

The next summer, I did feel too old to be building hay forts with the others. I decided to quit, but Mum forced me to continue going. Every day I snapped at Peter and groaned whenever a sweeping brush was shoved into my hand. I would wander off to ride Midnight on my own around the paddock.

'What's your problem?' Mr Murray said to me one day.

I was standing next to the paddock with one foot on the five-bar gate. He strode over, sweat on his brow, damp, thinning hair stuck to his head. Age seventeen was the height of my teen angst. I couldn't stand adults and the way they lauded their superiority over my generation. Mr Murray represented every authority figure I couldn't stand. That alpha-male stance. The brooding expression. There were rumours that he bullied his family, and I'd certainly seen snippets of evidence myself, often hearing his booming voice yelling at his sons from some other part of the farm.

'Don't want to be here,' I said honestly.

'Why are you, then?'

'Mum makes me watch my sister,' I said. 'I have to keep an eye on her.'

A smile played on his lips. 'Your sister can take care of herself, can't she? What's your mother worried about anyway?'

I just shrugged.

He allowed his gaze to roam casually up and down my body, then said, 'You remind me of your mother when she was young.'

I pulled away from the gate and faced him. 'You knew her?'

'Yeah,' he said. 'There was a group of us all friends at school.'

'What was she like?' I asked.

'You,' he said. 'Just another lost little girl.'

My jaw dropped stupidly as I reached for a reply and found nothing.

'Keep dressing like that and no man will ever marry you,' he said as he walked away. 'You'll be meat to them.'

I stared down at the strappy top that revealed a hint of midriff and tried to pull it down. Later, when I got home, I threw it in the back of my wardrobe and never wore it again.

CHAPTER SIXTEEN

Heather

Now

Peter and I arrive at Ingledown train station about ten minutes later. It's a small station with two platforms and a tiny ticket office. Aside from the small block of toilets, there isn't anywhere to hide. I've spent many an evening here, huddled up on a bench in the freezing cold waiting for my train.

It takes me less than ten seconds to see that Rosie is not on the platform for departures. Peter stays close as we check the ticket office, and then I head into the women's toilets and search each cubicle. She isn't here.

Peter sees the dejected expression on my face when I return. 'We'll try somewhere else.'

'Unless her train has already gone.'

He nods his head quietly.

Before we go, I describe my sister to the guy behind the counter at the ticket office, but he says he can't remember anyone tall with dark hair and light-blue eyes. He reminds me that she could always have bought her ticket on the train and might not have come into the office at all. It's not a particularly comforting thought.

I stare out across the car park to the pub opposite. The White Hart. We used to come here underage with ridiculous fake IDs. The staff didn't particularly care and served us our vodka and Red

Bulls anyway. Then we'd pile into a taxi and attempt an imitation of sobriety when we stumbled back into Ivy Cottage.

'What is it?' Peter asks.

I nod towards the pub. 'Maybe she's in there.' Warmth floods through my veins. Those memories of the White Hart make me feel strongly that I'm right. What if she came to the train station with the intention of leaving, but lost her nerve and went across the road instead? This is definitely something Rosie would do. 'Do you mind waiting here?'

'Sure,' he says.

I hand him the car keys and walk towards the pub. There are tingles like pins and needles working their way up and down my arms. *Please be here, Ro.*

It has always been a loud place at all times of the day. Ingledown isn't a tourist town, but people do tend to stop here once they're off the train. When I step in, I feel swallowed whole by the sounds of people chattering to each other.

I scan the place, starting with the bar, moving over to the seats by the window. Rosie isn't there. Unless she's hiding away where it isn't as loud; there's another room around the back, one that's much quieter. I hurry through, barely able to stand the suspense, every part of me hoping to be right.

Picking my way around the tables and chairs, I make my way to the back of the room, and relief floods through my body. My sister sits alone, her body hunched over the table, a full glass of white wine before her. She has her long hair pulled over one shoulder and the light catches the fluidity of it, making it shine. When I approach, she lifts her gaze before I even open my mouth to speak, as though she sensed I was there.

'I haven't had any,' she says, gesturing to the wine. 'I ordered it and then sat here staring at it for an hour …'

When I throw my arms around her neck, she stiffens, and then finally relaxes into the hug. 'Why didn't you answer your phone?'

I ask, letting her go. I grab a stool and pull it close to her, sinking onto it, my clenched muscles finally beginning to relax. The relief almost takes me by surprise, making me realise just how worried I was about her.

'I'm an idiot,' she says. 'I reached the station all in a huff, ready to get on a train, any train, but then I stopped and came in here instead.' One side of her mouth lifts in a crooked smile. 'I half expected someone behind the bar to recognise me from all those nights we used our fake IDs. But it's different staff.'

'I guess ten years is a long time. People move on.'

'But not me.' She sighs. 'I'm still stuck where I was ten years ago. What have I done with my life? Nothing.'

'You've come a long way,' I remind her. 'You've beaten addiction. You didn't drink that glass of wine and that is a massive achievement.'

'Whoop de do.' She rolls her eyes.

I don't take it personally. Instead I pick up the glass and return it to the bar. 'There. Now it's gone,' I say when I sit down again.

Rosie's wan expression relaxes into a slight smile. 'I'm glad.'

'Me too,' I say. The note is burning a hole in my pocket. I decide to just show it to her. 'I found this at the house.'

She takes the paper and scans the words, her brow furrowed. I watch her read it twice and then throw it down on the table in disgust. 'This has Ian Dixon written all over it. I bet he wants to buy the cottage.'

'He already has a decent house, doesn't he?'

Rosie's fingers clench and unclench. If this is an act, it's a good one. 'All I know is that I don't trust him. He's probably trying to frighten us, but it's not going to work. We're going to take our sweet time and I don't give a shit if everyone hates me.' She stares at the wall, her eyes burning fiercely. 'It should be Samuel they hate, not me. This is all his fault.'

'Samuel isn't here,' I remind her.

'So what?' She turns and fixes her ice-blue eyes on mine. 'It's still his fault.'

'I know,' I say quietly.

'It's not fair. Nothing has been fair since …' She drifts off and clenches her fists again.

'Do you think Samuel is dead?' I ask, sensing that part of her guard has dropped.

But she hesitates before answering, and her defences come back up. 'All I think is that I hope he got what he deserved.'

'Rosie,' I say, keeping my voice calm. 'Did you take Dad's gun?'

'What?'

'When I went back to the cottage, the door was wide open and some of Mum's things were gone. Dad's shotgun wasn't in the wardrobe.'

She seems as shocked as I was when I discovered the missing items from the house. 'Heather, it wasn't me. I didn't even go back to the cottage. I got in a taxi and came straight to the train station. Was someone in our house? Oh my God, someone broke in!'

Hearing her say it makes the realisation that someone broke into our house finally hit home. Dread spreads through me, leaving me cold.

'Should we call the police?' I suggest. 'I didn't when I thought it might be you. I just went out and started searching for you.'

Rosie drums the table with her fingernails before she answers. 'What if Ian Dixon takes the call?'

'I know he doesn't like us, but surely he would still investigate a crime,' I reply.

Rosie points to the letter. 'He's been nothing but nasty to us since Mum died. What if he wrote that note? What if he was the one to break into the cottage?'

I lean back. 'I dunno, Rosie. That seems … extreme. He's an arsehole but I don't know about breaking and entering. And *theft*. It would put his career at risk.'

'I don't trust him,' Rosie says again.

'Why not? Has he upset you? What's going on, Ro?'

She shakes her head. 'I can't stand the cocky bastard, that's all.' And then she rubs her finger with her thumb.

The drive home is somewhat awkward, especially when I have to drop off Peter at the farm. As soon as he jumps out of the car, Rosie raises her eyebrows, an unspoken question on her lips.

'What?' I say defensively.

'Nothing.' She shrugs dramatically and smiles, but I know my sister, and I know that the smile isn't genuine.

When we arrive back at Ivy Cottage, the quiet of the house has a threatening feel to it. Someone has been in our home, touched our things, stolen from us and invaded our space. Thankfully, the front door is still locked this time. I open it and step cautiously in. Now that it's been established that someone broke into our house and stole a gun, I can't stop thinking about all the hostile stares and words that have come our way since Rosie arrived in Buckthorpe. It could have been any of them. It could have been more than one, if I'm to take the letter at face value. *Sincerely, Buckthorpe Village.*

'Whoever it was stole a photo album and a gun, but they left the television, laptops and jewellery.' Rosie steps gingerly through the house and I follow behind.

'Yep.'

'Then it was motivated by some reason other than money. Those items were chosen specifically.'

'The only place they touched was Mum's bedroom. Everything else is exactly the way we found it, except …'

'What?'

'Well, I checked your room. I basically ransacked it. I thought it might help me find you.'

'You went through my things?' For the briefest of moments, she seems sixteen again, an incredulous expression on her face, hand on her hip. *Stop borrowing my clothes!* I almost laugh.

'Yeah, sorry.'

She waves a hand. 'Doesn't matter. Let's try and work out which album they took. If we know what's in it, we might be able to work out which sack of shit in Buckthorpe wants us dead.'

'Don't,' I say.

'What? It's true, isn't it? Why else would someone steal a *gun*?'

Though her words make my blood run cold, I try to keep a cool head to help us think through all the possible options. 'They could've just waited for us to come home and killed us.'

'Good point,' Rosie admits. 'Yeah, none of this makes sense.'

'I already know which album it was. It was one of the big leather-bound albums with old photos in it. I don't think we'd looked at the photos inside yet.'

'Weird. I guess there was something inside it that someone didn't want us to see.'

'And the gun?'

She shrugs. 'I don't know. They didn't want us to have it for some reason.'

'They don't want us to be armed?' I suggest.

I follow Rosie up the stairs and into Mum's bedroom, where she sinks down onto the bed. 'Just because they didn't try to kill us today doesn't mean they won't.'

'Maybe we should leave,' I say. 'Or maybe we should take a chance with the police.'

But Rosie shakes her head. 'No way. I'd say the police are the most likely suspects.'

'What's going on between you and Ian Dixon?' I'm not sure what's bothering me the most, that Rosie is obviously aggravated by the sergeant, or that she won't tell me why. What is she hiding?

'Nothing,' she says. 'But he as good as told us to get the fuck out of Buckthorpe. He hates us being here.'

'Enough to want us dead?' I raise an eyebrow sceptically. 'I don't think so.'

'Then he just wants to scare us. That's what all of this is, a scare tactic. The letter, the gun … it makes sense,' she says.

'Except for the photo album,' I remind her. 'Anyway, how would he know we were out of the house? He works in Ingledown most of the time.'

Rosie shrugged. 'Maybe he hired someone to watch us.'

'How did he get in without breaking in?' Her fixation on Ian Dixon is beginning to annoy me. I want to be free to think, to explore other possibilities.

'Oh, that's my fault, sorry,' she says. 'I was the last one out and I forgot to lock the door.' When my expression drops, she adds. 'Don't go off on one. We used to leave the house unlocked all the time.'

It's true, and I didn't notice her not lock the door, so I have to shoulder some of the blame. Buckthorpe always felt a million miles away from the dangers of cities. Most people left their houses unlocked. It was only after Rosie's accusation that Mum started locking the doors all the time. That was when our idyllic childhood was interrupted by danger for the first time. Someone threw a brick through the window and painted our house with abuse. There would be whispers in the school corridors. I remember finding a note in my school bag that said Rosie was a liar and I should disown 'the bitch'.

I always suspected Peter of that, but now, with hindsight, I think it's probably unlikely.

There were horrible incidents aimed at Rosie, but the truth was that most people believed her. A lot of the hostility came from the fact that she had rocked the status quo. It made people uncomfortable, unsettled the village. No one wanted it to be true, but at the same time people thought Samuel was a weird loner and exactly the kind of boy to attack the most beautiful and popular girl in Buckthorpe.

'What are we going to do?' I say, pulling my thoughts from the past to the present. I move a pile of clothes from Mum's little chair in the corner of the room, and sit down, exhausted by the eventful day.

She shrugs. 'Sell up and get out? Honestly, I just don't know whether I can see another solution.'

I rest my hands on my knees and allow my tired shoulders to slump. 'But this is our home.'

Rosie gets up and paces the room, fingers drumming against her thighs. 'Is it? We're not welcome here. *I'm* not welcome here. I'm still being punished for what happened all those years ago.'

I swallow, trying to force some moisture into my throat. What I'm about to say makes every inch of my mouth dry. 'Rosie, maybe we should talk about the past.'

She stops pacing and her body grows rigid. 'What do you mean?'

'The things that are happening to us are all connected with what happened with Samuel. Don't you think we should talk about it?'

'What is there to say?' she says quietly. Her fingers still drum against her legs, but the rest of her is still. She stands like a soldier; tense from head to toe. 'You know everything.'

I shake my head slowly. 'That's not true.'

Her chin lifts and her eyes widen as though warning me to stop talking. She doesn't say it, though. She doesn't ask me to stop. It's just her eyes that say the words she can't.

I open my mouth to speak, then lose my nerve and decide to try a different approach. 'What about the other girls? Rhona and Emily. Didn't they start that blog about Samuel?'

Rosie rolls her eyes. 'I didn't ask them to do that, and if you want to know whether I think they were telling the truth, I just don't know.'

'They accused him of some pretty weird things. Satanic stuff.'

She shrugs. 'And?'

'Well, you never …' I feel as though part of my insides have shrivelled up and died. Why can't I say it? I close my eyes and finish the sentence. 'You never accused Samuel of any of that.'

'I know.'

'Is that because he didn't do those things with you?'

'What does any of this have to do with someone breaking into the house?' There's that warning glance again, telling me to stop probing.

'Honestly, I don't know. If Rhona and Emily made up their accusations, maybe someone thinks you made yours up too. And they want to scare us away to punish us.'

'You mean like *you* think I made it up?' Rosie begins pacing again, her hands now clenching and releasing with each step.

'That's not what I mean,' I say.

'Are you sure, Heather? Because you knew Samuel better than anyone. You had a reason to hope I was lying. The two of you were best friends, after all.'

'You know I was always on your side. You're my sister. I'm always on your side.'

She shakes her head slowly. 'I don't think that's true.'

'It is,' I say. 'You know it is. You know that I never said a word about you leaving the house that night.'

Her face flushes red, and she stops, shifting her weight from one foot to the other. 'I never asked you to do that.'

'I know.'

'And I never told anyone about what I saw *you* do, either,' she says, eyes fixed on mine.

The blood drains from my face.

CHAPTER SEVENTEEN

Rosie

Then

It shouldn't have happened. I'd been walking around for hours trying to make sense of it all, but I couldn't. It would never make sense and it would never be okay.

My skin was dirty from where I'd hit the ground. There were scratches on my skin from the thorns that had caught my flesh. As night fell, I lost sight of the path that wound through the forest. Where was I? All I knew was that underfoot, the terrain had changed from the smoother footpath to the rough and rocky muddier part of the forest. With each step, the trees closed around me until I had to manoeuvre my body sideways to squeeze through.

What if he finds me while I'm here? I thought. What if he comes searching for me?

I'd figured that Mum and Dad must know I was missing by that point in the evening and I hoped that they might search for me. Heather would have gone home on Lady after I ran away from the Murrays'. I was worried that Midnight was still in the stable there. Dad would have to go and fetch him, and he'd be mad about that. But at least they'd know that I'd gone.

There was a rustle of leaves behind me. What was it? A fox? A pheasant? Did pheasants come out at night? Were there any wolves in Yorkshire? Don't be ridiculous, Rosie, I told myself. Keep going.

My ankle twisted when I took a misstep down a bank, and it was at that moment I realised I could hurt myself. I still remember the way the thought made my chest tight with fear. My breathing wouldn't come out properly and I felt light-headed and anxious, like I might keel over at any moment. Later on, I came to identify that feeling as a panic attack. I would come to understand panic again and again throughout my life. I sat down on the mud and the nettles and took a moment to steady myself. *What would Heather do?* She was always the best of the Sharpes in a crisis. She always had the answers. If Heather was with me there, she'd tell me to take a deep breath and calm down.

I examined my ankle. Twisted but not broken. Gently I tested my weight on it. I discovered that I could limp along just fine. It was going to slow me down, but at least I would have to go more carefully. That was a good thing, because then I wouldn't fall down any more banks.

I wish I could say that I knew the forest like the back of my hand. That was what the tough girls in the fantasy novels I loved would say. In that moment, I was the opposite of those girls. I'd never felt so powerless. Even though I spent so much time riding in the wood, I only knew the paths, and I definitely couldn't remember them in the dark. Later, I would come to know a path through the woods in the dark, but not that night.

What I did know – when I was seventeen and terrified – was that Buckbell was vast, stretching out past our village, eventually feeding into a much larger forest that continued through the county. I could end up lost for days if I wasn't careful.

There it was again, the rustle of leaves behind me. Was someone following me? Immediately I thought it was him, trying to find me in the dark. Or maybe it was Dad. No, it couldn't be Dad, he would call my name. Had they reported me missing yet? Were the police searching for me? If only I hadn't lost my phone I'd be able to call them, and then I'd know the time, too. All I knew was that the sun had set and I was lost. My limbs shook and my bottom lip trembled as I took each step.

Deep down inside, I felt shame.

One foot in front of the other, Rosie. Keep going. I might not have been a fictional warrior girl, but I still knew that I wasn't a coward. I thought about Mum, and how she always said that my bravery was half wildness, half stupidity. She was probably right. After all, I was stupid enough to get myself into this situation. I bit my lip and tried not to think about the scratches on my legs, the bruises, the dirt on my skin, my torn jodhpurs and my missing riding boot. I kept fighting back the tears. What was I going to say to my dad when I saw him? Would I have to live with this shame and guilt for the rest of my life, even though it wasn't my fault?

Every time the wind blew through the trees, my heart skipped a beat and I whipped my head around to check on the darkness behind me. There was nothing there but the hint of moonlight on branches, and nothing ahead but yet more trees. I thought I heard someone sobbing, until I realised it was my own ragged breath wheezing from my chest. Heather would never be this weak. I kept thinking back to four years ago when Lady had taken off down the road and she'd stayed quiet. She didn't even cry.

It was all Lady's fault. No, that wasn't true. It was all *my* fault. I was the one who went too fast that day and fired Lady up into such a fervour that she panicked. Lady was a good pony; she never misbehaved, apart from when I insisted on racing her with Midnight. If Mr Murray hadn't found us that day, we would never have ended up spending our summers at the farm. We wouldn't have made friends with Samuel Murray, and none of this would've happened. I wouldn't have been limping through the woods in the dark with all that shame inside me like a coiled-up ball of steel wire in my stomach. I felt, and still feel, like it might unspool at any moment and rip out my guts in the process.

The rustling came back, and this time I was convinced that it was footsteps behind me. A shooting pain worked through my ankle as I tried to speed up. I ignored it – thinking about my warrior heroines – because if I was being followed, I needed to get out of here fast. *What if it's him?* I thought.

There was no time to be cautious now that I'd heard the rustling of leaves behind me. I beat my way through the close-knit bushes and thorns, feeling thin twigs striking my face and torso. Weeds stuck to my feet and ankles. Up above, a sliver of moonlight helped me see my way through the woods, preventing me from running into a tree trunk or falling down a steep slope. I'd finally reached a point where there were fewer trees, which meant that I might not be as far into the woods as I'd thought. The path had to be around here somewhere.

Still ignoring the twinge in my ankle, I broke into a tentative jog, almost losing my sock in the process. Behind me, the rustling noise also sped up. There had to be someone there. It couldn't be a coincidence. And yet when I glanced behind me, still I saw nothing. Was there a ghost following my every step? Or was it him watching me from behind a tree? Following at such a distance that I couldn't see him. There were many shadows to hide in. Many dark places for a hunter to watch his prey.

The tears dried on my cheeks as I half jogged, half stumbled my way through Buckbell. There was only one aim in my mind: to get out of the woods alive. To get home and fold myself into my mum's arms. To get away from whoever was behind me. When the ground underfoot began to even out, I didn't even glance over my shoulder. Instead, I hurried on as fast as I could, letting adrenaline take over, ignoring the sharp stones beneath my unshod foot.

The moonlight allowed me to identify the path and make out the shapes of familiar trees and the place where the woods opened out towards the road. All I needed to do was follow that narrow road to Ivy Cottage.

But afterwards I had to face my family.

What was I going to tell them?

I started to slow down, tired, wary of what waited for me at home. There was no more rustling behind me, but even the slightest change in the wind frightened me. When my boot hit the tarmac of the road, I sped up again. I knew I was less than five minutes away from home. In the distance I saw the light from our neighbours' cottage. I dared to peek behind me one last time. The road was clear. Whoever had been in the woods was gone. But still I pressed on, just a few minutes away from home.

There were voices in the distance, but I couldn't make out what they were saying. My body hurt all over, but the sound spurred me on. A moment later, I heard the familiar sound of Dad's voice.

'You stay here. I'm going to drive around the village. Dad, do you want to come or stay?'

'I'll come,' Grandad replied.

'Wait,' I called out. I waved my arms around in the darkness until they saw me coming up the road. A car door slammed shut and Dad's shape hurried towards me.

Mum came sprinting down the drive, her long cardigan trailing behind her, Heather and Grandad following. But Dad was the first person to greet me at the gate, more panicked than I'd ever seen him. The whites of his eyeballs were all I focused on.

'What happened to you?'

Only then did I remember that my clothes were torn, that I was covered in mud and that thorns had scratched my skin. I started to cry. I didn't know what to say.

'Rosie?' Mum swung the gate open and pulled me into her arms. 'Wait, give her some space,' she said to the others. She manoeuvred me forward. 'Let's get you inside.'

Grandad peeled away his jacket and placed it over my shoulders. I saw Heather, standing back, her face almost translucent in the glow of our security light. Even her lips were pale. She seemed completely frozen by the sight of me. It was while looking at her that I began to cry.

When we reached the kitchen, I was positioned on a chair and a blanket was laid over my legs. I didn't deserve any of this. Mum's eyes were questioning as she fussed over the scratches on my face.

'Rosie, what happened?' Dad asked.

He didn't want to know what happened. Why would any dad want this for their children?

'He hurt me,' I muttered.

'Who?' Dad asked.

My lips trembled as I answered. 'Samuel Murray.'

CHAPTER EIGHTEEN

Heather

Now

'What did you see?'

Rosie pulls her legs onto the bed and crosses them. 'I saw you kissing Samuel in the woods after ... after the incident.' She lets out a long sigh. 'No matter what you say now, Hev, it doesn't matter. You still kissed him after I told you what had happened. That means you didn't believe me when I said that Samuel attacked me.'

I rub my palms along my knees and close my eyes, not sure which emotion to feel first. A few days after she'd limped home and told us what had happened, I'd met Samuel in the woods. Rosie must have followed me. I hadn't intended to kiss him. I just needed to know the truth. Since then, I'd always felt ashamed that I'd met him and the kiss had happened.

What I hadn't told my sister – what I hadn't told anyone – was that Samuel had been my boyfriend for several months before Rosie accused him of sexual assault. We'd kept it a secret between us.

'Why were you there that day?'

She rolls her eyes. 'Why were *you* there? You were supposed to be at school!'

'I needed to talk to him. He was my boyfriend,' I whisper.

Rosie smiles as though this revelation is important to her. It's true that I've never said it aloud, though I assumed that Rosie had figured it out.

'Secret boyfriend,' Rosie corrects. 'Sneaking around behind everyone's backs.'

'It wasn't like that,' I insist. 'I was, well, we were a bit shy about telling people. Samuel thought there'd be teasing at school, and I didn't want Dad to know. He hated us talking about boys.'

Rosie lets out a laugh. 'Forbidden dating. Yeah, I remember. I guess I didn't tell anyone when I went on dates in Ingledown. Not even Mum.'

'We didn't talk to them, did we?' I admit.

'Nope.' She sighs. 'But you could have told me. You *should* have told me. I'm your big sister.'

'I wanted to. It was Samuel who didn't.'

'Why not?'

But I don't want to tell her.

'Hev,' she insists. 'Why not?'

'Because he thought you'd be jealous.'

Rosie lets out another laugh, but this one sounds almost manic. 'And now Peter. The adopted brother.'

'Don't,' I say, flinching.

'Why not? It's obvious he still has a thing for you.'

The harshness of her tone riles me up again and I can't help snapping back, 'Yeah, well for most of our childhood it was obvious Samuel had a thing for *you*, and look how that ended up.'

'Jesus, we should just not talk about any of this.' Rosie gets up from the chair. 'Ten years later and you can't accept any of the shit that went down.'

'Explain it to me then,' I say. 'Tell me everything.'

'I can't,' she says. 'I can't tell you because you don't want to know. Trust me.'

'I *have* to know, Rosie,' I say. And I mean every word.

*

The atmosphere between us is icy for the rest of the day. I'm surprised the windows don't frost over. Rosie might have come back after almost leaving, but she still won't talk to me about the past, except to argue with me about whether I believe her or not. I'm now more convinced than ever that she knows what I've always suspected, but she won't do anything to assuage those fears. Why? Is it because she can't? Or won't?

I spend most of the afternoon in my room researching Emily and Rhona on Facebook. The argument with Rosie has made me even more determined to find out the truth. I don't think for even a second that she has ever believed either of those girls. In fact, aside from gossip, it was clear that most people didn't believe them. A lot believed Rosie, but they were more sceptical about strange blog posts rambling on about satanic rituals. After sending both girls a message, I root through my old belongings until I find the notebook where I wrote down everything I knew about Samuel and the accusations against him.

It was 3 April 2009. Rosie came home after being missing for several hours. She had cuts and bruises all over her and the seam on her jodhpurs had ripped somehow. One of her boots was missing, but we found that later in the woods. She told Dad that Samuel had hurt her. That he'd tried to force himself on her and that she'd eventually managed to push him off. She was sobbing, blood, mud and tears running down her face. I stood there transfixed, my stomach churning and churning until I finally ran upstairs and vomited into the toilet.

On 5 April, the Tumblr account appeared claiming that Samuel had sexually assaulted Emily and Rhona (though they didn't reveal their identities until later on) while using satanic imagery and language.

Then, on 7 April, another girl at school, Becky, claimed he'd done the same to her.

And then the floodgates opened.

Someone had seen him cutting himself on the football pitch after school and smearing the blood on the goalposts.

Someone else had seen him wearing reptile contact lenses while walking around Buckthorpe.

Someone else claimed to have seen him kill a cat.

Someone had seen him chucking a bucket of sheep's blood at his mother and laughing.

Someone had seen him dancing naked in the woods with Buckthorpe Jack.

The Murrays' farm was vandalised too. The road-facing wall was spray-painted with the words *SATAN WEIRDO*. A sheep had a pentagram painted on it.

On 8 April, a reporter called our house claiming that the story was about to make the nationwide news and we should get a statement out. In the end, a young girl went missing in Devon and all the rumours stayed local.

But it didn't stop the hysteria. We were the satanist village now. Backward weirdos that people from Ingledown made fun of.

Reading the details makes all the pain come flooding back. I close the book and press my fingers into my eye sockets, willing it all to go away. Maybe it's time to admit to myself that I want justice for what happened to Samuel. He didn't dance naked with Jack in the woods or hurt a cat or do anything with sheep's blood. Yes, he was an outsider, but he wasn't any of those other things. I knew him. I knew him better than anyone, didn't I?

Which comes back to the part about Rosie. What do I believe? Do I believe that my boyfriend assaulted my sister? Or do I believe that my sister falsely accused my boyfriend of assault? If Samuel never attacked Rosie, could she have killed him to keep the secret from coming out? If he did attack her, did she kill him as revenge? And if he did die, who helped Rosie murder a tall sixteen-year-old boy and hide his body? Because she could never have done it on her own.

On the other hand, what if Lynn Murray is right and her son didn't die that night? What if he's out there somewhere, living a new life with a wife and children? Or drug-addled and cold-hearted? If he is alive, why hasn't he contacted me?

It could have been suicide. If Samuel did attack Rosie, and then the other girls at school piled on with their accusations, it could have tipped him over the edge. There's a part of me that can imagine him running away to drown himself in a river and no one ever finding his body. But the chances of his body never being found, even in a river, seem slim to me. He didn't take a car, and there are no deep rivers near our village. If he'd cut his wrists or jumped from a high place, then surely someone would have found him, unless he went so deep into the woods that even the missing-person search failed to find him.

My phone vibrates before I can think of any more answers. Emily suggests that we should meet.

By the time I'm on my way to the Prince of Wales, Rhona has also been in touch and suggested that she comes to meet us too. The idea of dealing with both women at the same time fills me with some trepidation, but it's a good way to get this over and done with. All the way there, my stomach swirls.

The pub will no doubt be full of villagers, and it's possible that one or more of them wrote us the threatening note to try and frighten us. I don't think it could be Rhona or Emily, because they're still friendly with Rosie. At least they'll be allies while I'm there.

There's another reason why my stomach flips over. What I didn't tell Rosie while we were arguing was that Samuel wasn't just my boyfriend; he was the boy I loved deeply. The only person I've ever loved in that way. To Rosie, my lack of a love life is due to my primness. She blames my doomed relationships on my stand-offishness, but the reality is that true heartbreak takes a long time to heal.

I've allowed my other boyfriends to drift away because they don't mean even a tenth of what Samuel meant to me. Not the guy I dated on and off throughout university, not Simon, not the boss I slept with intermittently – none of them. My replies to their texts or voicemail messages would become less and less frequent until they gave up. Simon, a man so dull that Mum constantly called him Steven and on other occasions forgot he even existed, clung on a little longer than most men might in that situation, going as far as to once suggest we move in together, but everyone has a limit. I would push and push until I found that limit.

It wasn't my intention to distance myself from them; it was more of a subconscious thing, I think. After the first few weeks, or the first few months, my stomach would drop when I heard my phone buzz and saw the name on the screen. I'd clam up with tension at the thought of any sort of commitment. I threw myself into university work or my job as a distraction. And then, later, I threw myself into caring for Mum.

But if I can never love anyone in the same way I loved Samuel, does that mean I'll forever be lonely? Forever be a little bit sad? And what does it say about me that I still love the person my sister accused of sexual assault? What's wrong with me?

Reg glances up when I walk in, and then turns away. A line from *The League of Gentlemen* pops into my mind: *A local pub for local people.* I'm local, of course, but I'm as unwelcome as any outsider. And is it any surprise? It was Rosie's accusation that changed this village for the worse. Perhaps it's my family that's the rotten core everyone is trying to dig out. Or it could be the Murrays. Or Ian Dixon. I'm not sure I can think straight any more.

The two bleach-blonde women sitting on the corner couch stand to greet me.

'Oh my God, Heather!' Emily kisses me on the cheek. 'You look great. No mud on your face today?'

The reference to the nickname she gave me at school makes me grit my teeth with annoyance. 'Well, funnily enough, I do actually shower.'

She laughs, and it's the same boisterous cackle I remember. It dawns on me then that I'm here in part in the hope that they've somehow received some karma over the years. What a petty and bitter thought.

'Good to see you, Hev,' Rhona says, before sucking her drink through her straw. I can't help but focus on the fine lines around her puckered mouth. Smoker's wrinkles. 'It's been a long time.'

I take a seat on the opposite side of the table. 'Yeah, ten years, probably.'

'Well, I've seen you around a few times,' Emily says. Which is true, but I always crossed the street and pretended I didn't see her.

After I've ordered a Coke from the bar, we settle down to chat. I can't help but notice that both women appear to be drinking cocktails, despite it being early afternoon. That doesn't bother me. If they're drunk, they'll say more.

'So what have you been up to for the last ten years?' Rhona asks.

'Oh, you know. Uni. Job. I'm an accountant now.'

She grins. 'I'll send you my taxes then.'

I laugh, even though that joke makes me die a little inside every time. 'Actually, it's for a large firm. I wouldn't have a clue about individual taxes.'

Rhona nods, and the conversation lulls until Emily starts it again.

'We have kids now,' she says. 'Two each. I have a boy and a girl, and Rhona has two boys.'

'Oh wow, that's fantastic,' I say.

There's another break in conversation while they show me several photos of their children – Noah, Amelia-May, Jackson and

Asher – and by the time I've scrolled through them, both Emily and Rhona have finished their drinks. I politely order more, seeing as I'm the one wanting information.

'So what's the deal, Hev?' Rhona's habit of using my nickname makes my toes curl, and I think she knows that. 'No offence, but you've been coming back to Buckthorpe pretty much every week for months, and you've never reached out. In fact, we weren't really ever friends. It was your sister we knew better – not that we didn't like you.'

I want to say: *You didn't like me and I certainly didn't like you*, but I hold my tongue.

'I wanted to talk about Samuel Murray.'

I expected more of a reaction to that statement, such as a sharp intake of breath, or an uncomfortable shuffling in their seats, but neither Rhona nor Emily even blink.

'What do you want to know?' Emily sips her cocktail.

'It's been ten years since he went missing, and I guess I just wanted to think about it some more. And, I don't know, find out about the Tumblr blog you set up.'

Rhona shrugs. 'What is there to say? It's all on the site.'

'And it's all true?'

They both change their body language almost immediately. Rhona crosses her arms over her chest, while Emily juts out her chin.

'Yes, it's all true. What the fuck, Heather? Aren't you a feminist?' Emily says, her voice uncomfortably loud in the quiet pub.

'Of course,' I say, slightly taken aback by the sudden change in direction.

'Doesn't sound like it.' Rhona rolls her eyes.

'You don't blame the victim. *Ever*.' Emily flicks the top of her glass with her fingernail.

'I wouldn't,' I say, struggling to find the words to get things back on track. 'I would never do that. But we were young and the whole village went apeshit. There was such an abundance of weird accusations about Samuel that it's hard to remember what was true and what wasn't.'

Emily narrows her eyes. 'Were you and him fucking?' She takes another sip of her cocktail and breaks out into a grin.

'What?' I reply. 'No!'

'Oh my God,' Rhona says in delight, brushing back a lock of platinum-blonde hair. 'You were going out with the freak.'

'It makes sense,' Emily says, both of them ignoring me and speaking to each other. 'She was a freak too.'

A flush of hot anger spreads through my veins. 'You're both liars. Samuel didn't speak in tongues or harm animals. You made it all up to get attention. You gave interviews and walked around with tears in your eyes playing the victim when in fact it was all a complete fabrication.'

'That's why you wanted to meet. You think he's innocent of everything. Well, sorry, Hev, but you're wrong. He tried to rape your sister, and you're still defending him.' Emily leans forward, tapping a manicured nail on the tabletop, still with the same grin on her face, fascinated by me. 'Wow, what a mess that is.'

I get up. 'None of that is true.'

But Emily won't let it go. 'What isn't true? That strange little loner Samuel Murray attacked your sister? Or that you're still in love with him?'

I walk away without responding to her question, my hands shaking. Her words ring in my ears, echoing my own thoughts too closely.

CHAPTER NINETEEN

Heather

Now

It broke my heart when Rosie accused Samuel of attempted rape. And it shattered me into pieces when he disappeared and I found Rosie's bracelet in the woods. For a decade I've been dealing with that grief. I know how deeply I loved Samuel. What I don't know is whether I still love him, and whether I can love him and believe Rosie at the same time. Is that even possible? Is there something fundamentally wrong with me?

There have been moments when I've hoped he might come back and explain everything and tell me that all my suspicions are false: that no one killed him, that Rosie misunderstood what happened between them, that we can still be together. But my mind feeds on logic, and logic always takes me back to Samuel being dead.

After meeting Emily and Rhona, I've no doubt that they made up their ridiculous claims in order to get more attention. They might even have convinced themselves that they'd been hurt by him, but they aren't traumatised by whatever happened in their imaginations. There's no sense of shame or guilt. My sister is the one who felt those things. Rosie went through an event that turned her inside out and made her lose herself.

Rosie suffered. They didn't.

Is it possible for me to believe that the boy I loved hurt my sister? In one sense, no, it isn't. The boy I loved would never do that. But what if he was never the boy I loved? What if he hid a dark side from me? When we first started working at the farm, I saw the way he regarded my sister. She was always the more beautiful one – a curvy figure, skin the colour of cream, long hair, bags of self-confidence. I paled in comparison. I was mousy and plain. But what I had that Rosie didn't was a long friendship built on common ground. Samuel and I were both odd little introverts who preferred books and music to adventure. We were best friends who loved to talk to each other until the day we kissed and became more than friends.

But what if he always wanted my sister and couldn't get her out of his head? What if there was a darkness inside him that he hid from everyone until the day he couldn't hide it any longer? Just like Rosie … She wears her darkness in the scars on her arms, the dark circles beneath her eyes, the tired expression that clouds her features when she thinks that no one sees. What does she keep hidden away in her mind?

If I'm going to uncover the truth, I need to consider all the options. If Samuel didn't hurt Rosie, then it's possible that someone else did. I have always believed that she went through a traumatic event the night she came home injured and muddied. That part has never been in question. But if not Samuel, then who? And are they here in Buckthorpe?

I'm still sitting in my car, staring at the Prince of Wales, with its mock-Tudor exterior and faded sign. I can't seem to make myself start the engine and drive away. Rosie is probably at home, and I don't want to face her. Whenever I look at her, she sees the part of me still in love with Samuel, and I see the part of her that may have killed him, and neither of us can see anything else.

No, I don't want to go home and face that.

Ten minutes later, Emily and Rhona come stumbling out of the exit and make their way along the pavement into the village.

With them gone, I can safely go back inside without getting into a shouting match with two former school bullies. Alcohol is a bad idea right now, but it's also an excellent way to block out all the nonsense in my mind; to numb myself from all the pain. And God, there has been so much pain, and now there's not even Mum's shoulder to cry on.

Reg does a double-take when I return.

This time I sit at the bar. 'I know you don't want me here, but I want a double vodka and Coke, please.'

He doesn't disagree, just nods. 'All right.'

I've never been the person who drinks alone at the bar before. That spot is usually reserved for people escaping either their family or their loneliness. Right now, I'm escaping both.

There's no music in the pub and the glass scratches loudly against the top of the bar as he slides the drink towards me. I take it greedily, glad that the Coke masks the sharp, peppery taste of the vodka.

Reg leans back away from the bar, but his eyes travel towards me every now and then, even though he's pretending to watch the television.

'Sounds like you were asking a lot of questions while you were here with those two,' he says eventually.

A defensive retort rests on the tip of my tongue, but I don't have the courage to utter it out loud.

'Not really,' I say instead.

'The past is the past,' Reg replies. Whatever football match he was watching seems to have concluded, and he drags a wet rag along the bar.

Half of my vodka is already drained, and I'm beginning to feel a pleasant buzz. 'Sometimes the past interferes with the present.'

He nods almost approvingly. 'I can't deny that.'

We're silent for a while, me staring at my drink, going over the conversation with Rhona and Emily in my mind; him wiping down the bar, rearranging the glasses. At times I wonder whether Reg was involved with the note we received. Perhaps it was him and Ian Dixon and the Murrays, and maybe Joan and Bob Campbell too, all out to get us. I finish my vodka and order the same again. An alcohol-infused warmth spreads over my skin, daring me to stay put, even though the village hates me and my sister.

'You're going to get drunk,' Reg warns.

'Maybe that's my intention.'

He frowns. 'Take it from someone who knows, being pissed beyond all hope isn't a good place to be.'

I ignore his warning and pick up my phone, intending to avoid idle conversation by browsing the internet. But there's a text message from Rosie that I don't want to deal with. *Where are you?* Good question, big sis. I have no idea.

Avoiding conversation might be the wrong thing to do. I place my phone back down on the bar and lift my gaze to Reg, thinking about how much he has aged. Those fuzzy black eyebrows I remember as a teenager are almost completely grey now. When Dad was in a good mood, we used to come to the Prince of Wales for Sunday lunch.

'You must've overheard a lot of drunken things in this place,' I say, the alcohol beginning to loosen the tongue I usually keep so expertly in check.

'Aye.'

'Do you remember the night my dad got in a fight here?' It was after Rosie's accusation. Dad had been the target of some of the nastiness between us and the Murrays. Lines were drawn in the sand and sides were taken. Not everyone sided with us, especially after what happened with Emily and Rhona. Their over-the-top accusations cast some doubt on Rosie's story, which led to her being as much of a target as Samuel.

'Aye.'

I shrug. 'Well, what happened?'

Reg exhales loudly through his nose. 'Colin Murray came in and there were words.'

I almost roll my eyes. Reg has that typical laconic Yorkshireman stereotype down to a T. 'What were the words?'

'Colin thought your sister was lying. And he thought she had put those two' – he nods to where Emily and Rhona were sitting earlier – 'up to the claims they made.'

'Rosie did no such thing.'

'Never thought she did,' he says.

'And you don't believe Rhona and Emily either?'

'What do I know?' he replies. 'It all seemed a bit far-fetched, like summat two teenage girls with overactive imaginations would come up with. But like I said, what do I know?'

I nod and sip my drink, slowing down a little now that Reg has opened up. I need to remember anything important he might have to say.

'My dad and Colin seemed to make up eventually, though, didn't they?'

He shrugs. 'They became civil as far as I know.'

'Did you hear any of their conversations here?'

He shakes his head. 'There weren't any.'

'What do you mean?'

'Colin would be on one side of the pub and John the other. If there was a private reconciliation, I never saw it. They just kept themselves to themselves. But after Samuel disappeared, there was less tension anyway.'

It seems odd to me that they wouldn't ever speak again. Why would Colin contain his animosity for my family without coming to a friendly agreement with Dad? Colin Murray was an all-or-nothing person. He was either a friend or an enemy, and yet he and Dad had reached some sort of unspoken agreement to allow them to share the same spaces in the village. It did make sense in a way. It just seemed out of character for him.

The door opens and Peter walks in alone. When his eyes rest on mine, he grins. 'Hello again.'

'Are you a permanent fixture here?' I ask.

'I could say the same to you.' He nods at Reg and then glances down at my drink. 'Want another?'

'Double vodka and Coke, please.'

'You're not messing around, Heather.' His brown eyes widen but he orders the drink anyway, along with a pint of lager for himself. 'Didn't I see your car in the car park?'

'Yes, but I'm not driving home. I'll walk.'

'You were going to walk home on your own?' He frowns as he leans against the bar, one elbow bent to flex his upper arm, tightening the linen blue shirt he's wearing.

'It's still light out,' I say.

'I'll walk you home. No arguments.'

After being with me the day someone broke into our house and stole Dad's gun it's not surprising that he's cautious.

After a sip of his pint, he regards me with an intense gaze that makes me blush. 'Care to tell me what brought you here again? Or are you after some alone time?'

'Actually, I came to meet Rhona and Emily.'

Peter grimaces in a comedic way, and I laugh. 'Why on earth would you want to do that?'

'I know. It was a stupid idea. I wanted to find out once and for all if they were lying about Samuel. Turns out my interrogation technique could do with some work, because they got all defensive, called me a bad feminist and left.'

Peter bursts into spontaneous laughter that makes me feel lighter. 'They called you a bad feminist? Wow. That's a low blow.'

'Coming from them, yes, it certainly was. And now I'm back to square one.'

'Back to square one for what?' He climbs onto the bar stool next to mine, his body rotated in my direction, dangerously close to me. 'What is it that you're trying to find out?'

I finish my second drink and move on to the one Peter bought me. 'That's an excellent question. The truth, I suppose. I want to know where Samuel went. I want to know what he did.'

'Why? Isn't that my crusade? As the younger brother.' Long dark lashes brush the skin below his eyes as he blinks, and a warmth spreads through me. The kind of warmth that leads to bad decisions. The rare, addictive kind that feels even better when you're well on your way to being drunk.

We hold eye contact for at least ten seconds too long, and then he says, 'Oh.'

My gaze drops to the glass in front of me.

'You and my brother?'

I nod my head. 'He didn't want to tell anyone because of the bullying at school.'

'Why didn't I ever notice?' Peter says softly. Then he laughs. 'It's probably a good thing I never knew, because I had a huge crush on you myself.'

'Yeah?' I'm suddenly aware of Reg again, but he seems to have tactfully taken himself to the other side of the bar and is chatting to a middle-aged man I don't recognise.

'Oh, come on. You know I had a huge crush on you.' Peter has the kind of boyish grin that brightens up a room. 'In case you hadn't noticed, I was pretty jealous of my brother, even though he had all that trouble at school. And I had a thing for you, big time.' He laughs.

'Why were you jealous of Samuel?'

He shrugs. 'I guess it was because of the whole adoption thing. Samuel was the real son and I was the non-biological one. You could say I had a chip on my shoulder about it.'

I nod. 'Makes sense. I felt like that about Rosie sometimes.'

'Yeah?'

'It was always her the boys fancied. When I was feeling insecure back then, which was most of the time, I thought Samuel might only be going out with me because I was the closest version of Rosie he could get.'

Peter reaches over to touch my hand. 'Hey, stop selling yourself short, Hev.'

When Rhona called me Hev it set my teeth on edge. When Peter says it, my heart pounds.

'I should nip to the loo,' I say, pulling my hand from his, stumbling from my stool. But my legs have turned into a substance that can no longer support my weight. Embarrassingly, I fall against Peter, and he has to grab hold of my arm to keep me from falling to the ground.

'I think it's time to get you home,' he says. 'Shall we call a taxi?'

While I was drinking my third drink, I didn't notice that the pub was slowly spinning around me, as it is now. Peter takes my weight easily, an arm wrapping around my waist, leading me to the door while pink faces stare in my direction. The room spins faster and my stomach lurches, but I manage not to be sick. I get the odd sense that I'm mumbling, but I don't know what I'm saying.

Outside the pub, Ian Dixon's face comes into view.

'You should be gone,' he says harshly. 'Get out of my village.'

But as soon as I see him, he's gone again. Was he there at all? Did that just happen? And if it did, why didn't Peter get him away from me?

I blink, and then I'm in the back of a taxi. My head rests against Peter's shoulder and his lips are next to my ear.

'You're beautiful, Heather,' he says. At least I think that's what he says.

'God, I drank so much,' I mutter.

'That's what you get for ordering doubles.'

My hand rests on his chest, feeling the hard muscle of a farmer beneath his shirt. His finger trails along my arm but he doesn't lean in for a kiss, and that makes me feel disappointed even though I know I'm in no state to make good decisions, or even consent for that matter.

'How did it go wrong …' I mumble. 'Three drinks.'

'Six shots of vodka,' Peter reminds me.

I close my eyes because I can't bear to see the scenery blurring all around me. When I open them again, Peter is getting out of the car. Did I fall asleep? Did I drool on him? Please say no.

He opens my door and lifts me out. Suddenly Rosie is there and she's glowering at me.

'Seriously, Hev?'

Glower, glower, glower. Did I say that out loud? *Fuck. I think I said that out loud.*

'You're saying everything out loud.' She folds her arms across her chest.

Peter helps me into the house.

Mustn't annoy big sister. Got it. Big sister has been through enough without me wrecking everything.

'You're not wrecking anything, Heather. You're just drunk.' There's some shuffling, and then Rosie says, 'Just put her down there. Thanks. Sorry about this.'

'No problem.'

'I'm getting you a glass of water, Heather. Do. Not. Move.'

Peter's face drifts away. Another cold glass that does not contain vodka is placed in my hand. I drain it. And then the world goes dark.

CHAPTER TWENTY

Rosie

Then

In the week that followed the incident, which is what I decided to call it, the four walls of our bedroom become a prison. I couldn't decide if they were there to keep me in, or to keep everyone else out. For a week I watched my sister get up every day and go to school. And for that week I resented her more than I ever had before.

It seemed as though she was the perfect one because she got to remain the apple of Dad's eye. Whereas he could barely look at me. I'd disappointed him many times before, but this was the worst. In all truth, I wanted to die.

The house was more morbid than it had ever been. Even Grandad moped upstairs, and Mum always had tears in her eyes when she came into my room. I felt alone. No one talked to me, or at least not how they did before. They were scared of me. Scared of what I might say or do, I suppose, in the same way that people are scared to talk to people who have lost a loved one or received a terrible diagnosis.

Out of them all, Heather was the one I hated being around the most. She couldn't look at me either, and I knew why. Every day I saw the resentment on her face. I knew exactly what she was thinking. I'd ruined it all. I'd broken this family apart with what I'd said when I came home from the woods.

Heather has never been a person who's found happiness easy. She thinks I don't understand her, but I've always known her better than anyone else. She is her own worst enemy. She can't find happiness because she thinks her way out of it. Grandad used to say that if you asked her a question, you'd be able to watch her brain have an aneurysm trying to find the best response. Even with simple decision-making she'd end up stuck, not knowing how to proceed.

Every day I watched her trapped in her own mind as she tried to process what was happening. I hated it. I hated myself for putting her through it, and I hated her for making me feel like shit. She never said anything bad to me. She never told me that she didn't believe me. Yet her expression would say everything she couldn't articulate because of who she was.

In fifteen years, I'd only ever known Heather to truly enjoy one thing – going to the Murrays' farm. And now we could never go there again. I'd killed that part of our lives with just a few simple words. I'd ruined everything.

'Rosie, do you want pizza for lunch?' Mum called through the door.

After the incident, Mum fed me so many M&S frozen pizzas and lasagnes that I'd already started to gain weight. It was weird seeing her nurturing side come out for once.

'Just a sandwich, Mum,' I called back, not wanting to add any more pounds to my frame.

'What?'

'Just a …' I sighed and swung my legs over the bed. They were wobbly from my inactivity over the last few days. It was as though I had the flu or something. Everyone expected me to stay in bed. Since the police had completed their interrogation, I'd barely moved. I felt like Grandpa in *Charlie and the Chocolate Factory*.

I crossed the room and opened the door, making my way through the house to the kitchen. 'A sandwich is fine.'

'Oh, there you are, love. How are you feeling?' Mum put on a bright smile and tucked a lock of hair behind her ear. She wasn't fooling anyone with that fake tone of voice. She was a mess. She had dark circles underneath her eyes, and her cheekbones were sticking out from her usually full face. While I'd been guzzling down the pizzas and lasagnes, Mum had been practically starving herself.

'I'm okay, I keep telling you that.' It was supposed to be reassuring, but it came out all wrong, too harsh, too cold.

She stared at me for a long moment before walking over to the cupboard to fetch the bread. 'I'll get on with that sandwich then.'

The word 'sorry' was on my lips, but I couldn't manage to get it out.

Instead, I slipped out of the kitchen and switched on the television in the lounge. My phone, which had been found in the woods with my riding boot, vibrated and I pulled it out of my jeans pocket to discover dozens of unread messages that had been steadily accumulating since the incident. Now was as good a time as any to finally read them.

OMG, U OK?

Call me. I have to tell you something.

Always knew he was a psycho.

Check UR email.

He's done it before.

Have you seen it?

Seen wot? I sent back to Rhona.

An immediate response: *The website. Check UR email.*

Reluctantly I fetched my laptop from the coffee table and set it on my knee. I had no idea what Rhona was on about. After opening my inbox, I found the email in question, opened it and clicked on the link to a Tumblr site.

When I read the title of the site, my blood ran cold.

Samuel Murray the Satan Worshipper.

What. The. Fuck.

The more I read, the worse it became. The author of the site was claiming that several young women in Buckthorpe had gone to the police to accuse Samuel Murray of heinous crimes. In one case, he'd spoken in tongues while sexually assaulting a young girl. In another, he'd sacrificed an animal. I flinched as I scanned the gory details. The posts were already a few days old by this point and I couldn't stop thinking about the villagers reading those words.

Once I'd finished, I slammed the laptop shut and switched off my phone.

When Mum brought me the sandwich, my stomach flipped and I threw up on the carpet. A deep sense of shame washed over me. Mum stared in horror before hurrying out of the room. A moment later, she was back with a tea towel, dropping it over the puke.

'Come here, Rosie,' she said, wrapping an arm over my shoulder. 'Let's get you cleaned up.'

My legs wobbled all the way up the stairs to the bathroom. But Mum's arms were strong. She kept me upright till we got there.

'Do you want to wash your face?' she asked.

I sat on the edge of the bath and nodded my head.

'Take your time.' She patted me on the shoulder and filled the sink with water. 'Here, it isn't too hot.'

I got to my feet and splashed the water over my face. Mum helped out by putting a damp cloth on the back of my neck. Then she handed me a towel and sat on the toilet seat, her posture and expression much calmer than before.

'Do you want to talk about it?' she asked.

'No,' I said. 'I just want to get back to normal.'

'One day.' She smiled. 'But it's going to take some time. That's all.'

'I heard you talking to Dad. I know that Colin Murray blocked the planned building on his land because he knew Dad's company was involved. That's going to lose us money, isn't it?'

'We don't know yet,' Mum said, still calm and collected. 'Don't jump to any conclusions, okay?'

'He had that bruise on his face when he came home from the pub.'

Mum clicked her tongue. 'Don't worry about that. It was your dad's fault for getting into nonsense. Drinking too much.'

'What's going on in here?' The door opened and Grandad stood there, his tufty eyebrows drawn together like two bushy curtains. 'Is this a WI meeting or a bathroom?' He frowned at Mum and avoided eye contact with me.

'We're just leaving, Kevin.' Mum rolled her eyes when she had her back turned to him, and I almost cracked a smile.

Grandad moved away to allow us out of the room, wafting his arms, pretending to shoo us through the door. I think, in his own way, he was attempting to be funny, but it just set my teeth on edge.

'I hope you're not sulking,' he said to me.

'Are you an idiot? She's traumatised, Kevin,' Mum snapped. 'Just go and piss and leave us in peace, will you?'

It felt as though it was me and Mum against the rest of the world, and I couldn't help but smile for the first time in days. I'd been worried about how she'd react at first, but now I understood that she was my ally in this.

Finally, for the first time since the incident, I could see a way out. There was a future for me, one where the past could stay in the past and I could move forwards. I accepted that I couldn't control what was said on the Tumblr site. I had no control over anything that happened after that night. All I could do was try and move on with Mum's help.

At least that was how I felt for a fleeting moment, because the sound of a smashed window interrupted my hopeful thoughts. Mum rushed down the last few steps, almost tripping over her feet. Her breath came out in pants as I followed her into the lounge. In the centre of the room, on top of the carpet, was a rock with a piece of paper wrapped around it. Glass shards were scattered everywhere, on the floor, the coffee table, the sofa. Buster barked from the kitchen, and when he tried to run in, Mum shooed him back and closed the door.

Heart pounding, I bent down and picked up the stone. Grandad walked in and surveyed the mess, his mouth hanging loose with shock.

I unfolded the note.

CHECK OUTSIDE.

'Let's get it over with,' Mum said, taking my hand. 'Come on, Kevin. We're facing this as a family.' The matter-of-fact way she spoke gave me a modicum of hope that everything was going to be okay.

We made our way out of the lounge, through the hallway to the back door. Mum's hand was cold in mine. I was sweating all over.

'Bastards,' Grandad mumbled. 'John will have to deal with this. They can't get away with damaging our property.'

All I could think about was what would have happened if Buster had been sitting in the room. Or Heather. Or Mum and Dad. I took a deep breath to settle myself. What was out there? Had they hurt Midnight?

Mum opened the door and we followed her out into the small courtyard that led down to the stables. I quickly scanned the two ponies' heads bobbing over the door. Both of them were fine, and Midnight's ears pricked up when he saw me.

Cautiously I checked the rest of the area. The chickens seemed undisturbed; the house was okay. Nothing was out of place.

'They must mean the front,' Mum said.

Still gripping my sweaty hand, we walked around the side of the cottage, with Grandad now leading the way. His heavy boots plodded over the stone slabs.

'Well,' he said. 'This is it, then.'

'What is it?' Mum asked, her footsteps hurrying along. I had to speed up to stay with her, but my legs were heavy as lead and didn't want to move. Whatever was there, it was my fault.

Mum gasped when she saw the front of the house, and tears sprang into her eyes.

'I'll find the number of a good cleaner,' Grandad said briskly. 'Where's the phone book?'

I was about to tell him that no one used the phone book any more, but then I finally allowed my eyes to rest on the front of the house. Across the door and the brickwork either side, painted in black, was one word: *LIAR*.

CHAPTER TWENTY-ONE

Heather

Now

Eyelids glued shut, I regain consciousness. I blink them open and watch the room settle from spinning to stationary. The resulting headache forces me to close my eyes again. In the minutes that follow, I realise that I can't move a muscle without searing pain splitting my skull in half. Even twitching my fingertips makes me want to throw up. Eventually I'm able to open my eyes again and adjust to the light in my room. I haven't had a hangover this horrendous possibly ever, though a particularly awful morning-after at university springs to mind.

What did I do last night? What did I say? Most of the night is completely gone. I remember getting into a taxi with Peter, and that's about it.

This isn't me. The last time I let go like this was probably my last week at uni when I partied with my friends until I lost myself. The final release, and the one time I forgot to be apologetic about who I am like most other good little English girls from the countryside. And this is my punishment for allowing that side to come out. Pain.

The bedroom door opens and Rosie pads in wearing a summer dress, her hair pulled up into a topknot. Her bare arms reveal the scars that she never hides away, and the line of stars tattooed along her wrist. The scars give me a stab of guilt every time I see them. Rosie is trying to stay sober, and here I am passing out from too much booze.

'Morning, waster,' she says brightly, slamming a cup of tea on the bedside table. She places a packet of ibuprofen next to it. 'Breakfast of champions.'

'Thanks,' I croak. 'What time is it?'

'Six,' she replies.

'In the morning?'

She shakes her head.

'The evening?'

She nods. 'You slept all night and most of the day.'

This time I ignore the pounding pain, forcing myself to sit up. 'What the hell?' I wince as the room wobbles and my head seems to crack open. I lean over and put my face in my hands. 'Jesus. How am I still in this much pain after all this time?' Now that I'm aware how long I've been asleep, I know this is definitely my worst hangover ever.

'You woke up for a little bit about eleven this morning, drank some water and went straight back to sleep.'

I slowly lift my head. 'I did?'

She nods.

'But that's insane.'

'I agree. I was thinking of taking you to A and E or calling a doctor if you didn't wake up tonight.'

I rub my eyes, run my fingers through my hair. Mascara coats my fingertips, and is no doubt all over my pillowcase too.

'This has never happened to me before,' I say. 'I feel …'

'Paranoid? Self-conscious? Ill? Like you could drink a gallon of water and still be thirsty? Yep. I know the feeling, matey.' She reaches over and ruffles my hair. 'How much did you drink anyway?'

'Three double vodkas.'

'Huh,' she says. 'Thought it would be more than that.'

'I guess I drank them quite quickly. Within about an hour and on an empty stomach.' I take a cautious sip of hot tea. Did I even finish the last drink? Two and a half doubles would be more accurate. 'I don't know if I'm ravenous or going to puke.'

'Sounds about right.' She raises her eyebrows. 'Well, if I was thinking of having a drink, you've just cured me of that temptation with this display.' She lifts her hand and wafts it over me, the sad little specimen to prove her point.

I can't deny I've missed this side of my sister. This is how it used to be before everything that happened with Samuel.

'What were you doing yesterday, Hev?' she asks.

'I had this idiotic idea that it'd be good to meet Emily and Rhona.' I explain the ridiculous plan while Rosie frowns.

At the end of my story, she sighs. 'Sis, I don't get what's going on. Why do you keep bringing up the past? It's not as though you can ever go back and change it.'

I shake my head. 'I don't know any more.'

'You should be concentrating on grieving for Mum.' She sits down on the bed and shifts my leg with her bum. 'I think that's what you're doing, you know. You're avoiding grieving for Mum. And ...' She taps her thigh nervously and doesn't meet my gaze.

'What?' I ask, sensing that there's more.

'I don't think you've ever properly grieved for Dad, either. You idolised him. And then he let you down.'

I lift my knees underneath the duvet, making myself smaller. 'No, he didn't. It's not his fault.'

'He's the one who took the gun and put it in his mouth.'

I clamp my hands over my ears. 'Stop it.'

'And now someone has stolen that gun because they want us to go. Or they want us dead.'

The image of Ian Dixon's face comes into my mind. Did he confront me outside the pub, or did I imagine it? I have a vague recollection of him threatening me. And then I got into the taxi with Peter.

'What is it?' Rosie asks, noticing the change in my expression.

'I think I saw Ian Dixon when we were coming out of the pub. He told me – well, us – to get out of the village. But I'm not sure if I'm remembering that, or if I imagined it.'

Rosie frowns, creasing up the space between her eyebrows. 'You were seriously fucked up, weren't you? It's a little scary, Hev. Have you had this sort of reaction to alcohol before?'

I shake my head. 'No, but I've never pounded double vodkas like that before.'

'Listen to big sis, yeah? Have a break from the booze. I don't think it agrees with you. This is no normal hangover. People don't usually sleep for twenty-four hours straight.'

The next day is mainly made up of dealing with the aftermath of the ill-advised drinking session. My phone is missing, but when I call the Prince of Wales, surly Reg tells me that he found it underneath one of the tables. How did it get from the bar to the table? Did I drop it and someone accidentally kicked it there?

I arrive at the pub and sheepishly pick up the phone from Reg, who – thankfully, and tactfully – doesn't say a word. Then I drive home, eat jam on toast until my stomach stops grumbling, and help Rosie sift through some of Mum's paperwork.

'Here are the deeds to the house,' she says. 'We'd best keep them somewhere safe for when we want to sell up.'

'We haven't decided that, though, have we?'

'No,' she says, backtracking. 'I meant, if we decide to sell.'

I nod thoughtfully, watching as Rosie organises Mum's belongings. It seems an odd thing to say by accident.

'Did you say that you'd sold some short stories recently?' I ask.

She puts some old pens and pencils into a bag for rubbish and nods her head. 'Just a couple to some sci-fi zines.'

'I never asked how you paid for rehab.' I try to keep my voice light, as though the thought has just occurred to me. Of course, it hasn't. I haven't known how to broach it. Most of our conversations end abruptly when one of us annoys the other. But now that we have the deeds to the house here, and Rosie is talking about selling up, I realise that I need to know more about her money situation before making a decision.

'I found funding through the NHS,' she says, without meeting my eye.

I have no idea if that's possible, so I can't say much more.

'If you're asking whether money has been an issue,' she says, 'it has. I've had jobs, though. I write in my spare time.'

'Did you tell Mum about the published stories? She would've been proud.'

'I did,' Rosie says. 'In the hospital with you. It was nice to be able to tell her something good for a change.'

'I'm glad you inherited her talent.' I stand up from my uncomfortable position on the floor and walk over to the shelves on the other side of the office. Using one finger, I edge out a thin book and take it over to Rosie. The corners are frayed. The paper is yellowing. The cover almost immediately tries to curl up like those plastic mood fishes in Christmas crackers. It opens on the correct page, the spine already bent to that location. *The Road*, by Iris Sharpe.

Rosie reaches out for it with a smile. 'I haven't read this in years.'

It was the one and only published poem of our mother's. Now that I'm older, I can't imagine the rejection she faced just to have those few lines of words published.

'It's not my favourite of hers,' Rosie says. 'There was another. What was it? It started "Blame the blue" …'

'"Guilt the trees".'

'It was such an unusual one.'

'What do you think it means?' I ask.

Rosie shrugs. 'No idea. Maybe it's about regrets.'

Mum's last words to me: *I want you to know that I never regretted anything, and that I love you very much.*

Rosie might be right, and perhaps that's why the poem speaks to me too. As last words go, 'I never regretted anything' isn't so bad. And why *should* Mum have regrets? She was always true to who she was. Of course she had flaws, but she was a good person, as most relatively normal people are. Dad, too. On a scale of Mary Berry to Ted Bundy, they were both definitely closer to everyone's favourite baker.

Then why did I have such a strange feeling that the poem we're talking about is related to Samuel's disappearance? *Blame the blue.* The bluebell field? *Guilt the trees.* Buckbell Woods, where I found Rosie's bracelet? *We were complicit.* Who? Did Mum know that Rosie left the house that night? Wouldn't she have told me?

Maybe, a long time ago, before Rosie left Buckthorpe, she told Mum about the night Samuel disappeared. If she did, then that means something bad happened. The blue. The trees. It has to be Buckbell Woods.

And there is one person who knows everything about those woods. Buckthorpe Jack.

I have to admit, this isn't the first time I've thought of asking Buckthorpe Jack about that night, but I held off, forever hoping that one day Rosie would open up to me. Now I feel as though she will never tell me the truth about Samuel, and I have to find another way to move on from the past once and for all. That means going back to the woods, alone, despite the threat from the village. There's no other choice. I just need to be brave enough to do it.

CHAPTER TWENTY-TWO

Heather

Now

When we were little, Rosie and I had the run of the woods. Other parents would have a panic attack at the thought of their children walking through a forest on their own, but for us it was more akin to nipping to the playground across the street. There were rules we had to obey – we weren't allowed too far in – but from the ages of seven and eight we took Buster on little walks to the bluebell field and back, though only in spring and summer when the weather was nice.

Sometimes Grandad walked with us, complaining about us running too fast and his knees aching. He was a mutterer, always grumbling underneath his breath. Rosie used to say that she heard swear words amongst the muttering, but I think she was exaggerating. That was what she wanted to hear, so she heard it.

It was around that age that I first started sleepwalking. Mum would find me sitting on the sofa with the TV on, a strange, impassive expression on my face. Or I'd stand over their bed, resembling the possessed kid in a horror film. But it wasn't until I was twelve that I wandered into the woods.

To see Buckthorpe Jack.

As I'm doing today.

That night is one I don't tend to let myself think about because I lost control of myself. I made no conscious decision to wander into the woods, and that makes me feel ashamed for some reason. It's possible I'm just a control freak who can't stand losing the ability to choose. Unless the shame is an echo of whatever darkness was in my mind that night, because whenever I think about sleepwalking in the woods, that same sensation comes over me again.

But not now, walking through the trees with a gentle April sun dancing through the leaves. Gorgeous early spring light, delicately bright and accompanied by a breeze to ensure I'm not too hot while walking. This is my favourite time of year, and Buckbell is my favourite place to see it.

A few weeks ago, before Mum died, I was feeling as though my childhood memories were in a fog, or that they weren't mine at all. Maybe that's linked to Samuel and the way the village changed when he was accused of all those terrible things. It's only now, in this light, that I see those days more clearly.

The joy of Dad coming home after a job, but the moodiness of Rosie when he left. Mum's headaches, her insistence on 'me' time when she was writing, but her warmth on a good day. Grandad teaching us to ride our ponies and muttering under his breath when we stuck our toes out and slouched. Rosie always running. Running to school. Chasing Buster. Racing me. Always with a red flush on her cheeks and uncombed hair. Mum forced us both into dresses, which makes the memory romantic, with the pastel-coloured fabric catching the breeze. That is, until Rosie fell face first into a puddle and ruined the entire outfit. There was laughter then, until it made our ribs ache, and until we realised we had to go home and tell Mum what'd happened. 'One day you're going to pay me back for all this laundry,' she said, tutting and pacing the length of the living room. I'm not sure we ever did pay her back.

It doesn't take long to reach the edge of the bluebell field, which is where I stop for a moment. We've passed the anniversary of Samuel's disappearance, but I still crouch down and pick one of the flowers, tucking it into my pocket. *This is where I found the bracelet.* It was here, tangled up with the flowers, barely visible. Of course I saw it. I'm the one who sees the small details others miss. Sometimes I wish I didn't, but I do. I see the mistakes that other people make.

But that does not mean I'm immune to making my own.

There's a path leading through the bluebells, winding around the edge of the field to protect the beautiful flowers from being trampled. In summer, autumn and winter, the field is green, or covered in golden leaves, or a blanket of fluffy white snow. Those months seem stark compared to the softness of the bluebells. One recent problem that Buckthorpe has had is Instagram models coming to lie down in the field for a photo shoot. There's been talk of a fence being built to discourage such behaviour. I think we should tell them about Buckthorpe Jack instead.

I usually head home after reaching the field, but today I keep going around it until I reach the little dirt path that continues on to Jack's cottage. This part of the wood is darker, the trees positioned snugly enough to block out the sun. It reminds me of a movie where the protagonist rents a cabin in the forest. Those films are usually set in America, with bears and coyotes. The loner hunts with a fancy rifle and a funny hat.

Hunting is not allowed in Buckbell Woods.

Jack doesn't have any of those things. At least, I hope not.

I take a deep breath and continue on, trying to force my mind not to think about the night I went sleepwalking and the nightmare I had. But all I can see is Rosie's face when she teases me about my dreams about becoming Jack's bride.

It's cooler in this part of the woods, and I pull my jacket closer to my throat. As far as I know, Jack doesn't own a car. Whenever he comes into the village, or goes to the Murrays' farm, he walks.

The crumbling cottage comes into view up ahead. Tiles are missing from the roof and patches of brick show through the disintegrating rendering. What did Jack see the night Samuel went missing? I know the police talked to him, but I don't remember what was said, if I was ever told. I was two years away from being an adult, but neither of my parents treated me like one. They kept all the information to themselves, attempting to shelter us from the horrible truth.

When my jacket doesn't provide enough warmth, I fold my arms across my chest and continue walking. Did I see a shadow in the window of the cottage? Is that Jack watching me approach?

A loud crack, similar to thunder, but at a higher pitch, sounds through the woods. Several birds lift from the branches, their wings spread out wide as they fly away from the disturbance. My breath catches in my throat as I watch them, my mind slowly reaching a terrifying conclusion. Silence falls, and when I glance back at the cottage, there's no one in the window. Finally, I breathe.

There's no mistaking that sound. I've heard it coming from the farms before.

It was a gunshot.

The silence is broken by a rustle of leaves, but I don't wait to find out what it is. I spin around and run. My feet trip and slide on the uneven ground, but I push through my thighs, running as fast as I can.

When the second gunshot cracks through the air, my body jolts as though I've been hit. It was closer this time. I don't know where the bullet went. I don't know where the shooter is. But it's too close for comfort.

My arms stretch out for balance as I leap over stones and tree roots. My body warms, chasing the cold away. I run straight through the bluebells, trampling them, barely even noticing that they're there. I have no idea if the person behind me is still following me. I can't hear a thing over my own heavy breathing.

Back on the main path, my ankle twists and I almost fall, but I straighten myself up, moving on instinct, a primal feeling taking over. There's no one else in the woods today apart from me and my pursuer. No one to save me.

Even though the gunshots have stopped, I run all the way home. I open the door with shaking fingers and burst inside. The first thing I do is lock the door, and then I start moving through the house checking for open windows.

'Rosie? Rosie! Someone tried to kill me.'

My boots leave prints all over the house as I tramp through checking every possible entry point, even the windows upstairs. Rosie's room is empty. She isn't here. I try to think whether she said she was going somewhere for the day. But I know she didn't say anything.

Her phone goes to voicemail. She doesn't reply to my messages.

Sweat drips from my forehead as I strip away my outerwear and try to think about what to do next. Can I go to the police without Ian Dixon being involved? What if they send him to the house to take a statement? I don't trust him, and he is probably one of the most senior police officers in the area, which means he *is* the police.

Who was shooting? And were they really shooting at *me*?

If I'm being logical about this, then I would have to say that Buckthorpe Jack was spooked by someone coming to his house and fired a couple of warning shots. But I was sure I saw someone moving inside the house. I definitely saw a face at the window. If he'd run out of the house with a gun, I would've noticed.

I don't know much about guns, but I've lived in the countryside for long enough to recognise the sound of a shotgun or rifle. The Murrays used to run clay-pigeon shoots every now and then, and the crack of those guns would echo along to our house. It was the same sound today, only closer.

And then, most alarmingly, the person firing the gun chased me. I'm sure they were chasing me.

Were they trying to kill me?

Or were they just trying to scare me? Because if they were, it certainly worked.

CHAPTER TWENTY-THREE

Rosie

Then

Dad hired a pressure washer to remove the graffiti from the front of the house, but it took away the top layer of paint from the front door with it. That meant we needed to buy a new front door and he wasn't happy about that. The whole time I felt utterly miserable because it was all my fault. A new window and a new front door all because of me. Neither would be cheap.

The day after the rock came through the window, Rhona called me, crying down the phone.

'Samuel kept touching me when I told him to stop. He's a psycho. He tortures animals. He drew a pentagram in blood while reciting Marilyn Manson lyrics and then he started muttering in this weird language. Do you think he's some sort of witch who can curse me? Remember when he killed his lizard?'

'He didn't kill his lizard,' I said. 'He let the lizard loose into Buckbell Woods.'

'Fuck. Off. It's the same thing and you know it. The poor thing would've been eaten by a fox or starved to death.'

Samuel actually did let his lizard loose in Buckbell Woods. He told us about it once. He was six and his parents had just adopted Peter. He'd had his lizard for a few months. Mr Murray came home with it, tank and equipment included, after a poker game in the

Prince of Wales that later continued at someone's farm. Samuel decided to learn all about how to take care of it. But then Peter came along and was terrified of it.

Samuel bragged about his pet at school, which led to the kids teasing him. That, along with Peter's fear, made him decide to get rid of it.

He was only six. He didn't understand what he'd done when he released it into the woods.

Later, he grew fond of snakes and other reptiles too, which only added to his oddness. Rhona and Emily once stole his English workbook and wrote *FREAK* all over it, then threw it back at him, hitting him in the face. I cringed hard. But I'd done nothing.

'Have you told the police?' I asked her.

'Yeah, that guy from the village. Ian. I made a statement. Emily did too. We love you, Ro. We're with you. We'll take the freak down together, okay?'

After the call ended, I closed my eyes for a while and wished I could erase the entire conversation from my memory.

I wished I could go back in time to before the incident.

That would be nice.

Rhona had called during lunchtime at school. But I was at home, stuck in my bedroom, staring at the sunlight coming in through the window, falling on Heather's empty bed. I was pretty much alone today because Mum had gone back to work and Grandad was asleep on the sofa. Dad had never taken any time off work. He soldiered on, as did Heather. I was under strict instructions not to leave the house after the incident with the rock. Mum and Dad thought it might be dangerous for me to go out alone, seeing as someone had a grudge against me.

But I couldn't stand it. I'd never been good at sitting still, and this was torture. I'd scribbled down a few badly formed stories in my notebooks, and now I didn't have anything left to do. I needed to feel the sun on my skin. I needed air before I suffocated.

I left a note on the fridge telling Grandad that I was taking Midnight out for a ride. My pony needed exercise. None of this was his fault, after all.

I retrieved my hat from the tack room, carried the saddle and bridle to the stable, and got Midnight ready, gently pushing my thumb into his mouth to put on the bridle. He drooled on me a little, and I wiped it on his coat before the saddle went on, then led him out of the stable.

This was definitely the best idea I'd had for a long while. As soon as I was riding away from the cottage, all thoughts of Rhona and Emily slipped from my mind. Even Samuel seemed a million miles away. Spring sun was shining, and I wanted to see the bluebells in the woods. I wanted to go back to where it had happened, because I was afraid that if I left it any longer, I would never go there again.

But there were butterflies in my tummy at the thought of it. I took a deep breath and pushed Midnight into a fast trot. Nothing bad could happen to me when I was with him. No one could hurt me. Not even Samuel. My trusty steed would protect me the way loyal beasts did in fantasy novels. Whenever I was riding him, I was invincible.

With barely a breeze, Buckbell was quiet. It was perfect for strolling idly, listening to birdsong. I'd never been someone who enjoyed walking just to observe nature. It was boring to me. Not today, though, because anything that wasn't my bedroom felt deliciously exotic. Even the sound of your average blackbird chirruping from the branches above. I slowed Midnight to a walk to take it all in, closing my eyes and lifting my face to the sun.

The solitude was soon broken by the sound of voices. Of course, it was common to come across dog walkers and hikers, but they tended to stay in the western part of the woods, closer to the village. This part was our domain, the ones who lived outside the village in the middle of nowhere. The Sharpes and the Campbells and even the Murrays had relatively free rein in this part of woods. And then there was Jack, of course. Perhaps we were all trespassing on his territory.

Just as I was about to push Midnight into a trot to get past the chatty people, I realised that one of the voices belonged to my sister. Though it was unmistakably Heather, I had to admit that she sounded strange that day. It was as though she was upset, and that high-pitched whine was a tone I wasn't used to hearing from her mouth. She was the mature one who rarely became worked up over anything. Though she could give good silent treatment every now and then when I did something *really* bad.

I directed Midnight towards the sound of her voice, for some reason keeping him at a slow walk to stay quiet. But the closer I got, the more aware I became of his hooves snapping twigs underfoot. I quickly dismounted, wrapped the reins around a branch, and walked silently through the trees.

Why was I sneaking up on her? I can't explain it. There was some instinctual part of me that didn't want her to know I was here. A moment later, I realised why. The second voice, the lower one, belonged to Samuel Murray. A shiver of revulsion wormed its way up my back. But I didn't run away. I went a few paces closer, and hung back behind a patch of nettles. Leaning slightly to the left, I could see them through the tall weeds.

'You don't believe her, do you?' Samuel was asking. 'You don't believe those blog bitches either, do you?'

Heather was silent, neither nodding nor shaking her head. The way she was sucking in her lips told me that she was holding back tears. I leaned in, eager to know whether she truly did believe me or not.

'Heather, *please*.' He lifted one hand and slowly caressed her arm. She didn't stop him. 'You know me. You know I wouldn't do any of those things. I don't hurt animals. I don't hurt girls.'

'She's my sister,' Heather said at last.

But it didn't answer the question. She wasn't telling him who she believed.

Samuel took a step towards her, and I contemplated jumping out from behind the nettles to prevent him from touching her.

'Tell her to stop,' he said. 'Tell her that she's got it all wrong. I think I know why she's doing what she's doing, but ...'

'But what?' Heather asked.

Samuel dropped his eyes to the ground, and I got the impression that he was wrestling with some internal force, trying to decide what he could and couldn't say. Eventually he lifted his gaze, took my sister's face in his hands and kissed her.

My heart leapt into my throat as I watched them kissing. Heather wrapped her arms around his neck like they were at a school disco, and leaned into his body. He stroked her face, ran his fingers through her hair. I thought they might never stop, that they'd become part of the forest, their love rooted forever, until at last she wrenched herself away from him and he stumbled back in shock, his eyes red with tears.

'We can't,' she said. 'Not any more.'

He nodded once.

I moved away from the nettles and ran to mount Midnight, pushing him into a gallop to get me home.

CHAPTER TWENTY-FOUR

Heather

Now

Ivy Cottage is silent. All I can hear is the sound of my breathing, still ragged from the shock. I fill the kettle with water, my hands shaking.

Think, Heather.

Who would shoot a gun at me? Who wants me dead?

Rosie is the one who has attracted the attention of the village since she arrived. I've been back regularly for months, and no one has shown me any of the animosity they have since Mum died. The letter mentioned me as well as Rosie, suggesting that I'm as unwelcome here as she is, but why would that prompt someone to shoot at me?

The gas stove sparks up, and I consider what has changed since Mum died. I've been looking into Samuel's disappearance, that's the difference. Stupidly, I didn't consider the fact that someone would notice, and that they wouldn't want me to carry on investigating.

And that means that I can't rule out Rosie.

I slump down into a dining chair and place my head in my hands. My heart tells me that Rosie would never harm me, and that she couldn't have hurt Samuel either, because deep down she's a good person. But my head insists that there's evidence against her. She had a motive – Samuel hurt her, or he knew her secrets and lies – and she was unaccounted for the night he disappeared. She was unaccounted for when the shotgun went missing and she's unaccounted for now, after someone fired a gun at me.

This feels like a warning, but who is it coming from? Can I truly believe that my sister could do this to me?

I pull my head out of my hands, brush away a few self-pitying tears and go to get a mug out of the cupboard. My phone beeps. A text message from Rosie to say that she's at an addiction meeting in Ingledown. I chew on my bottom lip for a moment, considering whether to reply to her. A quick Google search doesn't come up with much information about addiction meetings in Ingledown, but she might have found out by word of mouth or a flyer.

The kettle boils and I consider what I should do next. If Rosie is telling the truth, she deserves to be warned about what happened to me in Buckbell Woods. If she's lying, then I need to protect myself from her. Head and heart are fighting one another again.

I don't want to be alone in the cottage knowing that someone just shot a gun in my direction. I consider leaving the house and going to the pub, but that means walking alone, unless I drive. But if someone did want to hurt me, what would stop them tampering with my car?

Not even a relaxing cup of tea can soothe my anxiety. After jumping at the sight of the neighbours' cat running through the garden, I decide to see if I can get someone to come to the cottage. If it's possible for my nerves to become any more frayed, they do when I send a text to the one person I'm comfortable inviting here. Peter.

I could be there in thirty minutes? He suggests. Then, a moment later, *Not that I'm keen or anything.* ☺

The smiley face is like warmth on a cold, dark day. Today, nothing makes sense except for the fact that a good man wants to spend time with me. His crush on me is sweet, but I can't decide how I feel about him. A new kind of nervousness tickles at my stomach. This is a dangerous time to bring a man into my life, especially a Murray, given everything that has happened in the past, and normally my renowned cool head would tell me that I'm at my most emotionally vulnerable. And yet I don't want to be alone. Who else can I turn to? I don't trust my sister. My mum is gone. My dad is gone.

I simply text Peter back *Thanks*, then move into the lounge and switch on the television for some background noise.

A few moments later he texts to say he's on his way, and my tensed muscles begin to relax. I push thoughts of his family connections from my mind. I make my way into the kitchen and put the kettle on again, take another mug out of the cupboard, and watch the Campbells' cat as it poos underneath the hedge.

Even though I know it's Peter, the knock at the door sends a sudden judder through my body, and I spin around. When the key scrapes in the lock, it causes another jolt of shock to course through me. Peter's eyes narrow when I open the door.

'What's happened?' he asks.

I suck in a deep breath and move back to allow him in. I have to squeeze around the bulk of him to lock the door again.

He's barely two strides into the house when I tell him about the woods.

'Fuck. I heard that,' he says. 'I thought it was the Bolton farm, out towards Ingledown. If the wind's right, I can hear them shooting. But it came from the woods? Are you okay?' He leans over and touches my arm.

'I'm fine.' I can't stop staring at his hand. 'I guess they were warning shots, but I think they chased me, too. I was on my way to see Jack.'

'Jack?' Peter leans back, removing his hand. 'Why him?'

I remember that he doesn't know about my suspicions about Rosie in the woods the night Samuel disappeared. 'He sees and hears a lot around the village. I thought maybe he might know more about Samuel's disappearance.'

Peter shrugs. 'My dad has tried to get information out of him before, but he claims not to have seen anything that night. Besides, there's no evidence Samuel was even in the woods.'

But there was evidence that my sister was there, I think. I wish I could tell him. I ache to get the words out of my mind and out in the open. But I can't. I can't betray Rosie.

Peter is shaking his head, his unfocused gaze directed towards the fireplace. 'Do you think someone was hunting?'

'No,' I reply. 'I think they were either trying to hit me or scare me.' I'm waiting for him to tell me I'm crazy but he just shakes his head slightly again.

'I don't understand,' he says.

'There was the note I received the day Dad's gun went missing,' I say, walking to the cabinet. I open the top drawer and and take out the letter from the village. 'Maybe the village doesn't just want us gone, they want us dead.'

'I remember you mentioning it,' he says. And then I pass it to him. He reads it quickly. 'Holy fuck. You're right, that is nasty.'

'You haven't heard anything? Any rumours? At the pub, maybe?'

'Nothing,' he replies. 'If this really is from more than one person, then the village hasn't involved my family at all.'

That surprises me. Surely the Murrays would be the first people to want us out? Well, most of the Murrays. Unless I shouldn't even be trusting Peter.

The kettle whines in the kitchen and I hurry back to take it off the heat, hating the sound of that high-pitched whistle. Even though my hands are still shaking, it feels good to keep them moving.

'Milk, no sugar, please,' Peter says as I'm taking the milk out of the fridge.

'I forgot to ask,' I say. 'Sorry.'

'Now what's that supermarket shite you have there?' He nods towards the carton. 'There's decent milk up at ours.'

'There is,' I admit. 'But I don't get a stern glare from your family when I go to the supermarket.' I let out an uneasy laugh. 'I do buy from your shop, but only on Thursdays when I know your mum isn't working behind the counter.'

'Mum's WI meetings,' Peter says with a grin, moving into the room to sit himself down at the breakfast bar while I pour milk into the tea. 'Very clever.' I can see that the letter has shaken him, despite his jokes. He runs his fingers through his hair and then under his eyes.

'Rosie won't go at all,' I say. 'She bought this pint, by the way.'

'Ah, I see. Well, I tell you what, I'll save you both the trouble and bring you a couple of pints next time I visit.'

My cheeks flush and my eyes burn with unshed tears at his kind gesture. I quickly blink them away, hopefully before he notices.

'Fine, but I have to pay you or I'll feel weird about it,' I say with a forced smile.

'I thought women appreciated gifts from handsome men,' Peter teases.

'I see you're as modest as most of the other men I've met.'

He laughs. 'I'm glad you're still in good spirits considering everything that's happened to your family. I'm sorry you're having to go through all this.'

I gesture for him to come through to the lounge, and he follows. Chatting to him is the best distraction I could have hoped for, and some of my fear slowly begins to ebb away. He's funny, good to talk to, and most of all, he makes me feel safe. Even though he's a Murray and has every reason to hate my family, I believe I can trust him. Yes, he reminds me of Samuel because of those childhood days on the farm, but he doesn't have the same intensity. Peter is lighter; he's one side of the moon and Samuel is the other.

'I'm sorry too.'

He sighs. 'Okay, so you've pissed off the village with your presence.' He settles into the sofa next to me. 'Someone broke into your house, stole your things and sent you a nasty letter, then fired a gun at you in the woods, and yet I don't see you packing a suitcase to get out. You're a brave lady, Heather Sharpe.'

'Or stupid.' I sip my tea before placing it on the coffee table. The warmth helps to keep me calm after the anxiety-ridden day I've had.

'I guess the arsehole with the gun is the same arsehole that sent the note.'

'They didn't send it,' I say. 'They hand-delivered it.' I sigh. 'Maybe you're right. Maybe it's time for us to go. Nothing is worth this kind of risk, is it? Not even finding out what happened to your brother.'

'Is that why you're staying?'

I can't read the expression on Peter's face. Is he impressed that I care that much? Or upset that I still have feelings for his brother?

'Well, yes and no. I'm also here because this is my childhood home and I won't be driven away by some idiot who can't aim a gun. There're all my parents' belongings to sort through. I'm not going to just throw away our precious things because I'm scared.' My eyes burn again when I think about Rosie, about the way my head keeps trying to make me believe she's guilty. I close them tightly, then open them again and focus on my surroundings. 'This is where all the memories of my parents are. I can never see Mum and Dad again, but I can live where they lived. Walk where they walked.' Nothing in my entire life has made me feel as helpless as the moment I heard that gunshot in the woods. Nothing has made me long for my dad so much. And then, running into this house, all I wanted was Mum. But they'll never comfort me again. 'I guess I'm an orphan now.'

Peter is quiet for a heartbeat or two, gaze directed towards me. He puts his tea on the coffee table and takes my hand in his. 'Come on. You need something stronger than tea.'

I resist him when he tries to pull me up from the sofa. 'Oh no! I'm never drinking again. Remember what happened last time?'

'I do,' he says with a grin. 'I remember you drooling on my shoulder. It was one of the cutest things I've ever seen. Come on. Show me where the hard liquor is. I know your dad enjoyed a tipple. There must be a bottle somewhere.'

Reluctantly I allow him to lead me back into the kitchen, where I open the cupboard and slosh whisky into two glasses.

'Here's to drowning sorrows.' Peter clinks my glass and winks.

'You're a bad influence.'

'I am not! I was the one who stopped you drinking the pub dry the other night.'

I almost laugh, but not quite. The whisky burns my throat as it goes down, forcing a choked cough out of me. 'Urgh.' This is certainly one way to dull my senses. One way to stop all the frightening thoughts from swirling through my mind.

'Have you never drunk whisky before?' The corner of his mouth lifts in surprise.

'Nope. Why didn't you warn me it was disgusting?' I take another sip, and this one goes down much more smoothly.

'I'm sorry,' he says with a laugh. 'I didn't know.'

'The other night gave you a bad impression of me. I don't actually drink that much.'

'No, that was what I thought. You were always more sensible than your sister.'

'Yeah, boring.'

'No. Never that.'

His eyes connect with mine, and there's a moment when I think we might kiss. Part of me longs for it. Another part of me isn't ready. I quickly cast my eyes downwards to break the spell.

'Do you think the person shooting at me did it with Dad's gun?' I say, trying to avoid any kind of romantic talk.

If Peter is frustrated by the missed opportunity, he hides it well. 'I suppose they could have done. You probably should have reported the gun missing.'

'What's the point? Sergeant Dixon lurks in every corner. He hates me too. Everyone's in this big conspiracy to get the Sharpe sisters out. Look at the letter. It says it's from the whole village.'

'You don't know that,' Peter reminds me. 'The person who wrote it might be lying. There are no names mentioned, just a vague suggestion.'

I drain the last of my whisky. My throat burns, but I manage not to break out into an unattractive coughing fit. 'No, but I can feel it. When I walk around the village, the animosity hits me in waves. I don't know how Mum could stand it. She must have felt it too.'

'The village has weird rules,' Peter says thoughtfully. 'The older generation are accepted because they're the originals. Despite being born here, the children are considered different because of their youth. And you two girls – sorry, women – have lived outside Buckthorpe, which means you're double outsiders.' He frowns. 'That's an odd phrase. This whisky has gone to my head.'

I laugh a little at his expression, but then I think more about what he's saying. 'I'm never going to be safe here, am I?'

'Were you planning to stay?' he asks softly. It's a pleasant change from the demanding tone everyone else in the village uses.

'Honestly, I just don't know. I think I fantasised about it. Settling down in the same place I was brought up. I could buy a horse and a few chickens. Maybe I could find a way to work from home, despite the patchy Wi-Fi. Find someone to live here with me. Consider having kids.' It all seems such a pedestrian fantasy. 'I'm sure Rosie wants to travel the world and see everything she can possibly see. But I want to stay rooted, like an old oak tree. It's pathetic.'

'No,' he says. 'It isn't at all.'

The expression on his face is one I haven't seen since I kissed Samuel in the woods that final time. Peter's eyes are open wide, jaw tense, hand gripping the edge of the kitchen counter. I have a few seconds to contemplate what I know is going to happen next, and my heart races wildly. Despite everything telling me not to do it, I realise that I want this.

I'm not sure who moves first, but in an instant, Peter's mouth is on mine, a faint taste of whisky on his tongue. His hands grip the back of my head, bundling up my hair, before trailing down to feel the shape of my body through my clothes. Every part of me wants him, and for once, I allow myself to give in.

CHAPTER TWENTY-FIVE

Rosie

Then

I watched the text message deliver, and then leaned back on the bed, closing my eyes for a moment. The police had finished questioning Samuel at this point, but they hadn't officially arrested him because they were continuing to collect evidence. The accusations that Rhona and Emily had made didn't help to validate my own; instead they had the opposite effect. More and more suspicion was cast on me instead of on Samuel. The village was divided between those who believed me and those who didn't.

It all had to end.

My stomach flipped over after I sent the message. I knew that what I'd done could not be rescinded. I had to see it through to the end. My skin went cold. I tried to remind myself that what I'd done was for Heather. I could be putting myself in danger, but it was all for her.

Finally I received a response.

I can do it. Where you said. At the time you said.

And that was that. The realisation began to sink in regarding what I was about to do. I wondered whether Heather would ever forgive me. Probably not. But if I didn't go through with what I'd started … I didn't even want to think about it.

It felt weird to go back to the living room knowing that I'd just set a potentially dangerous event in motion. But I did. They were all in there – Mum, Dad, Hev, Grandad –watching *X Factor*. All the seats were taken, so I sat on the floor with Heather. No one said anything when I walked in, but Mum patted me on the shoulder and stroked my hair.

Heather wasn't actually watching the show; she was reading a book. Edgar Allan Poe. Way too dark and depressing for me, but then that's Heather. Then I remembered that Samuel had lent her the book a few months ago, and the nausea came back again.

Why did it have to be Samuel? Of all the boys in Buckthorpe. Why was it Samuel that had melted her icy exterior with gothic poems and days on the farm? The whole thing was messed up.

But I was going to put it right, once and for all.

CHAPTER TWENTY-SIX

Heather

Now

Afterwards, the fog clears from my mind. My eyes roam around the kitchen and see the remnants of our momentary madness. I bend down and grab my jeans, bra and top. Where is the rest of my underwear? Socks? I can't look Peter in the eye as he dresses.

Finally, clothed, we face each other, and I'm all too aware of my mussed hair and flushed face.

'Hev,' he says. 'I think you're incredible.'

I close my eyes, waiting for the *but*. Of course there will be a catch; what we did was reckless and impulsive, not like me at all. What if Rosie had walked in?

'That was … unexpected, but also amazing.' He laughs. 'I hope you don't think I came over here for—'

'No,' I say quickly. 'I know you didn't. I really appreciate you coming over.' It feels as though my entire body is hot with embarrassment.

He runs his hands through his hair and moves closer to me, resting one arm on the kitchen counter. 'It's okay. I know how stressed out you are about what's going on in the village. I know that's probably the reason why it happened.'

'That's not true,' I interject. But I'm not sure I'm being honest with myself.

His eyes travel across my face, searching for more from me. I quickly glance away, but he takes a step closer and brushes some of my messy hair behind my ear.

'Let's go out tomorrow night,' he says. 'Me and thee. What about it?'

'Are you sure you want to go out with a pariah?'

'Fuck the village.'

'I'd rather not,' I say with a laugh.

He holds my face and plants a tender kiss on my lips. 'Seriously, Hev. We could go to a restaurant in Ingledown. Or go out in the village and show them all that the world has moved on since ten years ago.'

'Hmm, I'm not sure the village is ready for that.'

He laughs. 'Ingledown it is then. Maybe a romantic stroll in the woods after.'

The thought of walking in the woods makes my spine tingle. 'No. Not the woods. I don't want to go back there.'

He leans in for another kiss, pulling me close, and then whispers in my ear, his breath hot against my skin, 'I'd be with you. I'd keep you safe.'

I think he might be half joking. But I still feel cold at the idea of going into the woods.

When we break apart, I say, 'Maybe we shouldn't joke. Someone took a shot at me. There's a person out there with a gun.'

'Dad has a shotgun on the farm,' Peter replies. 'I could borrow it and walk around with you until the psycho reveals himself.'

I choke out a hollow laugh. 'I always forget just how many people in the countryside are armed.'

'Yeah, it's like the Wild West out here.' He takes me in his arms for another long kiss, then breaks away. 'I should get back. I told Dad I was popping out for a bite to eat. I'll pick you up about seven tomorrow, okay?'

I nod, wishing he wouldn't leave.

He winks at me as he steps out of the back door, and I quickly lock it behind me before checking the windows again. Then I head back to the kitchen, memories of what just happened flashing through my mind. I can't believe I allowed myself to be so impulsive. But then I feel as though I haven't been myself for days. I've let it all infect my ability to make decisions – the grief, the danger in the village, the torment of the past.

I can't deny that being with him brought me comfort when I needed it most. Yet what we did leaves a sour taste in my mouth, tainting the memory of his sweet kisses. By being with Peter, am I betraying the memory of Samuel? Or am I betraying my sister? Peter is stuck in the middle of all this, blissfully unaware of how much I loved his brother.

I didn't tell him my suspicions about Rosie, but if Rosie did play a part in Samuel's disappearance, then he has a right to know. Not only am I not opening up my heart to him, I'm not letting him into my deepest thoughts either.

After making myself a ham sandwich for lunch, cleaning up around the house and sorting through more of Mum's clothes, the afternoon sinks into its sunset. I wander through into the bedroom I once shared with my sister and allow my fingers to trail over the window she climbed out of that night. If only I'd woken up, I could've stopped her before anything bad happened.

I check my phone. Still no word from Rosie. Surely the addiction meeting is over by now. How long do these things last? An hour? Two? It has been several since I last heard from her. Do I even want her to come home? It depends on whether I believe she's a liar or not, and I still don't know. I want her to be my sister. And if she is telling the truth, I want her to be safe. I fire off a quick message to see how she's doing. Getting back from Ingledown can take a while, with cancelled buses and country roads to negotiate. And I'm worried about her coming home in the dark.

If it wasn't her in the woods, someone else is still out there.

*

With the setting sun pouring warm light through the living-room windows, I find myself drifting in and out of sleep on the sofa, with an old episode of *Friends* on the TV at a low volume. Soon I find myself falling into a deep slumber, dreaming about Buckbell Woods. There's Jack, waiting for me. I'm his wife-to-be, dressed in a floating white dress. Peter is the best man, and Rosie carries a bridesmaid's bouquet. Mum and Dad sit in the front row of the little gathering by the bluebell field, their skulls shining through their flesh.

I wake with a start, convinced that someone is in the house. Chest tight and muscles tense, I hurry around checking all the windows and doors. The nasty letter from the village sits in the middle of the kitchen table. Never have I felt so alone.

According to my phone, it's almost nine p.m. There are no messages from Rosie. I call her and leave a hurried voicemail about staying safe and watching out for anyone who might be following her.

Why hasn't she come back? I keep asking myself the same question over and over again: Am I in danger?

The last bus from Ingledown was 7.15. Which means she either lied about where she was, gave into temptation and is in a pub somewhere, or someone has hurt her on the way home. My heart flips over. No matter what, Rosie is my sister, and if someone has harmed her …

I let out a scream of frustration. For ten years I've fought and berated myself for believing that Rosie killed my boyfriend, but despite it all, I can't stay in this house if she's out there hurt. There's only one thing for it. I'm going to have to go outside and search for her. With a longing gaze towards my phone, I consider texting Peter, but our relationship is complicated now that we've been together. I don't want to continue intruding in his life by constantly asking for help.

The least I can do is ask the Campbells if they know anything. It's late, and Joan was downright rude to me last time, but what if they saw Rosie on her way back home? At least then I'll know if she tried to return. Fuck. Why did I fall asleep before darkness fell?

I grab my jacket and hurry out onto the drive, making sure to lock the door behind me. I don't want to come back and find someone waiting for me in the cottage.

The gravel crunches under the weight of my trainers as I hurry towards the narrow track that connects us with the Campbells. There's a fair stretch of land between us, which means I have to walk along the road in the dark for a few minutes, jumping at every change in atmosphere, every owl hooting in the distance. Anyone could be watching me. They could be waiting somewhere out there in the dark.

It's a little late for visitors, but I'm too desperate to truly care. They ignore the first knock, but I persist until Mrs Campbell opens the door, mouth set into a stern line.

'Heather. What do you want?'

'I'm sorry to disturb you this late, but I wondered if you'd seen Rosie coming down the lane? Or maybe heard a car? A taxi.'

'No,' she says. 'Nothing at all.'

As she's about to close the door, I reach out and try to push it open.

'Stop that,' she snaps. 'What do you think you're doing? Bob! Bob!'

'I need to check you don't have her,' I say, admittedly in a slightly deranged way.

'Why would we have your *slut* of a sister here?' Mrs Campbell shouts, pushing the door back with surprising force for an older woman.

But it's when I see her husband that I give in and back away. He comes to the door, visible through the gap I've managed to prise open, with a shotgun in his hand. My blood runs cold. Was he the one in the woods? Is that my father's gun? My eyes search the dark wood for any identifying marks, but I can't remember it well enough to say for certain.

'Go on back to your own house now, Heather,' he says. 'You're safe there. You're not safe out here.'

With almost robotic movements, I twist on my heel, move away from the neighbours I've known my entire life, who I thought were good people, and make my way back to my parents' cottage. The last of my resilience saps away.

Darkness spreads into the house until I can't bear it any more. I plod through each room closing the curtains, switching on every light. Dad would be furious about the use of all this electricity.

Rosie's phone continues to go to voicemail. I text Peter about the strange altercation with the neighbours, but he must be busy too. I retreat to the living room to bite my fingernails and stare at the television screen as the programmes move into evening viewing.

Ten p.m. comes and there's still no sign of Rosie. My wild mind won't stop conjuring images of her broken body in the woods. My sixteen-year-old self bends down to collect the bracelet tangled up in the bluebells, but instead I find her hair, which leads me to the rest of her, laid out with glassy, unfocused eyes staring up at me.

What is wrong with me?

I curl up on the sofa, too afraid to go to sleep. My phone is in my hand, plugged in for extra battery power, and I can't tear my eyes away from the screen. What if the Campbells are more violent than I've ever imagined? Another image flashes before my eyes. This time it's Mr Campbell shooting Rosie in the chest with the shotgun.

This isn't who I am. I'm not the one with the wild imagination. Rosie is the writer; I'm just plain old Heather. Apart from my Buckthorpe Jack dream, I don't have insane nightmares. Life is regular to me. There's a logic to everything that does and doesn't happen. Whatever strange occurrences there are in the world, there are always mundane explanations. *Samuel disappeared because Rosie killed him and buried his body.* I force the thought away and focus.

My sister lies. Does my sister kill? Did she hide Dad's gun in the woods? The thoughts keep coming. Did she write the note and slip it beneath the door? I have no idea what she is thinking …

I screw my eyes shut and rock back and forth on the sofa. I'm emotional, tired and making mistakes. I need to think about this logically. It was me who left first this morning. She would have needed to hurry through the woods to overtake me and then shoot at me. Unless she has an accomplice … She knows the woods just as well as me. She also knows that I always stop at the bluebell field for a few minutes, which might have given her enough time to find a shortcut to Jack's cottage and get there before me.

Which leads me to her motivation. If she was trying to frighten me, it would make sense that none of the shots would hit me. I can't say for certain that none were aimed at me, because I don't know enough about the sound of bullets when they come close, but I know that the first one seemed to be a warning shot. She knows that I'm dragging my feet about the potential sale. She knows me well enough to guess that I'm fantasising about staying here. She also knows that I can't afford to buy her out. She wants me to sell the house.

But the house was left to both of us. Surely she could force me to sell through lawyers? That would take time, though. What if she needs money now? What if she owes someone money? There's so much I don't know about my sister.

I start to pace my way around the room, stomach churning up sour bile. She knows I'm close to finding out the truth about her involvement in Samuel's disappearance.

I stop moving. Have I truly considered the implications of that, though? If Rosie is the person behind everything, then that could mean she wants me dead.

I start pacing again, chewing on a thumbnail, appalled by my own thoughts and yet unable to deny that they make some sort of sense. A gunshot in the woods could be put down to a hunting accident. There is the occasional poacher in Buckbell, though they'd be completely stupid to go near the path or poach in broad daylight. Maybe her plan was to keep hold of the gun, leave my body and feign innocence with some sort of phoney alibi.

God, no. Am I truly thinking this? My damaged, funny, smart sister surely would never try to harm me.

When there's a scraping at the door, a scream rips from my throat. I bend over, clutching my neck, desperately trying to calm my thudding heart. I hurry through into the kitchen as a wet-haired Rosie rushes in.

'Heather.' She grabs me by the shoulders and I flinch away from her. I've never seen her this wild-eyed. Her eye sockets are dark with mascara stains. Her freezing fingers dig into my bony shoulders. 'I've figured out what I have to do to make everything right.'

Despite the fear, it's disappointment that hits me the hardest when I smell the alcohol on her breath. She's been drinking.

She pulls a piece of paper from her jacket pocket and slaps it down on the sofa.

'I found your letter,' she says.

My heart sinks when I see the first line: *You'll never read this. Not while I'm still breathing.*

CHAPTER TWENTY-SEVEN

Rosie

Then

I was lucky that Heather had always been a heavy sleeper. I found that I could read with the light on, get up to go to the toilet, or send text messages with the sound on without her even stirring from her slumber. On the other hand, I was constantly woken by her sleepwalking and snoring. I never told her that the sleepwalking started again after we began sharing a room. But I found an easy way to stop her leaving. I just put a hand on her shoulder and led her back to bed.

She fell asleep quickly that night, with one earphone from her iPod still in place, the Cure playing quietly. I knew the playlist because it was one Samuel had made for her. The thought still makes me feel ill even now.

Even though I knew she wouldn't wake, I still tiptoed over to the window and gently opened it as wide as it would go. I knew the routine by heart now. One hop to get me up, then a swing of my legs to get out, followed by a second hop down. I propped the window open a few inches with the casement stay. Then I glanced up to check that no lights had gone on, or that no parents were visible in the upstairs windows, ready to bollock me for sneaking out.

It seemed the coast was clear.

I checked my phone and sent another text to say that I was about to set off into the woods. We were meeting at the bluebell field.

My heart was racing. I had no idea if I was doing the right thing, but it was too late to back out now. It began to rain. I pulled up my hood and set off into the dark.

I knew that he would be waiting for me.

CHAPTER TWENTY-EIGHT

Heather

Now

Rosie slumps down on the sofa, still in her coat and shoes. She picks up the letter again and holds it in front of me.

'When I first found it, I wanted to drink myself to death,' she says. 'But I went to a meeting instead.'

I want to interrupt her and point out that she's drunk now, but I don't. I give her a minute to explain herself. She seems upset and disorderly, but right now she doesn't seem dangerous.

'Do you honestly think any of this is a surprise to me?' she says, brandishing my own words in my direction. 'I've known all along that you never believed me. I've known all along that you still love him, which is *gross*, Heather. You didn't exactly make it hard for me to find out. You went for your secret tryst in the woods. You carried on reading the books he lent you and listening to the playlists he made you. God, Hev. Why him? Out of everyone, why him?'

My voice is small when I reply. 'We were the same, him and me. No one else understood us.'

She lets out a derisive laugh, her eyes glazed over. Finally she throws the letter down. 'I always thought you suspected I was involved. When he disappeared, you let your guard down, though I don't think you realised. Your disgust for me was plain. We barely talked between that night and when I left for university, did we?'

'No,' I say.

'That's why I spent all my time going out in Ingledown instead of studying. Ruined my A levels and barely scraped into my last-choice uni. Ruined my life, basically.'

'I'm sorry this happened to us,' I say.

'So am I,' she says. She leans forwards and rubs her eyes, before jumping to her feet and striding over to me, her hands outstretched. She grasps my shoulders again. 'I need to take you into the woods. I need to explain it all to you, otherwise it's going to haunt me forever.'

'What?' I wrench myself free from her grip. 'Why would you want to take me there?'

'You need to see,' she says, leaning over me.

'I can't,' I say. 'Someone shot at me earlier.' *Was it you?*

Her nose wrinkles in confusion, but I can see that she isn't properly taking in my words. Her gaze drifts vaguely from mine towards the front door. 'What? No, that's … No. We need to go now. You need to see it for yourself or you'll never believe me.'

'We can't go out there, Ro.' Slowly I take my phone from my pocket and rest it on my knees.

Rosie's eyes are distant. Has she taken drugs, too? Her mouth opens and closes as though she's at a loss, and she stares at various points in the room as if she can't remember where she is.

'What happened at the meeting?' I ask, trying to pull her back to reality. I'm finding it hard to believe that she could have orchestrated any sort of targeted attack on me, judging by her current state. How long has she been drinking?

'Typical rookie mistake,' she says. 'I went for one coffee with a guy there. I'd been talking about some heavy shit, you know? I needed a friend. Someone who isn't you. But he turned out to be a terrible influence. He had a flask of whisky, which we drained pretty fast.' It all sounds possible. I don't detect any hint of a lie and I want to believe that she's telling me the truth. My heart is reaching out for her, wanting her to just be Rosie and nothing else. 'Then we took a few pills.'

'What kind of pills?' My fear fades into concern. I get to my feet and slide my phone back into my jeans pocket. 'We should go to the hospital. Come on.'

'I don't know what they were, but finally everything is clear now. I know exactly where we need to go.' She begins walking towards the open door, but I pull her back.

'You're not in any state to go out there. How are you going to find what you want to show me when you're high?'

'Don't you get it?' she says. 'The forest is in my head now. What I did that night made sure of that. It's scratched into my brain. Deeper than a tattoo. I couldn't forget even if I wanted to, and a bit of booze and a few pills aren't going to erase it. Believe me, I've tried to do just that.'

She attempts to pull away, but I hold on tight.

'Let's sleep on it and wait until morning. It isn't safe to go out there right now.'

I expect her to fight me, but she doesn't. Instead, she goes still, regarding me carefully. 'You were right not to trust me, Heather. I have lied to you all these years, and I did go to meet Samuel the night he disappeared. Dad followed me.'

I let her go. It takes a moment for her words to sink in. My heart thuds and the sound of the television comes through a fog. *Dad* was there that night? What does that mean? An image flashes into my mind of my father leaning over Samuel as he lies dead and cold in the mud. Could Dad be the person who helped her kill him? Not him, surely. Not another member of my family who lied to me.

Rosie turns away from me and I watch her disappear into the darkness outside. For half a heartbeat I hesitate, and then I follow her, not even bothering to lock the door behind me. We're already in danger. So what if someone breaks in? This house cannot be any more dangerous than what lies in wait for us out there. I don't care any more. I just want answers.

Rosie is already wandering down the road, her arms wrapped tightly around her body. While she's preoccupied, I send a quick text message to Peter, telling him what's happening and where I'm going. He's the one person I can trust, and I'm relying on him to save me if I need to be saved.

Rosie stops and waits for me, looking back over her shoulder, body rotated, eyes searching out mine. I tuck the phone into my pocket and break into a jog to catch up. Her gaze is still unfocused. I hope I'm doing the right thing by following her. Every inch of my skin seems to tingle, and not because of the chill in the night air.

I have to know what happened to Samuel. I have to lay this mystery, and him, to rest once and for all.

We pass the Campbells' house, and I give it a quick scan. The upstairs lights are on and I'm almost certain that I see a curtain twitch. Are they watching us? I hug myself, sensing eyes all over in the darkness, waiting, watching.

A million thoughts rush through my mind. What if the Campbells follow us into the woods? Or worse, what if they call someone else? Ian Dixon, or Reg at the pub. Who else wants us gone? Colin Murray? It could be anyone. The pale faces of the congregation at Mum's funeral come back to me, and I imagine them all behind us now.

I glance across at my sister, who could easily be lying about Dad's involvement in Samuel's disappearance. I keep telling myself that I'm paranoid and finding enemies in all directions, but at the same time, I have to admit to myself that I'm still afraid of Rosie.

'Where are we going, Ro?' I ask, deliberately keeping my voice calm and unthreatening.

'We're going to find the answer to all your questions,' she says.

'Are you going to tell me how Dad was involved in all of this?'

She nods.

My stomach flips over. Samuel's face flashes into my mind. The answer could be his body, buried in a shallow grave. Morbid thoughts keep coming at me, faster than I can blink them away. Now I'm thinking about decomposition, and what Samuel might look like after all these years. I don't want to remember the boy I loved that way.

'Please,' I say, tugging on Rosie's hand. 'I don't want to see. Let's go back to the cottage and you can tell me what happened instead. Please, Rosie.'

Almost nonchalantly, she pulls her arm away and keeps walking. 'You don't understand, Hev. This is the only way I can get it all to end.'

'Get what to end?'

'The nightmares. The pain. The guilt. Your hatred.'

Fear pulls me one way, while sympathy pulls me the other. What has my sister carried all these years?

'I don't hate you.'

'Are you sure about that?' she replies.

'Okay, Rosie,' I say, as we begin our path into Buckbell. 'Take me to see whatever it is you need me to see.'

A few silent tears roll down my cheeks as we head into the darkness of the woods. Suddenly I realise that this could be my best opportunity to say goodbye to Samuel forever.

Rosie's cold hand finds mine. I didn't have time to put my coat on before we left, and I pushed my feet into flat pumps, which aren't much protection against the damp ground. She's shivering too. I put my arm around her, as though I'm the big sister.

'We didn't bring a torch, Ro. Do you know where you're going?'

Rosie pulls her mobile phone out of her bag and switches on the flashlight. My breath catches. For some reason I expected the spectral sight of a decaying Samuel to come into view.

'We never talked about me finding your bracelet the day after Samuel disappeared. Did we?'

'You didn't want to,' Rosie says. Her voice sounds as though it's a million miles away, soft and airy.

'I was too scared,' I admit.

'I thought I couldn't tell you the truth because you didn't want to know. Or because you couldn't handle it. I'm not sure which. But none of that matters any more. Mum told you that she didn't regret anything, and I don't want to die drowning in my own shame. If I show you everything, there'll be at least one thing I can stop regretting.'

'Rosie, what did you do that night?' My voice is choked. I can't stop thinking about what she's about to show me. My eyes fill with tears. With her slight frame pressed up against me, all I can think about is forgiving her for everything; hurting Samuel, wanting to hurt me, I don't care. I still love her, and the saddest part of all this is that my fear has blocked me from showing that love for a decade.

She begins to cry, a low whimpering sound. 'If I tell you, I don't think you'll ever forgive me.'

I hug her tighter, my own tears wetting my face. I haven't cried in front of her since I was eight years old and I broke my wrist falling down the stairs. I no longer believe that she shot at me in the woods, and I no longer believe she wrote the note. Her guilt comes from the past. I feel it emanating from her as she huddles next to me.

'You don't know that, Ro. I might have forgiven you already.'

She wipes away her tears with the back of her hand. 'No. You have no idea what happened. And you will never, ever forgive me. It's not in your nature, Hev. And maybe that's okay. Maybe we can both go on without your forgiveness.'

I don't understand what she means. How can two people continue a relationship if one refuses to forgive the other? I begin to open my mouth to tell her that I will forgive her no matter what, but she speaks again.

'Whatever happens,' she says. 'It ends tonight. Everything ends.'

'You're not making any sense, Ro.'

She pulls away from me and wanders forward, moving faster now. I have to hurry to keep up with her. The light from the phone caresses the plants and trees around us. Every now and then I hear the sound of an owl in the distance. The fast walk helps to rid me of that chilled sensation I had before, and soon a fine sheen of sweat breaks out on my forehead and the back of my neck.

The woods are beautiful at night. Like that sense of déjà vu I experienced when I first moved back to Buckthorpe, there's something familiar about the sight of the trees in the dark. Perhaps this is what I saw when I went sleepwalking through the woods that time Grandad found me.

Did I notice the stars above? The owls? The distant cries of foxes?

When we come to the edge of the bluebell field, a line from Mum's poem pops into my mind: *Blame the blue.*

'Was Mum there that night?' I ask, breaking the silence that has grown between us.

'No,' Rosie says. 'Just Dad.'

She takes a left at the edge of the bluebell field and begins to walk into a copse of close-knit trees. This isn't part of the path, and now my heart thuds harder and harder with every beat.

'Where are you taking us?'

She doesn't even check behind to see that I'm following her. She's moving with purpose, as though she knows exactly where she's going. Every step she takes winds us through the trees. Now, when I lift my head, I can't see the stars; all I see is branches. Nettles aggravate my bare ankles and wrists. My feet catch on ropes of thorny bushes.

'The stones,' Rosie mutters. 'Five stones.' She stops, finally allowing me to catch up with her, then raises her arm, pointing ahead. 'One.' A round, half-buried rock jutting out of the earth. 'Two.' A few feet away is a smaller stone next to a tree. 'Three.'

This one is vast, the kind you can sit on. 'Four.' Another few feet away, this one more like a step coming out of the ground. 'Five.' The fifth stone is half-covered in moss, barely peeking out from the undergrowth. The five of them form an irregular circle. Rosie takes two steps forward and stands in the centre.

'No,' I whisper. 'Please don't. I don't want to see.'

'This is it,' she says.

When she bends down, I reach out for her, one pale hand in the darkness extended towards her bent frame. But before I can touch her, she has her hands in the soil. I cover my mouth with that same pale hand. This is it, now. This is my answer. My body vibrates with fear and horror. *What is she digging for?*

Because I can't bear to watch, I turn away and close my eyes. It's as I close my eyes that I see him one more time. The boy I loved. Samuel. I see us together in the barn, holding each other, his hand on my cheek, mine on his neck. I feel the warmth of his face close to mine. I feel his lips on mine. I smell him. I smell the straw, dry and grassy. The absolute happiness that I've half-heartedly attempted to chase for the rest of my life.

'Heather.'

I don't want to see him, my love in a shallow grave.

'Heather. Look.'

Of course, I have to. Slowly I turn around and face my sister.

But what I see doesn't match the horrors in my mind. She stands looking at me with her cheeks flushed pink and her eyes open wide, as though she's about to hand me a prize. The effect reminds me of a cat that has just brought a dead bird into the house.

My eyes slowly work their way down from her face, finally stopping at her hands. They are black from the earth, and yet they glow. She has placed her phone down on the ground with the torch beam coming up to highlight her amongst the shadows. And as the light illuminates her form, it picks out the glowing white shards of a translucent object in her hands.

'This is it,' she says. 'This is what I wanted to show you.'

Tentatively I take a step closer. 'I don't understand, Rosie.'

But she merely nods towards the shards in explanation.

I lean over her hands, trying to ascertain the importance of what she holds. It's only when I pick up one of the pieces that I realise this is the same sort of strong plastic as from the headlight of a car.

'What does this have to do with Samuel?' I ask.

'I had to hide it,' Rosie says. 'They made me.'

She twists her body and begins to walk away.

'Wait.' I reach out for her, but my hand grasps at air.

Rosie stops, seems to remember the plastic in her hands, and puts it down.

'Where are we going now?' I ask.

'I need to show you the rest,' she says.

When she sets off again, I'm closer to her. Suddenly I see her foot catch the ground, and she trips. She grabs hold of me, with her weight tilting back. The world drops away and we fall, landing with a thump.

The earth is hard beneath us, and the wind is knocked from my body, leaving me gasping in cold air. It's pitch black here and stinks of damp soil. Next to me, Rosie groans in pain. I pull myself to my feet and quickly return to my senses. I feel in my jeans pocket for my phone, but it's gone. I grope around in the dark and find it in the spot where I fell, the screen completely smashed on a stone, unable to turn on. My hip and back are sore from the fall and I think I landed with my weight on top of the phone, adding to the damage. With my hands out in front of me, I feel my way around the hole and then squint up through the darkness.

'What the fuck?' Rosie mumbles.

We're in a square hole, maybe four or five feet across, at least eight feet deep.

Then it dawns on me. We're in a trap.

CHAPTER TWENTY-NINE

Rosie

Then

I met him on the edge of the bluebell field. My torchlight bobbed along the heads of the flowers, making me feel as though they were an audience. Witnesses to our pact. As I drew closer, the beam found Samuel's legs, his black hoodie, and finally his squinting eyes. I directed it back down onto the ground, where my shoes sank into the damp earth.

'I can't believe you actually came,' he said, blinking to recover from the sudden bright light. His hood was already wet from the rain, and he stood with his hands pushed deep into his pockets as though to keep them warm.

'Neither can I,' I admitted. The sight of him made me tremble with fear, but I forced it down, shoved away all thoughts of the incident.

'Why did you drag me out here?' he asked, jutting his chin out almost aggressively.

I'd felt a fearlessness on my way that fooled me into thinking I could actually do this. But now that I saw him, tall, muscular, twice as wide as I was, I wanted to run away. That would make it twice now that I'd run terrified through these woods.

'I … It's about Heather,' I said, my voice smaller than I'd hoped it would sound, made even smaller by the noisy raindrops pattering against the leaves. 'You have to stay away from her.'

'None of this mess is Heather's fault,' he said. 'You know that.'

'I don't care.' Hearing him say my sister's name helped me find that thread of anger that I'd been hoping would give me confidence. 'Stay away from her.'

Samuel shook his head slowly, with a small smile playing on his lips. I thought about how I'd found him attractive once, and how that had been a huge mistake. Maybe if I hadn't felt drawn to him, I would have made Heather stop going to the farm and none of this would have happened. I'd pitied him for being bullied at school, but now all of that had ebbed away. Instead, I saw an entitled, arrogant boy.

I felt ashamed of the way I'd enjoyed his attention, the way he often studied my body, and for failing to step in the moment I'd noticed him stop watching me and start watching Heather instead.

'What are you going to do to me if I don't stay away from her?' Samuel asked, his shoulders rising, his body tense. 'You've already ruined my life.'

I couldn't find the words to say in response and stayed silent instead.

'And now you just stand there with nothing to say. Nothing. You're a bitch, Rosie. You need to undo everything you've done.'

'Why? Are you going to hurt me if I don't?' I took a step towards him, reckless in my anger. 'You know exactly what you did, don't play the innocent with me.'

'That didn't give you the right to ruin my life!' He grabbed me by the shoulders, fingers tight as a vice.

'Get off me!' I tried to twist my body, attempting to wrench myself out of that relentless grip.

'They think I killed animals! I can't go to school any more. Mum cries herself to sleep at night and Dad drinks more than ever. Peter gets bullied at school. Peter! Remember him, my little brother, who looked after your pony when you were at the farm? Who followed you both around like a lapdog fetching you drinks?

He's thirteen years old and they painted "RAPIST" all over his football boots. He came home with a bloody nose. That's all because of you, bitch!'

'Stop it! Samuel, stop it!'

He shook me back and forth until my teeth smashed against my tongue and blood filled my mouth. Both my shoulders, still caught in his grip, throbbed with pain. His expression was focused, his lips pressed together and his eyes narrowed. For a split second I thought he might kill me.

But I couldn't allow that to happen. If it came down to him or me, I'd choose him. I lashed out, scraping my nails down his cheek. The sudden pain at least surprised him, because he finally released his grip and shoved me hard. I tripped over my feet, landed painfully on my backside, my torch bouncing on the forest floor.

'Hey!'

A tall shape rushed past me and collided with Samuel. Two men hit the ground, writhing around amongst the bluebells. The larger man was on top of the other, pounding him with his fists. I rushed to pick up my torch. It had powered down from the fall and my trembling fingers seemed to have lost the ability to switch it back on. Finally I got the light directed to the shapes writhing in the bluebells.

It was Dad on top of Samuel, punching and punching. Over and over. Pummelling his face into meat.

Fear turned me to stone.

I could stand there and do nothing. Or I could save Samuel. But I remember thinking that Dad was actually going to do it. He was going to kill Samuel. What happened next was in my hands.

CHAPTER THIRTY

Heather

Now

'We must be about eight, maybe nine feet down,' I say. I open my arms out wide and my fingertips brush soil on both sides. 'Maybe five and a half feet wide. The screen on my phone is smashed and I can't switch it on. What about yours?'

Rosie is sitting on the floor by my feet with her arms wrapped around her knees. She rocks back and forth, her eyes staring into the black. I can barely see her, with those dirty hands, dark hair and filthy clothing. She could be part of the earth. A broken version of Gaia herself.

I drop to my knees. 'Rosie, can you hear me?'

I've already checked myself over for injuries, but apart from a bruised hip, I seem to be unscathed. I just can't figure out if Rosie is hurt or not.

'I should've known,' she says quietly. 'We're going to die tonight, Heather.' Finally her eyes meet mine, and all I see is a haunted woman.

I can't stand the pain she's in. I wrap my arms around her and grip her tight. 'No, we're not. Just do everything I say and we'll live. And then we'll sell the fucking house and get the hell out of this village. Okay?'

She nods, and I'm relieved to see that I've beaten down whatever barrier was cutting her off from facing the reality of the situation.

'Good girl,' I say. Gently I help her to her feet and pat her down to check for broken bones. We establish that her ankle is sore, but she can put weight on it. There's a cut on her arm, too, and we use the sleeve of my top to stem the bleeding. I'm worried about the cut. It's not particularly deep, but it is bleeding profusely, and we're surrounded by dirt that could cause an infection.

'Can you try finding your phone for me?' I ask.

She gropes along the ground and then shakes her head. 'I put it on the ground while we were looking at the smashed headlight.'

'Shit. It's all right, that just means we need to get out and then find help. But we can climb out. You just need to give me a leg-up.'

She nods slowly, still not quite herself but beginning to come around.

'Okay, now cup your hands, Ro. I'll put my foot in it like we used to do when we were little. Remember when we'd ride the ponies bareback? Remember?'

'I remember, sis,' she says, and a hesitant smile brightens the terrified expression on her face.

I adjust my weight in preparation, but Rosie straightens up.

'Hev?'

'Yeah.'

'There's something else I need to tell you.'

'Tell me when we get home, okay?'

She shakes her head. 'No, I need to tell you now.'

'Then say it quickly.'

'Okay,' she says. 'I lied about Samuel. He didn't force himself on me.'

It hits me like a short, sharp jab to my abdomen. This is the exoneration I've always wanted for the boy I loved all those years ago, and yet there's no closure or comfort in hearing the words spoken.

'Why did you lie?' I whisper.

She glances up, and then back down to me. 'It's complicated. We need to go. If we get out of these woods, I'll explain everything.'

'Tell me,' I insist.

'I was wrong. I should have waited.' She puts her arms down ready to help me up out of the hole.

But I shake my head. 'Tell me, Rosie. What happened to Samuel that night?'

Before she can answer, a bright light floods into the hole. Both Rosie and I fall away from it, and I have to shield my eyes to avoid the pain of the blinding beam.

'Stay where you are, girls.'

The sound of the man's voice turns my blood to ice. I press myself up against the side of the hole, not that it will do any good. There is nowhere to hide, nowhere to go.

'When I first dug this little hole here, I figured I'd be catching just one of you Sharpe girls. But it's nice to have you both. Now, if you could throw up your phone.' He gestures with a wiggling of his fingers. 'Come on. I can see one over here, but there's two of you and I know you don't leave the house without them.'

Finally my eyes begin to adjust to the light and I can see our captor. Unfortunately, his features are obscured by shadows. But I can see the shotgun slung over one arm. He must be the one who fired the gun at me. Next to me, Rosie whimpers.

'Come on, I don't have all day.' He lifts the shotgun as a reminder that he's armed and we're not.

I fling the shattered phone upwards. It lands next to his feet and he bends down to pick it up, slipping it into his pocket.

'Good,' he says.

'Fuck you,' I say impulsively.

He stands at the edge of the hole for a moment until there's a buzzing sound and he walks away lifting a phone to his ear.

I lean back against the wall and let out a long breath. Since coming home, I'd figured we were being run out by the villagers, but it hadn't occurred to me that we were being hunted. Whoever is up there expected at least one of us to fall into his trap. I wouldn't have come here without Rosie, which means that this must all be for her.

'Do you know who that is?' I whisper to her.

Slowly she nods her head.

'Who?' I know I recognise the man's voice, but my exhausted brain doesn't seem to want to connect the dots.

'Colin Murray,' she says. 'It's Samuel's father.'

Of course it is. His voice sounds slightly different from usual, not quite as beaten down and defeated as the last time we spoke. The note of triumph threw me off.

'Who do you think he's on the phone to?' I whisper. Whoever it is, he's having an animated conversation. I can't make out the words, but I hear the sound of him hissing through his teeth in a seething kind of anger that chills me.

'I don't know,' Rosie says. There's an edge to her voice that makes me wonder whether she's telling me the truth, but then I have another thought that pushes the others away.

'Buckthorpe Jack!' I say, the fog of shock finally clearing. 'If we scream, he might hear us and call the police.'

'What if he's in on it?' Rosie says, face pale and drawn.

'What other choice do we have?'

I take a deep breath and signal for Rosie to do the same, before screaming '*Help!*' as loudly as I possibly can. If nothing else, I feel a tingle of pleasure when Colin turns back to us in alarm, his face thunderous. I scream again, keeping my gaze on his, hoping my expression remains strong enough to challenge him. This weak man, who hunts young women; I had no idea of the level of hatred he felt for us when I visited the farm. *I saw your pain. I felt sorry for you.*

He snaps the barrel and the stock of the shotgun together and raises it to his shoulder. 'Scream again and I'll kill Heather first.'

He means it.

The pleasure of our tiny victory ebbs away, leaving me hollow and freezing to my core. Are we going to die in this hole? Dirty and cold, like hunted animals?

'Heather has nothing to do with this. Let her go,' Rosie says. I'm surprised to hear the steel in her voice after seeing her fear and vulnerability. 'I'm the one you want.'

'Yes,' he says. 'You are. But I'm not against getting rid of her too.'

Rosie's face screws up in revulsion. 'Have you any idea how twisted that is?'

But Colin's voice doesn't sound twisted at all. If anything, he seems completely calm, almost businesslike about the situation. There's an air of detachment about the way he speaks, as though he's carrying out his plan with an attitude of unwanted inevitability.

'I don't care,' he says simply. And I believe him.

'Nothing you do will bring him back,' Rosie says. I suspect her attempts to talk him out of this are pointless, but I admire her for trying. 'Killing us won't make you feel any better.'

'Oh,' he says. 'You don't know that.'

'I know it was your fault,' Rosie continues. 'Everything that happened that night. You could've stopped it. But you didn't, did you?'

'Be quiet,' he says, still calm, but now with a vicious edge to his voice.

The two of them are talking as though they were both there the night Samuel disappeared. Which means Samuel, Rosie, Colin and Dad were all in the woods together. The pieces of the puzzle are finally coming together.

Nothing you do will bring him back. Rosie said that about Samuel which means that he's dead and Colin knows he's dead. But when I visited the farm, Lynn Murray stared me straight in the eye and told me she thought he was still alive. She *felt* that he was alive. I believed she truly thought that. Has Colin lied to his own family all these years? How can he go to bed at night with a woman who still doesn't know what happened to her son after ten long years? How could he carry on seeing her pain every day and not tell her what happened?

He moves away from the edge of the hole and stares at his phone.

'What are we going to do?' Rosie says. 'We can't climb out now, or he'll just shoot us.'

'I don't know. Maybe Jack heard us scream.'

'Maybe.'

She gives my hand a squeeze and we share a sad smile. Both of us know that our plan is wishful thinking. Who knows whether Jack would even want to help us, and who knows how many people from the village are in on this witch-hunt. And then I remember – Peter. I'd almost forgotten that I sent him a text about going into the woods.

I wish I could see my phone to check whether he saw the message or not, but at least it gives me some hope that we'll get out of this alive. Surely Peter can talk some sense into his father.

The freezing cold of the night air seeps into my bones. Colin's back remains a silhouette against his bright spotlight. He's been planning this revenge, waiting for an opportunity to trap Rosie in a cage. What else does he want to do to her? If we're to escape, I need to know more about this man's motives.

'What happened that night? You need to tell me, Ro.'

'Please remember that I only wanted to protect you,' Rosie says. 'Okay?'

'Fine. Just tell me.' If Peter doesn't make it in time, I refuse to die without finding out what happened ten years ago. I need to know the truth.

She takes a deep breath and begins. 'I snuck out of the house and went to meet Samuel in the woods. We couldn't meet during the day because if anyone saw us together they'd go apeshit. We met in secret near the bluebell field. As you know, it was April, and they were in bloom. Easy to find with a torch.'

'That was where I found your bracelet.' I glance up at the hole to see if Colin is listening in, but he still has his back turned to us.

'We were just going to talk for a little bit,' Rosie continues. 'He was upset with me because of the lie I'd told and I wanted to tell him to stay away from you because I'd seen you together in the woods.'

'But if he didn't try to rape you, why would you want him to stay away from me? I don't understand. Were you jealous of me and Samuel?'

Rosie's face contorts into something ugly as she relives her memories of that night.

'What the fuck have you done, Colin?'

The sound of another voice prompts us both to lift our heads towards the sound. A second man has joined Colin above the place where Rosie and I are trapped.

CHAPTER THIRTY-ONE

Rosie

Then

'Dad, no!'

The rain came down hard as I stood there frozen. It was as though my heart restarted when I realised that I had to stop him before he took Samuel's life. But even when I grabbed hold of him, I couldn't pull him away. I didn't have the physical strength against an adult man, and my hands were slippery with the rain.

'Dad, stop! You're going to kill him!'

He had his big builder's hands around Samuel's throat, and I was so afraid that I started to cry.

'I lied!' I blurted out, now almost shouting over the downpour. Tears ran down my face, washed away immediately. 'Samuel didn't attack me; no one did. I made the whole thing up.'

As he slowly let go of Samuel, I fell back into the wet bluebells.

'What?'

Now I was the one on the ground with my father looming tall above me. The shame of what I'd done washed over me in a wave and I thought I might throw up. But at the same time, relief flooded through me. I'd said it out loud. I'd finally spoken the words that had been in my heart ever since the incident. Ever since I stood in the kitchen in my torn clothes, tears dripping on the tiles, with the family staring at me asking me what had happened.

I'd lied.

And then Emily and Rhona had taken the lie even further. I think they'd wanted to be part of it. They saw the attention I was getting and wanted it for themselves. I'd always hated them for that, but to hate them was to hate myself, because I was the worst of them all.

'I'm sorry,' I muttered.

'What did you do, Rosie?'

He took a step towards me, face shadowed by darkness, hiding his expression from me. But I heard everything I needed to hear in his voice. He was disgusted. And I couldn't blame him.

Behind him I noticed Samuel climbing to his feet, unsteady and awkward after the beating. But I was too focused on Dad to say anything about it.

'I didn't mean it,' I said, wiping away tears and rainwater. 'It just came out. I didn't do it on purpose. And then everything kept going forward and I couldn't take it back.'

'Yes you could,' Dad said. 'You could've taken it back at any time. Do you know what you did to that boy? Do you know what you've done to this village?'

I buried my face in my hands. I always knew I would be the one to let Dad down. Out of me and Heather, it was always me who made the wrong choices and did the wrong thing. Deep down, I think he'd been waiting for me to mess up.

'What did I do wrong, Rosie? Why have you … Why are you like this?'

It was at that moment that the sound of my tears blocked out the rain. What *had* he done wrong? Was it the long absences from his family? Was it because he never asked me how school was at the end of the day? Or that he never seemed to care about any of us? Or was I making excuses for my behaviour?

'Now you know.' Hearing Samuel's voice came as a surprise. 'You can stop them all from lying about me. You can tell the police and everything can go back to how it was.'

'Get up, Rosie. We need to deal with this. You can't just cry and hope it's going to go away.' Dad's hands grabbed my elbows and hauled me to my feet.

But by the time I'd wiped the tears from my eyes and opened them again, Samuel was gone. Dad followed my gaze.

'Fuck!' he exclaimed. 'Now he'll go to the police and tell them I assaulted him.' He set off to follow Samuel, but I caught hold of his jacket.

'No, Dad. Don't. I want to go home.' I was tired and wet through and wished I'd never come to the woods. I had a terrible feeling that if we did catch up with Samuel, there would be even more arguing and someone would lose their temper and lash out. I didn't want anyone else to get hurt.

'He's running towards the back road,' Dad said, as though in his own world. 'He'll be back at the farm in less than half an hour. We need to stop him and convince him to work with us. I can't go to prison, Rosie.'

'Dad, please.'

He pulled himself out of my grip and backed away. 'Jesus, I don't even know what to think about what you've done.' He shook his head and began walking away.

My fingers withdrew. I folded my arms around my body.

That was when I heard the screech of brakes, followed by the crunch of metal, and then silence. Neither Dad nor I spoke; instead we started running towards the back road. I was younger and faster than him, and I took the lead, dodging between trees barely visible in the dark. My feet caught on the thorny undergrowth, slowing me down, but I pushed on. All the time my heart was beating as fast as my mind was repeating: *nononononono.*

When I reached the fence that separated the woods from the narrow road, I dropped to my knees and wriggled underneath the wire. As I squeezed through onto the road, Samuel's face was almost level with mine. His mouth was open, jaw slack, eyes glassy, body bent at the kind of angle you instinctively know is wrong. There was blood, but the rain was coming down in sheets, washing the red stain away.

It took me less than a second to realise that I was face to face with a lifeless body.

Samuel was dead, and it was all my fault. If I hadn't lied. If I hadn't arranged to meet him …

And then I thought of Heather, and of how much she loved him. She was going to be heartbroken. I closed my eyes, but it didn't stop me from seeing his bloodied body in my mind's eye.

I felt hands help me up, and when I opened my eyes, Dad was next to me. He didn't linger, instead he sprinted to the body and dropped to his knees beside Samuel. But he knew as well as I did that there was nothing he could do. He placed two fingers beneath Samuel's chin and then rose and stumbled away.

When I heard the sound of a car door open, I tore my eyes away from the body. It was the passenger side, I remember that clearly, and it was Colin who stumbled out, almost tripping onto the tarmac. He rushed towards his son, but Dad caught him and held him back.

'There's nothing you can do, Colin,' Dad said, his voice hoarse with shock.

'Sammy!' Colin cried helplessly.

And then he sobbed. Deep, body-racking sobs. It's the sound of his sobbing that I hear at night even now. The kind of heartbreak that I wouldn't wish on my worst enemy.

'We need to call someone,' I said. 'The emergency services. The police …' My voice trailed off. 'I don't know …'

Dad simply nodded at me, then went back to comforting Colin.

Not wanting to look at Samuel's broken body any more, I turned away from the road. As I took my phone out of my pocket,

I was vaguely aware of a second car door opening. There was the sound of heavy boots on the tarmac before the phone was slapped from my hand.

'No one is calling anyone.'

CHAPTER THIRTY-TWO

Heather

Now

When Ian Dixon comes into view, his pointed face shadowed by the backlight, I don't feel any surprise. This is what I suspected as soon as Colin answered his phone. But what I don't know is why he's involved with Colin in the first place. It's not unfeasible that Ian is the first man people call when things go wrong. I've always suspected that he's a dodgy copper who enjoys controlling the village. I'm sure he turns a blind eye to minor infractions when it's convenient to him, and calls in favours in return.

'You've fucked everything up, Colin, haven't you?' He talks to Samuel's father as though he's a child to be admonished. 'Why couldn't you stick to the plan? They were about to up and leave before you fucked everything up!' His voice rises on the last few words, revealing a violent temper beneath his usually calm exterior.

'If you let us go we'll sell the house and get out,' Rosie says. 'We won't say a word about this.'

'That's right,' I chip in. 'We'll leave Buckthorpe and get on with our lives. I swear we'll never come here again.'

If only Rosie had been able to tell me the full story, I could try and use that knowledge to our advantage. My only hope is that she can do it for the both of us.

'Shut. Up.' Ian leans over the mouth of the hole and his spittle flies down in our direction. I cringe away from his ugly angular features.

The revulsion I feel for both of these men is unlike anything I've ever felt before. I almost don't recognise myself as I hope from the bottom of my heart that I get an opportunity for justice.

'We're not letting them go,' Colin says, stepping forward. He points at Rosie. 'She started this whole thing. She killed my son. She ruined everything we have in the village. She's a lying little bitch and I'm going to kill her no matter what you say.'

Ian shakes his head and begins pacing around, both hands balled into fists. His manic anger is a stark contrast to Colin's detached brutality. 'You're an idiot.'

'How is this so different to what we did to John?'

Next to me, Rosie gasps. I feel a stab in my chest. *Dad.*

'We had time to set that up,' Ian says. 'We did it properly. No one suspected a thing.'

Rosie runs and leaps at the muddy side of the hole. 'You killed our dad!'

Ian barely even glances at us, and I realise we're utterly worthless to him.

I just mouth, 'Why?'

'They have lives outside Buckthorpe,' Ian says. 'They have jobs. Boyfriends. People will notice when they stop answering calls and messages.'

'We'll make it look like they've run off,' Colin says. 'They're young and flighty. No one will care. No one gave a shit when my son went missing.'

'Why did you kill Dad?' I try again. This time my voice is louder, directed straight at them both. 'What did he do to you?'

'He helped you.' I don't need to see Rosie to know she's crying as she forces the words out. 'That night he put himself on the line to help you. He wanted to call the police too, but you wouldn't let us. And this is how you repay him? You put a gun in his mouth, pulled the trigger and left him for our mother to find.' She beats the soil with her fists. 'I thought it was because of me! I thought he killed himself because I wasn't a good daughter.'

I take my sister and fold her into my arms.

'See,' Colin says, arm out towards us. 'This is why they have to die. No one can keep these secrets except for you and me. John was about to crack before we put an end to him. She's a fucking alcoholic. She can't keep her mouth shut either.'

Rosie pulls away from me, wipes her eyes with dirty hands and turns to face Colin. 'I've kept that secret for ten years. I didn't even tell my sister.'

'Until tonight,' he says with a grin. 'Why do you think I dug the hole here? I remembered more about that night than you thought, didn't I? I knew exactly where you buried the headlight. See that tree behind you? There's a camera there. I've been waiting.'

Next to me, I feel Rosie's body go completely rigid. She knows he's telling the truth. I look up at the tree to see the trail cam fitted against the trunk.

'I knew you'd come back here, because keeping the secret is eating you from the inside out. All I had to do was wait for the camera to record you falling into the trap I set.'

'Fucking hell, Colin. You're recording this?' Ian says.

Before Colin can reply, Rosie screams, 'You're a monster! You haven't even told your wife what happened to her son! She thinks he's alive!'

Colin smirks. 'And you never told your sister what happened to her boyfriend. We're all monsters here.'

'That's enough,' Ian says. 'We need to decide how we're going to handle this. The girls can't live. They know too much now. They know about John and they know about the crash that killed Samuel.'

Even though I already knew he was dead, hearing those emotionally detached words is still a blow. When I let out a small gasp, Rosie takes my hand in hers and squeezes it.

'I'm sorry,' she says.

The night Rosie met Samuel in the woods, he was somehow killed by a car. Dad, Ian and Colin covered it up. Rosie hid the broken headlight. She too played a part in all of this.

'Where is he?' I whisper to them all. 'If you covered up his death, then there must be a body. Where is he buried?' I pull my hand away from Rosie's grip and tighten it into a fist. 'You could at least tell me that before you kill me.'

'What do you even care about my son?' Colin says. There is the first glimpse of emotion in his voice. It's small, but it's there. A slight thickness to the sound of his words.

'I loved him,' I say.

Rosie's chin drops to her chest while Colin merely lets out a hollow laugh. I don't know whether he's always been this monstrous, or if the years of grief have brought it out of him, but here he is, as evil as any person can be, standing over his quarry with a gun.

'And yet you're fucking his brother,' he says.

'How do you—'

'I saw you together.'

The thought of Colin stalking me, watching me with Peter, leaves me feeling nauseated. But of course he's been following me. He's no doubt been following both of us.

'You enjoy sneaking around with my sons.' His voice becomes lascivious, but I can't decide whether the idea of me with his sons turns him on, or whether he's using that tone to say something about my lack of virtue. 'You and Sam thought you hid what was going on at the farm, but I knew. I always knew.'

'Fuck. You.' Rosie says the words with a quiet kind of power.

Colin glares at my sister before nodding to me. 'She isn't telling you the full story.'

'Why? What more is there to tell?' I ask.

'Enough!' Ian lifts his hands in frustration. 'Samuel's buried on the moor. Now let's get on with this. Murder and suicide. Rosie, you're the fuck-up. You're going to kill your sister and then yourself. We'll get them out of the hole, kill them and fill it in.'

'No you won't.' Rosie stands up straight.

Ian rolls his eyes. 'Couldn't you have just sedated them? This is a mess.'

'It is now you're here. Let's kill them, then get ourselves an alibi. It's not hard.' Colin turns, the barrel of the gun now pointing towards the sergeant.

'And how am I going to deal with that? I can't stop a murder investigation.'

'I don't give a shit,' Colin says.

'You're an idiot, Murray. What kind of alibi are we going to get? I had to sneak out while my wife was asleep. It's not like I can pop into a fucking party and show my face on the way home.'

While the two men are arguing, I cup my hands close to the wall on the side away from the men. 'Get out,' I tell Rosie. 'Run as fast as you can. Don't go to the Campbells. Either call Peter, or go to the pub in the village.'

'Are you sure we can trust Peter?'

'Yes,' I say, hoping that I'm right. 'But if you don't want to, the Prince of Wales has a lock-in until two.'

She nods and puts her foot into my hands. She's slight, but even so, there's some weight to her.

'I don't want to leave you,' she whispers.

'If I go, they'll kill you without any hesitation,' I say. 'But I haven't got a part in this. I think Colin will hesitate to hurt me.'

Rosie opens her mouth as though to speak, but she thinks better of it and hauls herself up the dirt wall.

There's a shout from the two men. The shotgun goes off, but I can't tell whether it's aimed in our direction or not. I shove Rosie up as far as I can, and she grabs hold of a root.

One of the men lets out a groan and a ragged scream. Rosie makes it over the top of the wall and scrabbles away out of sight.

I'm alone in the trap.

I force myself to face the light. Ian Dixon stares down at me from the top of the hole, blood dripping from the hand casually hanging over the edge. Colin stands over him.

'Help me,' Ian mumbles, his skin turning grey and his eyes rolling back in his head.

I can see that he's been shot and is probably bleeding out, but there's nothing I can do even if I wanted to. Colin walks into the light. His hands are empty. Where is the shotgun?

There's no shotgun because it isn't Colin.

The man standing over the hole is Buckthorpe Jack.

CHAPTER THIRTY-THREE

Rosie

Then

'No one is calling anyone.'

I reached down to pick up my phone, but Ian Dixon got there first. He snatched it and held it out to me.

'Do you understand?'

'Yes,' I said numbly.

'Do you know who I am?'

'Police officer,' I said, a child stumbling over her words.

'That's right.' He handed the phone back to me and moved to face the others. 'I'm sorry, Colin, I truly am. But your boy came out of nowhere and I'm not going down for this.'

In the midst of his sobbing, Colin wiped away tears, pulled away from Dad and stood up straight. 'What do you mean?'

'I'm over the limit. You dared me to race down this road, remember? After spending two hours drinking whisky at Reg's. I'm a police officer and I've got a good fucking career. I'm not going down for this.'

'But ...' Colin stared down at his son, then back at Ian. 'I can't ... We have to ...'

'It won't bring him back, will it?'

I walked towards them, still avoiding the sight of Samuel's body. 'You can't be serious.'

'And what about you?' Ian jutted his chin towards me. 'You accused the boy of sexual assault. It doesn't look too good, does it? Him ending up dead after you met him at night. What if you pushed him into the road? How about that?'

'But I didn't!'

'Don't you dare threaten my family.' A vein bulged from my dad's temple. I went to stand by his side.

'And you, John,' Ian continued, unmoved by Dad's anger. 'What were you doing in the woods? Did you have a calm conversation with the boy who tried to rape your daughter?'

Dad's face fell.

'No, Dad,' I said, twisting my body to see his face. 'Don't listen to him. This is wrong.'

But Dad turned away from me and shook his head. 'Don't talk to me about right and wrong.'

A slow, knowing smile spread across Ian's face. He turned away from Dad and back to me. 'So you did make it up after all. I thought you did, right from the start.'

'What?' Colin's voice was small. Tentatively I met his gaze and saw hatred shining from his wet eyes.

'I'm sorry,' I said, shifting my gaze so that I didn't have to see him.

A sense of cold dread spread over my skin and I fought off the urge to turn around and run. I didn't want to be there with these men because I knew what they were about to do and I couldn't stand it.

Colin's attention returned to the police officer. 'Ian, this is my son. My wife deserves to know. We need to hold a funeral.'

'Are you forgetting your own problems?' Ian said, voice low, dripping with a sly charm that added to the cold sensation running up and down my arms. 'The assault charge. The suspended sentence. The domestic violence, too.'

'What about it? Those offences have nothing to do with this. I wasn't driving.'

'What if I say you were?'

'They … they'd figure out a way to prove you're lying. There'd be an investigation.' The shock registered in Colin's voice. It was whiny, desperate.

'I'm a copper. Who would they believe?' The rain ran down Ian's nose as he lowered his chin, and I thought I'd never seen such an ugly man in all my life.

Dad twisted slowly towards him. 'If you're planning on lying anyway, what difference does it make if we call the police or not?'

'I don't want this on my record, do I? Coppers involved in the accidental death of a teenage boy don't tend to fly up the ranks!' He flung his hands out of his pockets to gesture at Samuel's body.

'You're doing this because you want a promotion?' I say. 'You're disgusting.'

He took a step closer to me and I saw the spit fly from his mouth as he spoke. 'And you're a lying little bitch, so shut up.'

Dad flew for him then, but Colin yanked him back. The action had gravitas, seeing as he'd lost his son, and Dad calmed at once.

'Okay,' Dad said. 'Say we do cover this up. How are we going to do it?'

Ian's voice was soft as he began to explain. 'John, you can come with me. We'll take Samuel out to the moors, bury him there. We'll do it respectfully, Colin. We'll use a marker so you always know where he is. Some stones maybe.'

'How are we going to dig a hole?' Dad said. 'You got a shovel?'

'We'll stop off at the allotments on the way there. I have a shed with all the tools we'll need,' Ian said.

Dad nodded, eyes cast down in grim acceptance.

Ian turned to Colin. 'You and the girl need to clean up the scene. Get rid of every speck of glass. Every fleck of paint. The rain will do the rest.'

'What are we going to *say*?' It was Colin who spoke. 'What am I going to tell Lynn and Peter?' I had no pity left for him.

'We'll say that he ran away,' Ian said. 'The boy was about to be arrested for the sexual assault of half a dozen girls in the village. As far as he knew, anyway. And as far as anyone else knows, he's guilty. Most of the village *believe* he's guilty. People will be relieved. Never mind the fact that he was actually innocent.' He turned to me. 'I guess I have you to thank for that.'

I twisted the sleeve of my coat in my hands until the material dug painfully into my skin. It took every last bit of willpower not to throw up on the ground.

CHAPTER THIRTY-FOUR

Heather

Now

'Come on.' Jack extends a hand down towards me, but I can't reach, no matter how much I stretch myself.

Frustrated, Jack kicks the dead body of Ian Dixon into the hole. I watch it land with a disgusting thud, then stand on his chest for the extra height. With Jack on his front, reaching into the hole, I'm just tall enough for him to grip my forearms and heave me up.

'That's it.' His gruff voice comes out even deeper with the exertion of lifting my weight.

I dig the toes of my shoes into the malleable soil and push myself up as hard as I can. Jack hooks one hand under my armpit and together we manage to get me over the mouth of the hole and onto the surface. I use the palms of my hands to push the rest of my body onto the grass.

My chest rises and falls as I inhale the cold night air. My hair is a tangle of sweat and dirt. Every part of me aches. I can't even speak until I have a moment to collect myself.

'You heard us,' I say, still gasping slightly.

'Aye.'

'Thank you.'

This is the first time I've seen Jack close up, and the blinding light highlights every wizened wrinkle. He doesn't meet my gaze; instead his eyes roam the woods. He climbs to his feet and helps me up.

'Did you shoot Ian?' I ask.

'No, it was the farmer.'

Colin must have shot Ian and then gone running after Rosie. That means my sister is in grave danger and I need to find her.

'Do you have a phone with you?' I ask. 'Colin took mine, but it was broken anyway.'

Jack shakes his head and I swear in frustration.

'There's one at the cabin,' he says.

He leads the way as we step around the floodlight and the mouth of the hole. I never thought I'd feel safe with Buckthorpe Jack, but after seeing the face of a true monster, I'm ashamed of my younger self for being afraid of the lonely man in the woods.

'Jack, do you know who was shooting at me the other day? I saw you in the window of your cabin.'

'I heard the gunfire but I didn't see anyone. I called the police for you, but I guess it went through to the fella in the hole.'

He's probably right. Ian will have intercepted any calls relating to Buckthorpe and pretended to sort the investigation.

'I was coming to see you that day.'

'I know.'

'You do?'

'Aye. It was about the night the lad went missing, wasn't it?'

'The night Samuel died, yes. Did you know? About the car accident? About Ian and Colin covering it up?'

'This and that,' Jack replies. 'You'll be wanting to know about your mother as well, won't you?'

'What do you mean?'

A crack of gunfire prevents him from saying more. I drop to the ground and Jack drops with me. But he falls differently. Limply.

I grab him, feel for a pulse. My fingers come away bloody. It takes me a moment to realise that his chest is open with a gaping wound.

'You need to run now, girl.'

I can't leave him. He'll die.

But if I stay, I'll die.

'Go on now,' he says quietly.

If Colin Murray managed to shoot Jack in the chest, then he can't be far away, and I don't have an awful lot of coverage down here in the tangles of the thorn bush. Jack's right. I need to go.

'Thank you,' I say softly, unsure whether he's even still alive or not. But vowing I will try to get help for him as soon as I can.

I reposition my body into a half-crouch and propel myself forward as fast as my legs will carry me. Another gunshot goes off. I duck down and nearly run straight into a tree. When I swerve to avoid another one, I almost trip. But I don't. By some miracle I stay upright.

The ground beneath my feet changes sharply, and I tumble down a steep slope, slithering on the loose soil. I hold my breath for a moment or two, standing straighter and stabilising my core to stop myself falling. I'm all too aware of the panic building within, but I can't allow myself to lose control. Not now. I need to keep hold of my senses.

Crack.

He's further away now and I'm not sure he knows where I am, because that didn't sound as though it came in my direction at all. But then again, *I* don't know where I am. I'm just flailing through the dark with no direction, no purpose, nothing but survival keeping me going. There are already two dead bodies in the woods. I could easily be a third.

'Heather!'

Colin calling my name is a clear sign of desperation, but it doesn't mean I can allow myself to become complacent. However, there is a possibility I can figure out from the sound of his voice how far away he is. He could be closer than I thought.

The thin branches of the beech trees slap my face as I run. The undergrowth is mostly ferns and thorns, slashing at my jeans, catching my ankles. It makes the ground uneven and unpredictable. The swishing of the plants mean that I can't listen out for Colin any more.

Without warning, the ground changes again to a harder, beaten-down surface without grass or thorns or bracken. It feels as though I'm on a path, which could be a good or a bad thing depending on which path it is. There are many tracks in the woods, some flat and easy to navigate, others full of stones. They go up and down, winding through the trees, and take a lot of concentration to navigate even in daylight. I'm running almost completely blind, with my arms out, groping my way forward.

'I have Rosie.'

I stop dead. Somewhere behind me I can hear Colin moving through the forest. If he really did have Rosie, she'd make a sound. She'd shout to me.

Listen.

Is that one person moving? Or is it two?

I think he's lying.

'I'm going to kill her, Heather,' he taunts. His voice seems to swirl around me.

He's getting into my head. I slip down a slope, find a rock and huddle there, still straining to listen. It forces me to control my breathing and quiet myself. Colin's heavy footsteps tell me that he's coming up behind me. I carefully twist my body around the rock for a better view. I can see torchlight bobbing up and down as he moves.

If he has a torch, that means he doesn't have to worry about bumping into trees or tripping over roots. He has every advantage over me. He has a weapon, and he can see.

But he's alone.

Rosie isn't with him.

CHAPTER THIRTY-FIVE

Rosie

Now

Don't look back, Rosie. Don't look back.

There's nothing like the sound of a gun to sober up a person. The reverberation of the loud crack vibrates through my ribcage. It almost feels as though the bullet has hit me, but I know it hasn't. I'm still on my feet and I'm still running. My heart still beats. My mind is sharp and I'm focused at last.

Behind me I hear shouting, along with the shuffling of feet. I'm not sure if I imagine it, but I think I hear Heather yell at me to keep running.

Heather.

I'm the big sister. I should stop and take care of her, but I'm more likely to die if I do. While I'm unhurt, I can get help. That's our best chance.

Colin won't kill Heather, no matter how hard he tries to make us think he will. She's not his target. I am. There's a chance he might hurt her to get to me, though. And for that reason, I have to move fast.

On the night Samuel disappeared, Ian and Dad bundled his body into the boot of Ian's car while I crawled along the road collecting all the pieces of headlight. Colin sat on the grass verge with his head in his hands, moaning and muttering to himself. A man lost in sadness and guilt. Ian gave me a carrier bag from his car and I put the hard plastic into it, thinking how he had wrapped Samuel in the same carrier bags to try and stop the blood staining his car.

'We can't leave any trace of evidence behind,' he'd said, and told Dad of his plan to find a mechanic out of town to fix the headlight before anyone noticed.

After I'd collected all the pieces, Colin walked with me through the woods in silence until we came across the stone formation. I'd wanted somewhere far from the path, to ensure that no nosy dogs would disturb the evidence, but with a unique marker so that I could come back if I needed to move it. I hadn't realised that Colin was watching my every step with great care.

I think I memorised my tracks and the formation of the stones to protect myself. To make sure that I had a hold over the others. Perhaps there's a dark recess of the mind that goes into survival mode when threatened. No doubt the same dark recess that encouraged my father to go along with Ian's disgusting plan.

I went along with the plan too. Let's face it, I'm part of it. Ian gave me my phone back after he stopped me from calling the police, and I can only imagine that it was an oversight not to take it off me again before he left. I could have called 999. Whether Colin would have let me or not, I don't know, but it wasn't fear that stopped me from trying. At least, not fear of Colin. I'd watched my father lift a dead body into the boot of a car. When it came down to it, I didn't want Dad to go to prison, and I didn't want to get into trouble either. About the lie, about the cover-up, any of it.

Now that lie is coming back to punish me. There would be poetic justice in me dying in the woods just as Samuel died in the woods, and at his father's hand, too. But if I die, Heather will stay Colin's prisoner while he tries to figure out what he's going to do with her, and I need to try and save her. She is innocent in all this.

While the adrenaline of the last few hours has banished any groggy feeling I had from the alcohol and the pills, my mouth is bone dry. But at least I can concentrate as I hurry through the trees. Everything around me is quiet except for my own footsteps. No one seems to be following me.

I was convinced that one of the two men would chase me after I climbed out of the hole. But there's no one. Another gunshot sounds out, but it's further away in the woods. I stop and consider returning in case Heather needs me, but by now I'm almost at the back road. And then I just need to sprint along it as fast as I can to the village.

Trying not to think about Samuel's broken body, I drop to my knees when I see the wire fence and shuffle underneath as I did that night. A sense of relief washes over me. I'm out of the woods at last. My body is tired and some of the adrenaline is waning now that I'm no longer in immediate danger, but I push on, running as fast as my legs will allow.

I let my sister down once before and I never want to do that again. What she doesn't understand is that I've always known that she knew I was lying, and that she's afraid of me and has been since the night Samuel died. Nothing in the letter I found surprised me; I was only shocked by how much pain I read between the lines. The regret for not helping me through my addictions. God, I don't blame her for that. I don't blame her for anything.

I knew that the trust between us had broken as soon as she found my bracelet. I'd always thought that broken trust was irreparable until I read her letter and decided to finally let her in.

There's just one final part she doesn't understand.

I promised myself I would never tell her.

But as soon as we're back together, I'm going to break that promise.

And that's why you need to survive, Hev.

For at least five minutes the road is silent apart from the sound of my shoes slapping against the tarmac. The run could take twenty minutes or forty, I'm not sure. I jog on occasion, but I'm no runner and my lungs burn with every step. My hair is plastered to my forehead with sweat, and every part of me wants to slow down now that there's no one chasing me.

I don't hear the car at first because I'm panting from the run. It's only when I notice the illumination of headlights behind me that I know there's someone there, which is strange, because only villagers use the back road, and even then, rarely at this time of night. I don't know whether to hide or flag them down. Surely Colin couldn't have got to a vehicle in such a short amount of time? Unless he'd found a spot to hide his car somewhere along the road close to the forest.

At the last minute, I duck down into a ravine next to the verge, but it's too late. The driver sees me and pulls over.

A man opens the door and climbs out.

'Rosie?'

I allow myself a peek over the grass verge. The man driving the car is Peter Murray.

'Rosie? Where did you go? I got a text from Heather about two hours ago and I haven't been able to find her. Is she okay? What the hell is going on?'

My heart beats so loud and so fast that I'm surprised he can't hear it. He's less than ten feet away, and I can see the brown work boots he's wearing.

Can I trust him? I know that Heather thinks she can, but I don't trust anyone, especially a Murray.

He starts walking and those boots come closer. *Thump. Thump. Thump.* His steps match the pattern of my heartbeat.

Two feet away, he squats down.

'Why are you hiding?'

For a brief second I'm embarrassed to be crouching down in the grass, with mud stains and sweat all over me. He holds out a hand and I allow him to pull me out onto the verge.

'I don't know who to trust,' I say honestly. 'Your father just tried to kill us.'

Peter leans away from me and lets out a short, sharp exhale. 'He did what?'

'You have to believe me,' I say, talking quickly, still panting. 'He's been planning this ever since I came back. I went into the woods with Hev and he'd dug a trap for us to fall into. It's all because of what I did all those years ago.' In desperation I reach out and take both his hands in mine. 'You have to help Heather. Have you got a phone? I need to call the police.'

Peter frowns. 'My mobile is dead. We'll have to go to the farm and use the landline.'

I shake my head. 'It isn't safe at the farm. Your father might go there.'

'It's closest,' he says. 'I don't understand. What do you mean, he dug a trap?'

I sigh. 'It's a long story. I just need to get to a phone. Can't you drive me into the village?' I glance warily in the direction of the Murrays' farm.

'Come on,' he says gently. 'I'll protect you from Dad.'

I'm about to protest, but he puts one arm around my back and leads me to his car. That arm is solid and firm. If I decide not to comply, there's not much I can do against his strength.

He opens the passenger door and helps me in, then slams it shut and gets into the driver's seat.

'Dad wouldn't hurt Heather,' he says. 'You, on the other hand …' He glances at me sideways and frowns, then puts the car in gear and performs a fast three-point turn to head in the opposite direction, back towards the farm.

'What did Heather text you?' I ask.

'That you were heading to the woods. That you seemed unhinged. That she was afraid.' He raises an eyebrow in my direction. 'Heather doesn't trust you, Rosie. She thinks you're dangerous. How do I know you're telling the truth about my dad?'

'Because you more than anyone know what an arsehole he is. I saw him yelling at you and Samuel on the farm.' I saw a lot on the farm that I shouldn't have seen.

'Yes, I know.' Peter frowns more deeply, exaggerating the seriousness of his expression.

'How did you receive my sister's text if your phone was dead?' I ask.

'It was low on battery before I came out,' he replies. 'I didn't think to charge it. It died ten minutes ago.'

'You've been driving up and down here, then? Searching for her?' I ask.

'I walked through the woods, too.'

There's no emotion in his voice at all, and that's something I always remember about him. I don't understand what Heather sees in him, and I can't help but wonder whether I should've stopped whatever is happening between them. It's too late now, though, and none of it matters. But I hope she's right about him. I hope we can trust him.

Because he's our only hope.

CHAPTER THIRTY-SIX

Heather

Now

In my dark part of the forest, I shiver next to the rock, aware of the fact that I have nowhere to go. Colin's torchlight sweeps over the surrounding area, always just a few feet out of range of me. But with each step, that distance shortens. Soon he will find me.

I can't run, because any movement would catch his eye. But if I stay here, he'll see me anyway. My error was stopping to check that he didn't have Rosie. If I'd trusted my instincts, I would've managed to escape.

And that, of course, has always been my problem. I never listen to my instincts. I use my head every time. My instinct told me that Dad would never kill himself. If I'd shared that thought with Mum, maybe we could have insisted on an investigation into his death and Ian and Colin wouldn't have got away with his murder.

My head told me to never say a word about Rosie's bracelet. My instinct was to tell my parents. If I had told them, maybe we could have dealt with the issue as a family rather than basing our relationships on destructive lies.

My head told me that Rosie was involved in Samuel's disappearance, that she might have killed him. I should have listened to my heart and reached out to her.

When the torch sweeps ever closer, part of me wants to give up and reveal myself. Instead, I shrink down, making myself as small as possible. I screw my eyes shut in the childish way I used to as a kid, mistakenly believing that if I can't see him, he can't see me.

I'm holding my breath as the yellow beam moves on and footsteps rustle further along the undergrowth. Finally I dare to open my eyes. Inching out slowly, I peek from behind the rock. The forest is silent now; maybe he's gone. But no, he's still there; he's just stopped and is speaking on his phone again. With Ian dead, I have no idea who it could be this time. Perhaps he's been forced to check in with his wife, or Ian's wife. But at least he's distracted and facing the other way. This could be my one chance to make my escape before he goes back to sweeping the area with the torch.

I scramble out from behind the rock and begin my descent into the woods. I try to keep as low and as quiet as possible, but I still find brittle twigs snapping beneath my feet. When I hear Colin's voice cry out, I don't stop, I keep going. He's seen me.

As soon as I'm at the bottom of the slope, I set off running as fast as I can, but the forest is dense here. Stones shift beneath my feet as I try to sprint. The thin soles of my pumps slip, and this time my luck has run out, because I can't right myself. I crash to the ground, smashing a tooth on a stone, blood bursting from my lip.

When I hear the shuffle of feet behind me, I know that Colin has almost caught up. It's now that I need my muscles to obey as I try to push on, but I can't physically do it. I can't muster the strength to keep going. A hand closes around my ankle while I scrabble uselessly against the ground.

Colin yanks me back, pulling me roughly towards him. As I'm scraped along the undergrowth, my top catches on a branch and tears. My fingernails drag through the dirt. He grabs me by the neck of my shirt and forces me up. The material digs into my neck as I clamber to my feet, leaving me gulping and gasping through my bloodied mouth.

I feel him behind me, his hot body pressed against mine, and I shudder. He releases some of the hold on my shirt, which allows me to breathe again. And then he whispers into my ear.

'Come on.' He jams the shotgun into my back. 'You need to move.'

CHAPTER THIRTY-SEVEN

Rosie

Now

'How does it feel to know your sister trusts me more than she trusts you?' Peter asks, and I swear there is a smarmy, slippery feel to his words.

'I think we have more important things to worry about.' No, you can't convince me that there's a good soul amongst the Murray men.

'Oh yeah.' He rolls his eyes. 'You think Dad is trying to kill you. Or at least that's what you're trying to convince me of. Not sure I buy it, to be honest.' He flashes that grin at me again. It doesn't strike me that he's worried about Heather. Worried people don't try to goad their lover's sister into a fight when she's missing in the woods. Heather could be hurt or dead for all he knows.

He notices me watching him and the boyish grin fades from his face. A slack expression replaces it, and I feel the sensation of bugs crawling over my skin. Is this who he really is? I know he isn't related to Colin by blood, but he reminds me of his father now.

'I think you should pull over and let me out if you don't believe me,' I say, trying to sound more offended than scared.

'I thought you needed that phone.'

'I'll walk back to the cottage.'

'That's a dangerous walk for a young woman,' he says. 'You don't want to be raped.'

I yank the door handle, but nothing happens.

'Child locks,' he says simply.

'Let me out.'

'No.' When his eyes meet mine, there's nothing in them. No pain, no sadness, no joy, nothing.

'Heather only wants you because you remind her of Samuel.' Hopefully provoking him will at least spark some kind of emotion. And if he's emotional, he might make mistakes.

But he just shrugs. 'Worked out for me. I got her trust, which was the main thing, and I got to screw her over your kitchen counter.'

'Why did you need to screw her when it's me your dad wants?'

'Because we needed to know how much you'd told her about the night Samuel died.'

My heart sinks. That confirms it. Peter knows all about Samuel's death and has been working with Colin to help him get his revenge. All this time he's been playing Heather and spying for his father.

Another thought clicks into place. 'You drugged her the night she came back wasted. What did you give her?'

'Something to help her loosen up,' he says. 'Figured it'd be a good way to find out what she knew and steal her phone in the process. If you want the gossip, I'll fill you in. She thinks you killed Samuel but she can't figure out how you hid the body, what with you being a scrawny girl and everything.'

'If I find out you did anything to her that night …'

'I enjoy the chase,' he says. 'But it's no fun if they're unconscious.'

'What are you going to do with me?'

'I'm going to take you back to the farm, of course. Dad's joining us once he finds your sister.'

'And then what are you going to do?'

'We're going to end this. We're going to kill you – like we should have done years ago.'

CHAPTER THIRTY-EIGHT

Heather

Now

It seems fitting that the story that began at the Murrays' farm should end there too.

Once Colin has me on my feet, he forces me to walk through the woods to the spot where he parked his Land Rover. It's in a lay-by next to the back road. The gun is never more than an inch away from my back, meaning that I have no choice but to obey his every command.

'Is this all because I came to the farm and asked questions the other week?' I say, climbing into the car. 'Would you have left us alone otherwise?'

Colin gets in, and for a split second I consider leaping out and running away, but the moment is fleeting. He's close enough to me that he can grab me, and I'm tired and bruised and not strong enough to fight him off.

'No,' he says. 'I wouldn't kill Iris's child while she still lived. A long time ago I made a pact with myself that if your mother died before me, I'd finally end it the way I wanted to.'

'What if she'd never fallen ill? What if Rosie had never come back to Buckthorpe?'

'Then you wouldn't be sitting in my Land Rover right now.' He places the gun between him and the door and reverses out of the spot.

I try to find another way to keep him talking, but I can't think of anything. To my surprise, he begins to speak anyway, which is out of character for the incredibly laconic man I remember from my childhood.

'You left,' he says. 'You don't know what it's like out here with nothing. I'm out there every day in the fields, breaking my back. And for what? We can't sell owt. Supermarkets sell milk for less than it's worth. The meat trade is on its knees. There's little footfall in the shop. We can drag ourselves round to farmers' markets every month, but there's only three of us and we're tired. I've sold most of the tractors for a pittance and borrowed more from the bank than I can pay back in this lifetime.' His fingers wrap around the steering wheel, squeezing the leather as though it's someone's neck. 'We've been bleeding ever since your sister accused Samuel of that awful crime. He was my firstborn son. The farm would be his when I went. But when your sister tainted it all, folk wouldn't come near us. We were dirty. It took years to earn back some of the reputation she ruined, but by then we were in a huge amount of debt. The farm continued to bleed and bleed until its veins ran dry. I've had enough. It's time for it all to end.'

'I'm sorry,' I say, somehow controlling my voice, because now that I know the full extent of his psychological issues, he has become even more dangerous to me. It's clear what he wants from tonight. He wants to complete a suicide mission. 'You're hurt, and I understand that. But hurting other people isn't the answer to your problems.'

'It's an answer.' His voice has a vague, distracted sound to it.

'What about Peter?'

He directs his face away from me, staring at the wing mirror. 'Peter has no future here, and he knows that.'

'Your wife, then? She doesn't even know that Samuel is dead.'

'I'll tell Lynn before it ends. I'll tell her where he is.'

So that confirms it. Colin plans on committing suicide after he kills me and Rosie. I lean forward and place my head in my hands.

It's not often I allow the tears to come, but there's no hope left. Nothing. I can't fight this man. I can't talk him out of his plans. There's nothing I can do.

If only I hadn't allowed Lady to spook at that tree all those years ago. If only I'd kept my nerves under control, none of this would have happened. Rosie would never have spent any time with Samuel and we would all have gone on with our lives as normal. I caused all of this. My fear set everything in motion. Now I'm overcome by fear again. It's in every pore, and in the tears flowing between my fingers.

When the car comes to a stop, I lift my head to see that we're in the courtyard of the farm I used to love. The door opens and Colin drags me out. My body tingles with the anticipation of what's to come.

He's gentler than before, perhaps because he thinks he's broken my spirit. He doesn't grip me as hard as he could. He assumes that I'm compliant now, but he's wrong; there's still a part of me that's willing to be brave. I wrench my arm out of his grip and start to run. The gun goes off, but the bullet doesn't hit me; instead it hits the flagstones, sending up a cloud of dust.

'I have your sister!' he yells.

No, he's lying. I won't make that mistake again.

'I'll kill her,' he shouts.

'Actually, *I* found her.' The voice makes me stop short, and I glance back to watch him come out of the same stable I used for Lady time and time again. He has Rosie by the collar, and I can tell from the pallor of her face that the tight grip is causing her pain.

'Peter,' I breathe.

He nods slowly.

A few hours ago, his mouth was on mine and I wanted him deeply. I felt something; not love, but more than lust: a connection. I stupidly thought we'd formed a connection. All this time I've been berating myself for using him for comfort, but what I haven't even considered is that he was using me. I close my eyes, desperate for the images of our afternoon together to stop running through my mind.

'It's okay, Hev,' Rosie says. 'You didn't know.'

Colin walks slowly towards me with the gun still trained on me. There's a cautionary expression in his eyes, a warning for me to behave.

'Come into the stable,' he says. 'There's a lot to talk about.'

I make my way back from the gate and stand closer to Rosie. Her eyes are filled with tears, as are mine, because there are two of them and they have guns, leaving us with no option but to do what they say. As we move closer to the open stable, a figure dressed all in white stumbles into the courtyard. Lynn. I'd forgotten all about her in the madness.

She hurries towards her husband in her slippers and nightdress. Her hair is dishevelled, her eyes startled.

'Colin! What's happening?'

Colin casts a cold glance at his son. 'I thought you gave her the pills.'

'I gave her sleeping pills,' Peter says warily.

'What about the Rohypnol you used on *her*?' When Colin nods his head towards me, a jolt of shock jumps up my spine.

I turn to Peter in disgust. 'You drugged me. The night we went drinking.' My mind goes back to the day I spent sleeping and out of it. I remember how I left my phone in the pub that night. 'You stole my phone. And then you took it back to the pub knowing I'd think I'd forgotten it because I was drunk.'

'You were already drunk,' Peter says. 'It was the perfect opportunity.'

'What did you expect to find? Messages about Samuel?' I ask, confused as to why he'd go to these lengths.

He shrugs. 'It was Ian's idea. He wanted to know how much you knew.'

'So that's why … that's why we …' I wrap my arms around my body. Despite the immediate danger, this betrayal hits me hard.

'Will someone please explain what's happening?' Lynn rubs the side of her head as though she's suffering from a terrible migraine. Or a nightmare. It feels like the latter for me. 'Do I need to call the police?'

'No, love,' Colin says, with a gentle tone to his voice. 'Don't do that.'

'I don't understand, Colin. Why do you have the Sharpe girls here?'

'Because it's time to end this,' he says, eyes focused on her.

Colin kept all of this from his wife, but he chose to include his adopted son. Why? Is Peter as crazy as Colin? He's right that there's no place for Peter here if there's nothing to inherit. But surely Peter doesn't need to die because of his father's failing. It's possible that he will attempt to talk himself out of a prison sentence by making sure Colin takes the blame for everything.

'Were you always going to bring me here to die?' I ask, my gaze directed towards Peter. 'The date planned for tomorrow. The suggestion of the woods. Is that why your father dug that hole?'

'That was always for your sister,' Colin says. 'She would've gone there eventually.'

Peter gives me one of those boyish grins I was once attracted to. 'The walk in the woods was just a joke. I wanted to keep you busy while we organised things for Rosie. That didn't work out, but I'm glad you sent me that message earlier so we knew tonight was going to be the night. It's a shame Ian lost his nerve, though.'

'He was more amenable when it was only Rosie. It would have been much easier to make just one of you disappear,' Colin says.

'What do you mean by disappear?' Lynn says quietly.

'Why don't you go back to bed, Mum?' Peter says.

'Colin, I think you should give me that gun.' Lynn reaches out towards her husband, but he yanks the gun away and pushes out an elbow that catches her in the ribs.

When Lynn folds in half, clutching her side, Peter winces.

'Your dad is a violent man,' I say slowly.

'That's not even scratching the surface,' Rosie says. She glares at Colin. 'Is it? Are you going to tell your wife everything? Or shall I do it?'

'Lynn, whatever she says, don't believe a word of it,' Colin tells his wife.

But it doesn't stop Rosie.

'He lied to you,' she says, her voice cold and hard. 'He knows that Samuel is dead. Ten years ago, on the night he disappeared, there was a car crash. Ian Dixon, drunk, driving dangerously, ploughed into your son and killed him. He wouldn't take responsibility for it. He convinced your husband, and my dad, to bury Samuel's body on the moors. I had to hide the broken headlight because I was there too and I saw everything. The next day Ian had his car fixed out of town and no one was ever the wiser. If you go into the woods, there's even a camera recording Colin shooting Ian in the chest.'

Lynn staggers back, finds an old milk-bottle crate and collapses onto it. The motion sensor floodlight comes on, momentarily blinding me. When my eyes adjust, I see that her face is blank with shock. She believes Rosie. That, at least, is one good thing.

'But that's not all,' Rosie says. Colin gives her a sharp glance, but my brave sister goes on. 'He cheated on you.'

Peter grips the back of her neck and Rosie lets out a yelp. Her knees bend and I take a step towards her, but Colin moves the gun in my direction.

'He had an affair with our mother,' Rosie says, almost shouting through her pain. 'Heather is his daughter.'

CHAPTER THIRTY-NINE

Rosie

Then

It's fair to say that there have been many contenders for the worst day of my life. Facing down Colin Murray with his shotgun is one of them, but the first one occurred when I was thirteen years old and I discovered a secret I was never supposed to know.

Heather was just twelve at this point. She was chasing hens with Samuel in the field behind the farm, but I'd gone back to Midnight to check that he'd settled into the stables. It was our second trip to the farm, and Mum had stopped for a cup of tea before leaving.

I thought she'd gone, but it turned out she hadn't. As I always did, I moved quietly around the farm, and slipped into Midnight's stable. There were two voices coming from the stable next door, and I realised quickly that they didn't know I was there. I also realised that the voices belonged to my mum and Colin Murray. I noticed a tiny hole between the bricks on the connecting wall with the other stable. I placed my eye to the hole and watched them argue.

'You need to figure out a way to get us out of this,' Mum said. 'The girls can't keep coming here, it's impossible. It's ridiculous, considering everything that's on the line.'

'Lynn is already suspicious,' Colin replied in a hard voice. 'Unless you can think of a decent explanation that doesn't offend her or piss her off, she'll keep digging and eventually find out.'

'We haven't been together for twelve years,' Mum snapped. 'Why is she still suspicious?'

He shrugged.

'Oh, I know why,' Mum said. 'Because you still can't keep it in your pants.' From my tiny slit in the bricks, I saw the twisted shape of her sneer. I'd never seen my mother make that face before.

'There's a lot at stake here,' Colin continued. 'There's Heather to consider. And John. Imagine him finding out that Heather isn't his daughter. Twelve years of lies.'

'Don't,' Mum said.

'Bit late for that, isn't it?' Colin said. 'Just leave things as they are, Iris. Let the girls come. They'll soon get bored. They don't want to be working on a farm every summer. Let it play out.'

I heard Mum sniff loudly. 'How am I supposed to do that?'

'Just do nothing.'

She let out a hollow laugh.

'I need to go now,' he said. 'And so do you.'

As he walked past the stable, my body trembled from head to toe. Heather wasn't Dad's daughter. I wished with every part of my body that I could have stopped myself from listening to that conversation, but now I was burdened with the truth. A terrible truth. One I never wanted to know.

I moved closer to the door as Mum emerged from the neighbouring stable. Behind me, Midnight rubbed his nose on my shoulder as though he sensed my emotions. I froze, angry tears in my eyes, not knowing what to do or say. When Mum saw me, she started, and then her eyes grew wide.

'Rosie,' she breathed. 'Rosie, what did you overhear?'

'Everything,' I admitted.

Her hand flew up to her mouth. 'You know the truth?' she asked.

I nodded and wiped tears from my eyes. Then I unlocked the stable door and moved slowly towards Mum, trying to pull myself together in case Heather came along.

Mum took me in her arms and held me tight. 'I'm sorry, sweetheart. You shouldn't have found out like that. And I'm sorry to ask this of you, but I need to know that you won't tell your dad.'

As soon as I rested my head on her shoulder, the sobs came out. In a high-pitched voice I answered, 'I won't.'

She stroked my hair and let out a long sigh. 'I know this is a big ask. I know that it means you might have to lie to your sister, and I know how close the two of you are. But Rosie, I can't help it, I'm relieved someone else knows.' She pulled back, crouched a little and stared straight into my eyes. 'I need your help.'

And from then on, our relationship changed.

I became Mum's spy. It was my job, as the older sister, to be my mother's eyes and ears at the farm. *Did Colin talk to Heather today?* She would ask me all kinds of questions in Midnight's stable when Heather wasn't around. Her primary focus was on Colin, because even though she knew that Heather played with her half-brother Samuel, I don't think she ever imagined that anything could happen between them.

And to be honest, neither did I. Heather had that air of the angelic about her, and I didn't expect teenage hormones to affect her in the same way they did other kids. While I had been going through those changes, Heather had always seemed untouched by them.

They hid it well. At first I thought they'd had a falling-out, and that was what I told Mum. She was now a little more concerned about Samuel than before, but because they'd only ever come across as friends, she still didn't think anything bad would happen.

Until the day of the incident.

We were working there on the last Saturday of the Easter holidays and Samuel and Heather were stacking bales of hay in the barn while I was collecting the eggs. Colin was at a farmers' market with Lynn, and their part-timer was minding the shop. Halfway through my collection, I realised that one of the hens had died in the night. Not wanting to touch a dead bird myself, I decided to go and get Samuel to help. But when I reached the barn, I heard a sigh followed by a kissing sound.

Heather had her back to me, but Samuel was facing me and his eyes flicked open. He had one hand tangled in her hair, the other on her hip. Their bodies were pressed close together.

He saw me hovering by the entrance to the barn. He saw the disgusted expression on my face. He pulled away from Heather, but before she could turn around, I ran away.

I didn't know what to do. I'd just seen my sister kissing her half-brother. I knew Heather had no idea who he was to her. I felt revulsion shudder through my body, like I might vomit, but I also felt weirdly jealous. As Mum's faithful spy, I was expected to tell her, and I was dreading it. How long had this been going on? Had they gone further?

In a daze, I found myself wandering into Buckbell Woods, near to Jack's house. He didn't frighten me in the way he did some of the kids my age, but at the same time I also didn't want to be around him on my own. No seventeen-year-old girl would want to be around a man they didn't know in an isolated place. I started walking quickly away from the cabin, trying to make sense of everything in my mind.

And that was when I heard the sound of footsteps behind me. I spun around to see Samuel running towards me along the path.

'Rosie, wait,' he said.

I turned around and carried on walking, because I didn't want to face him.

'We love each other. It isn't anything seedy,' he insisted.

Finally, I stopped. Samuel was panting from the exertion, and his forehead was shiny with sweat. He wiped some of it away with his forearm.

'You don't know how disgusting it is,' I snapped. 'You have to stop. You can't be with her.'

I expected him to be angry, to demand to know what I was talking about. Instead, he calmly placed his hands on his hips and said, 'You know, don't you?'

The words took me by surprise, and I remained silent.

'Did your mum tell you?' he asked.

'No,' I said. 'I overheard. You *know* that Heather is your half-sister?'

He nodded his head slowly. 'Dad saw us kissing and he told me. He said I should keep away from her. I'm pretty sure he's going to stop you both from coming to the farm soon.'

I covered my mouth with my hand and moved away. My stomach lurched and I dry-heaved. When I'd composed myself, I faced him again. 'You carried on the relationship even after finding out you're related?'

'Half related,' he said. 'I don't care. I love her. She's my soulmate.'

I shook my head. 'You're an idiot.'

'Love is love,' he said.

'How far has it gone?' I demanded.

Samuel smiled. 'We were thinking of taking things further soon. Heather wants to lose her virginity.'

A red-hot flash of rage coursed through me. 'No, she won't,' I spat. 'Because I'm going to tell her everything and she'll finish with you.'

'You're going to break your family up then?' He smirked. 'Your dad doesn't know. My mum doesn't know either. How would you feel knowing that you're the reason two families have been torn apart? When your father moves out of the house and your mother has to sell because she can't afford the mortgage, will it all be worth it?'

'Maybe it's for the best,' I mumbled, feeling unsure of myself.

'It's all right for you because you'll be going to university in a year or so. But your mum will be alone. Depressed and alone.

What if Heather is so angry that she never speaks to her mother again? What if she never speaks to you again?'

'She … she wouldn't do that.'

'How do you know?' he goaded. 'How would you feel if you found out that your dad isn't your dad?'

I took a step away from him and shook my head. 'Why are you being like this? You never used to be so … so … cruel. I don't understand you.'

He recoiled as though he'd been slapped. 'You know nothing about cruelty. I've been bullied my entire life, just for being myself. I don't fit the Buckthorpe cookie cutter and I've been punished for that. Were you there in Year Ten when Rhys Turner put pig's blood in my pencil case?'

I shook my head and briefly closed my eyes, repulsed. 'No, I wasn't there.'

'But you heard about it?'

'Yes.'

'And you went out with him. You even had sex with him.'

It was true. But it hadn't meant anything. It was expected.

'Why do you care so much about being popular in Buckthorpe? It's a tiny village school, for fuck's sake,' Samuel said. 'You do realise that once you go to university, you'll be completely insignificant. None of this will matter any more.'

'Will the bullying matter to you?' I asked.

'That's different.'

'Is it? Maybe this is all I'll get in life. I just want to be part of something, okay? I like how it feels.'

Samuel took a step forward and kissed me. Not forcefully, but confidently. I placed both hands on his shoulders and pushed him away. 'What the fuck?'

'Sorry.'

I turned to leave, but he shouted after me, 'Don't tell Heather. Please.'

'I have to.'

He grabbed me by the arm. 'Please don't tell her. I love her.'

'You just kissed me!'

'I didn't mean it.' He shook his head back and forth, and those dark blue eyes I had always considered gentle suddenly seemed manic. He was frightening me.

I tried to prise myself out of his grip, but he held onto me tightly. He was too strong. I remember shouting 'Get off!' He slapped me once around the face and I kicked him then dashed away into the woods.

After running for a while, I fell down a bank, ripped my breeches and lost a boot to the mud. I just sat down on the ground then and wished I could turn time back and right all the wrongs that had happened around me. But I couldn't.

Eventually I got to my feet and tried to find my way back to the cottage, abandoning my boot and, without realising it, my phone. As I walked, I couldn't shake the feeling that someone was following me. Watching me. I thought it was Samuel. Sometimes I wonder whether he was considering hurting me that night, and that's why the lie popped into my head. Dad looked me in the eye and asked me what had happened, and I blurted it out:

Samuel hurt me.

And then my life became even worse.

CHAPTER FORTY

Heather

Now

When Peter throws Rosie to the ground, I fly at him, my body connecting with his. But he's twice my size, and I barely knock him off balance. He grabs my wrist and bends it back until I'm screaming in pain, my body slowly crumpling to the ground. Once I'm on the hard concrete, he smirks and lets me go. I pull Rosie close to me and we huddle together.

'I'm sorry you had to find out this way,' she whispers.

My heart beats twice before I remember what she means. *Heather is his daughter*. The words haven't sunk in yet. I know that it means I was in love my half-brother, that all this time my father was someone else, and that our mother betrayed our family in a way I never thought possible. *I want you to know that I never regretted anything*. Was that a callous admission during her last moments? Or did she mean that she didn't regret her affair because it resulted in me being born?

How selfish of her to die without telling me the truth.

'I never wanted you to find out,' Rosie says.

Standing above us both is the man who is my biological father. Do I resemble him? Do I have his eyes, his smile? That calm, resigned expression I see on his face now?

'Yes,' he says. 'This all started because of my mistake. That's why I'm ending it now.'

'You won't kill her.' Rosie moves out of my arms and sits back on her heels, facing Colin. 'She's your daughter. You won't be able to.'

But Colin simply stares at her, and then at his gun.

My gaze drifts over to Lynn, who hasn't said a word. Is this news to her too? Her face is like a Halloween mask, ghostly white and blank. With her nightdress and her dishevelled hair, she could be mad Miss Havisham, ready to set herself alight.

Mum had no way of knowing that her actions would bring us here, to the cold courtyard of the Murrays' farm, with the threat of death looming over us. Colin could kill all of us. Even Peter. Even Lynn. Would they fight him if they were threatened?

'He would kill me,' I say to Peter. 'And he would kill you too. And your mother. He has nothing to live for any more. Lynn, do you know about his debts, or is that something else he's kept from you? Do you know anything about what this man is capable of? Ian Dixon lies dead in Buckbell Woods because your husband shot him in the chest. Together, Ian and your husband put a gun in my father's mouth and made it appear to be suicide. If you don't believe he's capable of murder, then think again.'

'Someone get that girl out of my sight,' she says in a low hiss. 'All I see is you, Colin. I don't know why I didn't see it earlier. You look just like each other.'

Peter snorts. 'Bullshit.'

'And you.' Lynn regards her son. 'What happened to you? You were such a sweet boy. Now I see that Samuel was the kind, gentle one. He was the one who loved his family. You're nothing to me now. What have you turned him into, Colin? Why have you made him a monster?'

Colin says nothing, and I watch as the blood drains from Peter's face. 'Mum?'

'What did you expect, Peter?' I say. 'She just saw you try to break a woman's wrist. But as the saying goes, like father, like son.'

His eyes flash with anger.

'How many times has he beaten you, Lynn?' Rosie says. 'I remember the night Samuel died. Ian reeled off a few of the crimes your husband had committed. One of those was domestic violence. He's been beating you your entire marriage, hasn't he?'

Colin glowers, but he remains silent. Lynn stares at Rosie and then at me, her body completely rigid.

'Dad, just shoot her,' Peter says. 'She deserves to die for what she did to our family. Her lies tore this village apart.'

'Has he raped you?' I say to Lynn, ignoring Peter. 'I bet my mother wasn't his only affair. Does he like to take what he wants no matter the consequences?'

Colin drives the butt of the gun into my ribs and I land heavily on my side. 'That's enough,' he says quietly.

He levels the gun at us, and Rosie grasps my hand. There's no getting out of this situation. Colin made up his mind long ago, and his wife and son are either in shock or brainwashed by him.

'Where did you bury him?' Lynn asks.

'It's in a letter,' Colin says. 'I left it next to the fridge. It explains everything. They took him to Ingledown Moor, drove a mile up the east road. Then they walked for ten minutes with his body until they found three stones together nestled within the valley. They dug between those stones and buried him, then laid the moor grass back on top. Ian took a photograph of the area the morning after and he's had it ever since, probably in case he ever felt like blackmailing me.'

'Did he?' Lynn asks.

'It started with a few hundred here and there when he needed it,' Colin admits. 'And then sure enough I was paying him monthly. It was only when John Sharpe decided he was going to talk that things began to unravel. There's not a day goes by that I don't regret it, Lynn, and that's the truth.'

Lynn gets to her feet and walks over to her husband. 'If I told you I would forgive you, would you stop this nonsense and live, instead of giving it all up and dying?'

There are tears in Colin's eyes as he answers. 'It's too late, Lynn. Like the girl said, Dixon's body is in the woods. I think I killed Jack, too. There's no way I can come back from that. Not now.' His chin wobbles and I watch my biological father as his carefully constructed control begins to unspool.

Gently, Lynn takes the gun from her husband's hands.

'Mum?' Peter says. 'What are you doing?'

She turns in our direction, with the gun facing us.

'I can't bear to look at you,' she tells me.

'None of this is Heather's fault,' Rosie says fiercely. 'She's the only innocent person in all of this.'

'The lass is right,' Colin admits. 'And she was right before. I wasn't going to shoot Heather. Just her sister.'

Lynn wipes away her tears, relaxes her hold on the gun and turns to her husband. 'Thank you for telling me where Samuel is buried.' Then she raises the gun and pulls the trigger.

CHAPTER FORTY-ONE

Heather

Now

'You should go now, girls.' Lynn steps away from her husband's body and faces us. Her nightdress is splashed with a red spray of his blood. The glint of life has gone from her eyes, leaving glazed marbles inside a pale, expressionless face. Before me I see a woman who has let everything go. A dangerous woman. Without hesitation, I take Rosie's hand in mine and quietly lead her away while Peter sinks to his knees next to his father.

'We have to call the police, Ro,' I say, as we hurry along the back road. 'And that means we have to tell them everything.' I hate to say it, because I know what it means she'll have to do, but the truth needs to come out. It's what's right.

'It's okay,' she says. 'I want to tell them.'

It was on that long walk home in the cold that Rosie finally told me the entire story. It began with her overhearing our mother arguing with Colin Murray, and ended with Dad driving away with Ian Dixon to bury Samuel's body on the moors, leaving her to tidy up the last of the evidence. We stopped at the place Samuel died, just for a moment, and I wondered whether I truly was better off knowing the truth, or whether I should have let it all lie.

We walked through the woods to see if we could find Jack. His body lay lifeless on the forest floor. I checked for a pulse, but he was cold. Then we went back to the cottage and called the police, no longer scared that Sergeant Ian Dixon would control the investigation. In a sense, two evils had perished. In another sense, three souls were lost. Four, if you counted Peter Murray.

I was right that Buckthorpe village had a rotten core, I just didn't realise that the two people at the heart of it were Ian Dixon and Colin Murray.

Once we went to the police and the truth came out, it was clear that half the village were aware – or at least had their suspicions – that Samuel's disappearance was connected to Ian. Most thought that he'd arranged with the Murrays for Samuel to escape arrest. Others believed that Rosie had killed Samuel and Ian Dixon had made it go away. He was known as some sort of fixer around the village. Caught drink-driving? Pay Ian and he'll make it go away. Want to sell some not-so-kosher produce? Ian will make it happen for you. Keep the pub open until two a.m.? Not a problem, as long as you pay Ian a percentage of the profits.

And then everything came out about Peter. Not only was he under his father's influence, but he was a drug dealer. He sold horse tranquillisers, prescription pills and hard drugs. They caught up with him twenty miles out of Buckthorpe, asleep in his car; later, in the interrogation room, he claimed that everything he had done was to save the farm. But nothing worked. Colin drank away a large portion of the money and gave the rest to Ian to keep him quiet.

If they hadn't killed my father, I would pity them.

'I'm going to ask one more time,' Rosie says. 'Are you sure you want to do this?'

She raises her eyebrows questioningly, and in her expression I see hesitation. We're not the same as we were before. We're not full sisters. I'm not my father's daughter. And yet, we're closer. The barrier of our secrets has finally been broken down, and I see her and feel nothing but love. No fear, no guilt, no anger. Rosie carried our mother's secrets with her until they broke her down into little pieces. Smashed like the headlight she buried in the woods.

'I'm sure,' I reply. 'We're going to stay in Buckthorpe. Even if the village hate us, we're staying.'

Lynn and Peter are both awaiting trial. Ian Dixon is dead. Colin is dead. The Campbells finally admitted to us that they'd stolen an old photo album and Dad's shotgun out of the house because Ian had threatened them. They'd been storing them and were terrified we'd come in and see what they'd taken. Joan brought them back to us in tears. Rosie hugged her until she stopped crying.

The photo album contained pictures of Ian with Dad and Colin before the accident. He didn't want us connecting him to Dad's death. The shotgun was the murder weapon, now given over to the police. I'm certain Ian was too clever to leave any DNA evidence, but as I was poking around about Samuel's disappearance, he probably wanted to keep us away from it. The Campbells had a spare key to our house; when I thought I saw someone slip out of the door, it was Bob hurrying away.

'If I end up in prison, you'll have to live here alone,' Rosie says.

'You're not going to prison,' I say. 'You were just a kid, Ro. They'll focus on the real criminals. Like Ian. And, I guess, even Dad.'

I was always Dad's favourite; that was what everyone said. Rosie used to say it all the time. But he never knew the truth about me. He believed all his life that I was his, and I'll never know how he would have reacted if he'd found out. Would he still have loved me?

What I do know is that there were problems between him and Mum. At least now I understand why he often worked away from the family. One comfort is that there must have been some real love between them. Otherwise they wouldn't have stayed together after Rosie and I moved out.

'I hope you're right,' she says. 'Anyway, I have to catch this train if I'm going to be back tomorrow.'

I give her a hug and watch her leave. Because we've decided to keep the house and live together, Rosie is travelling back to Brighton to collect more of her belongings. I need to go to London soon, too. It's time to quit my job, give notice on my flat and pack up everything I have, which isn't a lot. I don't know if I'll find a job up here, but the mortgage is paid off on the cottage and I have some savings. Rosie is going to write a novel. I don't know what I'm going to do. Just stop and learn to be me for a change.

When I came back to Buckthorpe, I didn't feel as though my childhood had truly existed. It was akin to a blurry film watched years ago and barely recalled. I couldn't remember the plot. Maybe that's a good thing for me now, because almost all of it was a lie. I wasn't Dad's daughter; I am the daughter of a violent man. My existence caused problems for everyone around me. And yet my mother told me that she had *no regrets*. She never regretted the fact that I was born.

And then I complicated things further by falling in love with my half-brother. Rosie told me how Samuel knew that we were related and decided that he didn't care. I don't know what to think of the boy I once loved. Over the last ten years I've gone through Rosie accusing him of assault, backed up by other girls from school, the revelation that we were related, and now the revelation that he knew and didn't tell me.

I can admit it to myself now, but I never believed that Samuel tried to rape Rosie. Not even on the night she ran home from the woods bruised and upset. No, I never believed it. I thought she must have become confused after someone else hurt her. I thought she might have mixed up a different monster in her mind with the boy I loved.

I never believed that he hurt her, but I convinced myself that she might have killed him. Her lies got to me. I twisted her into the villain when I should have focused on the adults around us. I'll have to come to terms with the fact that I didn't trust my sister, and why that might be.

Rosie and I are in the process of sorting through our parents' belongings and deciding what we want to keep and what can be binned or given away to charity. Neither Mum nor Dad lived extravagantly. Mostly the house is full of books, which Rosie wants to keep. I walk up the stairs in the same way I did as a child, stepping carefully amongst the dusty piles.

Today I've decided to be brave enough to enter the attic armed with a can of spider killer. All I need to do is pull down the last boxes and take them into the living room to begin sorting the contents into piles. Rosie hasn't much interest in the stuff in the attic, because we know that Mum and Dad stuffed their old bits of crap up there.

I open the hatch, climb in and grab the first box. It takes me a while to carry them all downstairs, and by the time I've finished, I could do with a shower. But it's worth the extra effort so that I can stick a sitcom on Netflix while I work.

As I suspected, they're mostly full of junk. I find our old Halloween costumes: Rosie was a pumpkin, I was a fairy. I take some of Grandad's old records and pile them to one side. I don't know much about records, but these might be interesting to play, or potentially worth some money. Then I find Mum's old jewellery box, which, I realise now, I haven't seen for ten years. I open it up, expecting to find her old costume jewellery. I know I'm not going to find any old diamonds or gems; her most expensive item was her engagement ring.

But there is a shiny object nestled within. I pick it up and hold it to the light, and as I do, all the blood drains from my face. It isn't a forgotten diamond; it's a shard of hard plastic from a headlight.

And beneath that shard of plastic is a note.

Heather, you were always John's daughter. Whatever you may learn, I did it all for you.

I hear Jack's words in my mind: *You'll be wanting to know about your mother.*

Mum was there that night. Rosie didn't know, but Mum was there.

Shaking, I put the piece of headlight back in the box, pick up the note and read the rest. It explains everything.

CHAPTER FORTY-TWO

Iris

Then

You may think after reading this that I regret the things I did. But I don't. It's true that as a young mother, I made a terrible mistake. I mistook a weak man for a man with a good heart. He charmed me, spun me silly with compliments, and made me believe that I was worth loving. And no, that man was not my husband.

While I love my husband, and always have, he is not an easy man to love. He's not a man who makes a woman feel special. He's a good man and he will do anything for his family, but words don't come easily to him. At first I knew he loved me because he woke me up with a cup of tea each morning, despite the fact that he hated getting up early. He knew how I appreciated being woken up and he did it for me. Then it was just at the weekends. Then he stopped altogether.

The small changes became big problems. We wouldn't kiss as often. Then we barely embraced. There were times when we didn't touch for days. And then he started taking jobs further and further away because they paid more. Away for weeks at a time.

I thought he was trying to get away from me. In my mind, my marriage was over because he had grown bored of my company.

Colin showed me the affection I'd become starved of. It was all a lie, but I fell for it in the same way many of us do when we're desperate for love. Of course, when I found out I was pregnant, he dropped me so fast I hit the ground with an almighty thud. There was no discussion of us leaving our partners and being together. Lynn was already pregnant with Samuel. I had Rosie and John to care for. There was no romance in the end, only a mess.

Yet out of that mess came you, Heather. My calm and considerate daughter. I loved you just as much as Rosie, I want you to know that.

Buckthorpe has always been its own contained world with its own set of rules. With the forest surrounding us, we're cut off from much of the rest of the country, and we deal with our problems on our own without going to outsiders. But it's a tiny village, and when there's a huge secret, that's when lives become complicated. Neither Lynn nor John knew about the affair and I couldn't bring myself to tell either. Which is why, when you girls started working at the farm, I was furious with Colin. I also knew I couldn't stop it, because it would raise too many questions.

Could I lie and claim you had other things to do in the summer? Lynn knew you didn't. She knew I was often at my cleaning job and you girls would run around in the garden or ride your ponies in the woods. Like a bloodhound, she would sniff out a lie within moments. And then questions would be asked. *Why won't you let your girls associate with my sons? Aren't we good enough for you? What's really going on, Iris?*

The solution came by accident. Rosie overheard the dreaded secret, and for once I had an ally. Oh Rosie, I am sorrier than words can express. I knew in my heart that you were too young to handle such a huge responsibility, and yet I piled it on you anyway. I needed you, but I shouldn't have put all that pressure on you. I wrongly thought that with you watching over Heather and Samuel, you could step in if anything blossomed between them. What I didn't anticipate was them falling in love. It felt as though nothing could stop them after that.

I'm sorry, Rosie. Everything that happened to you after was because of what I said to you. I saw the conflict on your face when you made that false accusation. Later that night, you confessed to me in secret that you'd seen Heather and Samuel kissing, and that in your shocked state you hadn't known what to do. And then you told me how Samuel knew and didn't care. He frightened you, Rosie, and you panicked.

It was at that moment that I considered suggesting you come clean and exonerate Samuel. But you know that I didn't. Even though Samuel didn't hurt you, he intended to hurt your sister. He was going to pursue you, Heather, even knowing what he knew. That was inexcusable to me. He did not deserve to be free. In my eyes, he was dangerous. He was everything you said about him, Rosie.

And Heather, I knew he would never stay away from you.

The night Samuel disappeared, I was woken by John getting out of bed. I quietly followed him into the woods, a few minutes behind him. He had no idea I was there. Buckbell is full of shadows. When I saw the two of them fighting, I panicked. I ran down towards the back road with the intention of going to fetch Colin. But then I heard the fighting stop.

By this time I was close to the road, next to a break in the fence. There'd been a crash a few weeks ago and someone had knocked part of the wire down. I hadn't planned it that way, but that's how it happened. Samuel came running down to the same part of the woods. It's possible that he'd seen the broken fence on his way to meet you, Rosie, and had used it to enter the woods as a shortcut.

'What are you doing here?' he said.

'I followed John.'

His face was all beaten up, but he still seemed to me as arrogant as always. I hated him. He was Colin's double.

'You're never going to stay away from my daughter, are you?' I said.

'You mean my sister?' He laughed. 'Why would I? I love her. No one knows we're related. What's the harm?'

'What's the harm? You're hurting her! You can't get married or have children. You can't do any of the things that normal couples do.'

'Tell her that,' he said. 'Tell her that you fucked my father. Tell her what you did.'

I didn't get a chance to respond, because we both became distracted by the car careening down the back road. The driver must have been going at least sixty, seventy miles an hour on that narrow road. Someone was whooping for joy in the driver's seat.

I saw an opportunity to end this sorry situation. Samuel had made his intentions clear: he was happy to carry on an incestuous relationship with you, Heather, and I knew it would break you to find out. You were the most proper young woman, completely different to the other teenagers in the village. You followed the rules to the letter. At that age, knowing this secret would have broken you, and I had already broken one daughter.

Better to grieve for a lost love than to lose your identity.

I pushed him.

There was a terrible screech of brakes. Samuel went flying up into the air before he landed. I staggered back, amazed by my own actions, before running away. I ran and ran and ran until I stopped and dry-heaved, the realisation of what I had done beginning to hit home. I couldn't hear a thing behind me. No talking, no shouting, no panicking. Nothing but me, alone.

I knew I had to get out of there, and a will to survive emerged from the shock. The silence of the forest enveloped me as I picked my way back to the cottage.

I felt ashamed and horrified by what I'd done. I stared up at the trees and I saw guilt. Moonlight illuminated the bluebell field through the darkness and I saw blame. I used to meet Colin here. The woods have a lot to answer for, giving us this seemingly safe space to indulge in our desires.

Samuel was connected to me, like a stepson in some way, and I threw him in front of that car with hate in my heart. I'm sorry, Heather, but I don't regret it.

I set you free when I pushed him, but I also imprisoned my other daughter. Rosie, maybe this will now set *you* free, my love.

I'm sorry I couldn't tell you while I was alive.

I love you both.

A LETTER FROM SARAH

I want to say a huge thank you for choosing to read *The Liar's Sister*. If you did enjoy it, and want to keep up-to-date with all my latest releases, just sign up at the following link. Your email address will never be shared and you can unsubscribe at any time.

www.bookouture.com/sarah-denzil

I am so thrilled to be able to share this book with you all. I hope you enjoyed reading it as much as I did writing it!

I hope you loved *The Liar's Sister* and if you did I would be very grateful if you could write a review. I'd love to hear what you think, and it makes such a difference helping new readers to discover one of my books for the first time.

I love hearing from my readers – you can get in touch on my Facebook page, through Twitter, Goodreads or my website.

Thanks,
Sarah A. Denzil

ACKNOWLEDGEMENTS

Books don't get any easier to write, and although this might be my twentieth completed novel overall, I went through as many of the usual issues while writing it as even the first one. This process never gets easier! But it is helped by the people around me.

As always, thank you to my husband for being my first reader and supporter. And thank you to my family and friends for buying and reading twenty books you probably wouldn't unless I'd written them!

Thank you to my editor, Natasha, for your fantastic insight. And thank you to everyone else at Bookouture for all the hard work that goes on behind the scenes.

Lastly, thank you to caffeine for getting me through this process.

Printed in Great Britain
by Amazon

56402939R00163